The Vampire's Former Flame

Nocturne Falls
Book 16

USA Today Best Selling Author
Kristen Painter

THE VAMPIRE'S FORMER FLAME:
Nocturne Falls, Book Sixteen

Copyright © 2024 Kristen Painte

All rights reserved. No part of this book may be reproduced in any form or by any electronic or mechanical means, including information storage and retrieval systems—except in the case of brief quotations embodied in critical articles or reviews—without permission in writing from the author.

This book is a work of fiction. The characters, events, and places portrayed in this book are products of the author's imagination and are either fictitious or are used fictitiously. Any similarity to real person, living or dead, is purely coincidental and not intended by the author.

ISBN: 978-1-941695-89-0

Published in the United States of America

Welcome to Nocturne Falls, the town where Halloween is celebrated 365 days a year. The tourists think it's all a show: the vampires, the werewolves, the witches, the occasional gargoyle flying through the sky. But the supernaturals populating the town know better.

Living in Nocturne Falls means being yourself. Fangs, fur, and all.

Ephelia Moreau doesn't know she's in danger. All she knows is that her mother's up to something. Nothing new there. Her mother has been trying to dictate Ephie's life since the day she was born. So when an old boyfriend suddenly appears and tells Ephie about the cool little town he lives in, Ephie jumps on the chance to take a trip, not realizing she's doing exactly what her mother wants. Or what kind of trouble is headed her way.

Remy Lafitte wasn't supposed to be in New Orleans. He was only there to see a sick friend, but then the mother of a former girlfriend finds him and asks for his help. He can't refuse, and not just because her mother is threatening him. If Ephelia's in danger, Remy will do anything he can to protect her (and her cat). She was, after all, the only woman he's ever loved.

Ephie and Remy have a lot of catching up to do, but they

may not get the chance when a real threat comes to Nocturne Falls. Suddenly, Ephie's life hangs in the balance and Remy must make a decision. Even if it means breaking his own heart again.

the bustling port of New Orleans as his personal playground. Wine, women, and song, he'd lived the life.

He leaned forward again, ate the last bite of beignet, brushed his hands off, then crumpled up the bag and set it next to him to throw away later. He stretched his legs out and leaned back, taking in the night air and enjoying the music.

People-watching wasn't bad, either. Some of the outfits the women had on could barely be described as clothing. The drunk people were pretty entertaining, too. More than half the crowd carried a hurricane, a daiquiri, or a yard of beer.

He shook his head. Some of those people were going to have a bad night. He'd seen it plenty of times.

A man fell into another man, sending both of their drinks flying. The two men laughed. Those around them who'd been splashed with the drinks didn't think it was so funny. Sharp words were exchanged, and some of the men squared up.

"And so it begins," Remy muttered.

A uniformed police officer on horseback quickly intervened. He separated the men, defused the situation, and sent them on their way. Crisis averted. Having a twelve-hundred-pound partner certainly helped.

Remy nodded all the same. As an officer of the law himself, he appreciated the man's quick response and obviously effective words. Beautiful steed, as well.

They didn't use horses in Nocturne Falls, even though it could get hectic sometimes, like during parades or festivals. Anyplace that had a large influx of tourists was susceptible to such nonsense. But nothing really compared to the French Quarter after dark. In his day, tourism hadn't been anything like it was now.

Mostly the Vieux Carre had been filled with men looking to drink, gamble, and carouse with the women who worked the gentlemen's clubs. Because all of that was so readily available, the Quarter attracted its fair share of shady characters. Men specifically looking to take advantage of the first group.

And, of course, it had been a haven for vampires in search of an easy dinner.

His stomach rumbled, and his fangs protruded. He ran his tongue over them before retracting them. He would need to feed soon. There were plenty of places to get legal blood in town.

But that would mean announcing his presence. He'd only come to New Orleans to say goodbye to Professor Boudreaux. The man was suffering with cancer in St. Boniface's Hospice. Remy could not let the man pass without seeing him one more time.

Remy had never gone to college, but he'd sat in on Boudreaux's evening classes at Tulane for three years. Lemuel Boudreaux had known Remy wasn't registered, but he'd said nothing, letting him attend whenever he liked.

Boudreaux had taught forensic science, something Remy had been fascinated with even before he'd gone into law enforcement. Maybe it was all the blood.

Or maybe it had been the girls on Tulane's campus. He knew that wasn't true. It had been one girl in particular.

Remy rolled his shoulders, an odd heat rising through him. Funny how an old memory could evoke such a response.

Didn't matter why Remy had found the man's classes so interesting. Boudreaux had been kind and understanding. They had developed a friendship. Especially after Boudreaux had sussed out what Remy truly was.

Unlike most, Boudreaux had not been terrified. He'd been fascinated and full of questions. Blood became their common ground.

They had kept in touch over the years. Boudreaux's last correspondence had come from his daughter, telling Remy about her father's failing health.

And so, Remy had used some of his accrued vacation time to see the man once more. He'd spent as much time as he'd been able to with his friend. Last night, around 3 a.m., Lemuel had slipped into a coma.

Brokenhearted, Remy had left. Humans didn't live long enough. Not the good ones, anyway. And going to Boudreaux's funeral wasn't possible, as it would be during the day. Even if Remy could go, there was a chance he might be seen and recognized by someone who would have expected him to age the way everyone else did. There would be questions.

He wasn't here for any of that. He did not need to anger the other vampires in town by causing problems, nor did he want to get himself into trouble with the local vampire council.

He would send flowers, though. That was at least something he could do.

His stomach rumbled again. Going to one of the sanctioned blood banks was really his only option. Wouldn't do for a Nocturne Falls deputy to get pinched for treating a tourist like a walking juice box. Not only that, but that kind of behavior was no longer who he was.

With a soft sigh, he picked up his beignet bag and stood. The closest blood bank was several blocks away and fronted by an unassuming used bookstore.

As he stood there, a group of obviously intoxicated women dressed in all shades of pink and wearing feather boas went by. A bachelorette party in full swing. The bride-to-be, easily identified by the tiara and white sash she wore proclaiming her status, smiled at him, as did several of the other women.

He smiled back. None of them were his type, and a woman promised to another man already wasn't even a possibility, but it cost nothing to smile.

When they stopped, he realized he shouldn't have made eye contact. The alcohol was making them bold.

He used a little vampire speed to slip away, disappearing into the crowd. The only woman he'd ever truly felt something for was in his past. It was no wonder that visiting Boudreaux had brought her to mind again. More than usual, anyway. She had a way of sliding into his thoughts when he least expected it.

sugar on the beignets off of his person. It was working. Mostly. No one ate Café Du Monde's beignets and came away unscathed. The dusting of fine sugar was a small price to pay for a taste of the delicious fried doughnuts.

His position by the fence meant he was looking at the backs of the musicians, four energetic teenagers and one older man, maybe their teacher. Teachers were good people. The man seemed to be encouraging the boys as they played.

Remy leaned back. He liked having the wrought iron behind him and a good view of the swirling crowds. There was a sense of security in his positioning.

Nighttime in New Orleans meant keeping an eye on those around you. Regardless of whether or not you were a two-centuries-old vampire.

The city was nothing like it had been when he'd first arrived. Then it had been much wilder, much more dangerous, and a lot less civilized, in some ways.

In other ways, it had been a little *too* civilized, but he hadn't been one to socialize with that crowd. They wouldn't have accepted him even if he'd wanted to join their ranks. Might have been interesting, but even then he'd had to be careful about becoming too familiar with anyone. Which wasn't to say he hadn't done his fair share of socializing.

He'd just associated with a much different crowd. One that didn't care about status or breeding, just that you had money to spend and were willing to do so.

As the grandson of pirate Jean Lafitte, Remy had seen

1

April probably wasn't the best time to return to New Orleans, what with the Jazz Festival going on along with various other street fairs, music events, and general exuberance that spring brought to the Big Easy. But Remy Lafitte was still happy to be in his hometown, despite the reason he'd come.

The crowds and noise and raucous atmosphere were a welcome distraction after the sterilized quiet of the hospice facility. The chaos was as much a part of the city as he had once been, and it put a smile on his face.

The beignets he was currently eating helped his mood, too. He'd needed something comforting, and beignets did the trick. He was a vampire; he didn't need food. But it could still bring him pleasure.

He sat with his back against the fence that surrounded Jackson Square so that he faced the St. Louis Cathedral. He was closer to St. Peter Street than he was to St. Ann, a spot he'd chosen so that he could enjoy the music being played in front of the gates of Jackson Square.

He sat slightly hunched over, his knees bent, his upper half leaned forward between them as he ate. All in an effort to keep the copious amounts of confectioner's

Losing her was his fault, too. He'd fallen hard and scared her off. She'd already been a shy thing, unaware of her own beauty and charm, struggling with her fledgling powers as a new witch.

He'd professed his love and offered to turn her to keep them together for eternity. He'd proposed with a gold ring designed to look like a pansy made of sapphires and diamonds. It was a sweet, delicate piece that had seemed a fitting tribute to her beauty and refinement.

The ring had been selected from his grandfather's pirate horde. Which had not been buried in the bayou, despite what the legends said. The entirety of that treasure had been divided amongst the remaining family. Remy's share resided in a safety deposit box at the Nocturne Falls branch of the Georgia Federal Credit Union.

Not surprisingly, his love had bolted like the devil'd been chasing her. He often found himself wondering what had happened to her. Probably married with kids by now. Probably never thought about him.

And why should she? He was the one who'd made a mess of things. She'd probably sold the ring, too. He didn't mind. Especially if the money had helped her in some way.

With a sigh, he tossed the crumpled bag into a trash bin, shoved his hands into his pockets and headed for the nearest blood bank. He could get blood at the hotel, but the prices were nearly double what the bank charged.

Just because he had a healthy bank account didn't

mean he was going to spend it unwisely. He preferred to live on the salary his job with the sheriff's department paid and leave his reserves untouched. So the blood bank it was.

What he needed was a full belly and a good sleep. He had an eight-hour drive home tomorrow night, which couldn't be done comfortably in one shift, since there were just barely enough hours of darkness. He didn't like to cut things too close, not when something unforeseen like a traffic accident or car trouble might happen.

That meant spending the day in a cheap motel along the way. Not his favorite thing to do, but it couldn't be helped.

Soon enough, he'd be home and back at work, thoughts of old friends and former flames tucked away in his memory banks, where they belonged.

Louisiana Supreme Court Associate Justice Leonie Moreau turned on the lights in her chambers. The warm glow of the brass chandelier over her desk filled the space. The walnut desk and paneling gleamed, and the light reflected off the windows.

It was early. Her daughter probably wasn't even up yet, as it was still nearly dark outside, but Leonie liked to get a good start on the day. Court wasn't for another two hours, so she'd review the cases on today's docket, go over any outstanding requests, check in with her clerks, and answer any mail or email that awaited her.

There was always plenty of both.

A stack of mail sat on her desk, delivered by one of her clerks after she'd left yesterday. She paused by the door. Would there be another letter?

The two that had already come could be ignored, for the most part. But a third? Three had to be taken seriously. That was the number of bodies it took for a murderer to be classified as a serial killer.

Death threats were nothing new. Judges got them. That was part and parcel of the job. At least if you were doing it right. It wasn't her responsibility to make people happy, just to dispense justice, something she took very seriously.

No matter the outcome of a trial, someone was going to get bunched up over it.

She carried her travel mug of coffee to her desk and sat. Putting things off was pointless, no matter what the thing was. She turned on her computer, then shuffled through the stack of mail, looking for the one particular envelope she hoped she wouldn't find.

It was second to the last item in the pile. Cheap ivory paper, the computer-printed address label smudged from its travel to her office, and yet there was no stamp, no postmark, so it hadn't come via standard routes.

That was worrying, obviously. She'd pondered this since receiving the first letter the same way.

Someone was getting these letters to her without using the United States Postal Service. Which meant ... what? They worked in the court system? Had access to someone who worked in the court system?

The mail room was a big place. It could be someone there. But it could also be someone who worked on the janitorial staff. Maybe one of them had been paid to drop the letter off in her office.

It couldn't be one of her clerks. She refused to believe that. They were good, trustworthy people, and all had worked for her long enough that she felt she knew their characters. Each one had been through intensive background checks, as well.

Besides that, none of them had any reason to threaten

her or her daughter's life. None she could think of, anyway. And Leonie had done nothing *but* think since receiving the first letter last week.

She turned the envelope in her hands. She should take these letters to the police, but the letters had said specifically not to or there would be consequences. She wasn't a woman who was easily scared off. She was an Associate Justice of the Louisiana Supreme Court. If she'd been timid in any area of her life, she'd never have made it this far.

But it wasn't herself she was concerned about. It was her daughter, Ephelia. Ephie was a sweet young woman. She did charity work and minded her own business. She'd never done a thing in her life to deserve this kind of vitriol.

Whoever was behind these letters sounded serious. And Leonie had a pretty good idea who that was. Which meant that as much as she'd like to keep ignoring them, she couldn't.

What Leonie needed was a way to protect her daughter first. Then she could go to the police. But Leonie didn't know quite how to protect her child. She couldn't take time off. It just wasn't feasible with the current docket.

She'd thought about sending Ephie to her grandmother's in Metairie for some plausible reason, but that would only put Leonie's mother in danger as well. And if they could get to Ephie in New Orleans, they could get to her in Metairie.

Leonie sipped her coffee, not ready to open the envelope and see what new threat had been leveled against her and her daughter. The hot chicory coffee fortified her. She used the letter opener from the top drawer of her desk to slit the envelope and dump the contents onto her desk.

Just like before, a sheet of plain white paper, triple-folded. The computer-printed words visible through the paper but not readable.

She unfolded the paper.

Time is ticking. Soon it will be too late. Support Abraham Turner's parole at his next hearing or what you value most will be taken from you.

Leonie drew in a ragged breath. If that wasn't a direct threat, she didn't know what else to think. Ephie was clearly in danger. But there was no way Leonie would support the man's parole. He was a criminal and a killer. She'd helped put him away. Whoever was sending these letters obviously thought they could convince her to help, but they were wrong.

Was there a chance it was Turner himself? He was currently serving a lengthy sentence for manslaughter. Appeal after appeal had been filed on his behalf, but those things took time, and if there was any justice, they would all be struck down.

In the meantime, he was up for parole. Ridiculous, in Leonie's mind.

But Turner was a powerful figure steeped in the dark aura of voodoo. At six-four and nearly three hundred pounds, his stature had little to do with why most people feared him. The Haitian immigrant was a self-proclaimed voodoo priest. He'd used that to build his reputation.

That and a crew of degenerate associates who would do whatever he told them to. Regardless of whether or not he was in prison. But prison was definitely where he belonged. If he were freed ...

She shook her head, not wanting to think about that.

Despite his incarceration, he still had plenty of friends on the outside, and his name carried weight with a great deal of people. If he wasn't doing this directly, he was certainly behind it.

Leonie felt confident of that.

A soft knock came through the heavy wood office door.

She tucked the envelope and letter under her blotter and glanced at the time. "Come in, Mervin."

Mervin Cross, her senior clerk, entered. "Morning, your honor."

"Morning, Mervin."

He had a white cardboard envelope in his hands. It bore the insignia of an overnight delivery service. He brought it to her and held it out. "This just arrived for you by special messenger."

She took it from him. "Thank you."

"Fleur's about to make the breakfast run. Your usual?"

"Yes, please," Leonie said. She wasn't especially hungry at the moment, but she didn't want the slightest hint that something might be wrong or out of sorts. The egg and cheese croissant sandwich could sit in the refrigerator. The café au lait she would drink.

"Very good. I'll be back when it's here."

"Thanks." As soon as the door was shut, she pulled the strip at the top of the envelope to open it. A single sheet of paper was inside, a photocopy of a registration book. Scrawled in black ink beneath the photocopy were three words.

Hotel Du Palais

She read the names listed on the registration, which was the reason she'd been sent this information. One immediately popped out.

Remy Lafitte was not the name she'd been looking for, not the vampire she'd been dreading to find, but he might be exactly the vampire she needed. She made a quick phone call to confirm he was still in town.

He was.

Now all she had to do was wait for sundown, then try to convince him to help. It wouldn't be easy. They had no love for one another.

But they did share a love for someone else. Ephie. Leonie just hoped Remy still had those feelings for her daughter. Otherwise, she wasn't sure what she'd do.

With her mass of curly hair wound up on top of her head, Ephie Moreau logged into her client's website and began working on the updates they'd requested. She had three websites to update today, and once that was done, she would immediately return to the new website she was building.

She tugged at her T-shirt. It was a little smaller than she would have liked and not one of her favorites, but she needed to do laundry.

There was no real timetable for completion on the new website, as it was a volunteer project she was doing for one of the local cat rescues. Even so, she felt an internal pressure to finish it and have it up and running as soon as possible.

The sooner that could happen, the sooner more cats could find their forever homes. She was designing the site so that each available cat could have their picture and bio posted. Anyone interested would be able to click through to an information form and even set an appointment to come visit the cat in question. She thought that would help tremendously.

People shopped for everything online. Why not let them shop for a pet that way, too?

Made sense to her. Adoption was the way to go.

Although that wasn't how she'd ended up with her cat. Jean-Luc Beauvoir had chosen her. Sometimes it happened like that.

Well, maybe not for most people. But then, most people probably didn't spend as much time in cemeteries as she did. And even if they did, they had probably never befriended an animal like Jean-Luc Beauvoir.

Jean-Luc was indeed a very special creature.

She frowned as she scanned the apartment for him. Where was he? Usually by now he was on her desk, trying to bat a pen off or something. She had started her day a little earlier than usual. Maybe he was still curled up on the bed. "Jean-Luc? *Bebe*, where are you?"

A little trilling meow answered her, and Jean-Luc came trotting sleepy-eyed out of the bedroom.

Ephie grinned. "There you are, my love."

He jumped up onto her desk, which was actually a door blank supported by two sawhorses painted black. Not fancy but cheap and spacious. He landed on her computer, but it didn't matter. Jean-Luc was as light as a feather.

Lighter, probably. In fact, she wasn't sure he truly weighed a thing. After all, he was a ghost.

He had form and shape but no substance, unless he materialized. He seemed to be able to control that, enough that he could bump his head against her hand or leg and she could feel it. Some nights, he'd curl up on her pillow or tuck against her back, his weight and presence as real as any other creature.

But he could walk through walls when he wanted to. When she showered, he often stuck his head right through the curtain to meow at her.

The first time he'd done that, she'd nearly had a heart attack.

It was all for attention, because unlike any living animal, he didn't require food or water. He had no need for a litter box, either.

So while he could appear solid at will, at the moment, he was in his usual state of translucency. Her little ghost cat. She loved him regardless of his quirks. Maybe even a little more because of them.

He was genuinely the ideal animal companion.

"Pets?"

He materialized, his way of saying yes.

She scratched under his chin. He stretched toward her, his head going up as his eyes closed. A low, grumbly purr emanated out of him. She leaned forward and kissed his head. He was so soft. Sometimes, it made her sad that he was just a ghost. She would have loved to have found him sooner.

It made her sad to think about what had caused him to become a ghost, too. But at least he'd be with her forever. "I love you, *bebe*."

She scratched him a little more. "Now, I have to get back to work. Sorry, *mon petit bout*." Her grandmother had called her that when she was little. Now Ephie used it for Jean-Luc when he was being particularly cute. Which was pretty much always.

He jumped down and went to lie down in a ray of sun coming through the living room windows. She wouldn't have thought a ghost could feel heat or cold, but he definitely liked lying in the sun, so he must be able to feel those things.

Unless that was just a habit from his previous life?

She shrugged, sipped her coffee, which was rapidly growing cold, and went back to work. She turned on some working tunes, just soft instrumental beats meant to help improve focus and productivity.

One by one, she knocked out the changes her client had asked for, all while tracking her billable hours. As soon as they were done, she sent him a note to have a look and approve the work or let her know if there were any other changes.

Once that email was sent, she prepped an invoice, then went to work on the next client's changes.

She kept at it, stopping for more coffee and a bathroom break, but by lunch, she'd sent the first invoice. One more approval and she'd send the next one. Her last client had requested not only updates but a new page for a product they were about to launch.

She built a preliminary page, sent the client an email to have them look at it, then went to get herself some lunch. Nothing much. Soup and half a sandwich made with what little remained of the chicken salad she'd bought from the deli down the street.

First, though, she put a load of laundry into her stack unit and got that going. Otherwise, she'd be scraping the bottom of the closet for something to wear tomorrow.

Washer started, she got a can of soup out of the cabinet and fetched the can opener from a nearby drawer.

Hopefully, she'd soon be able to work on the rescue's website. The three paying jobs would take care of her bills. She wasn't rich, but she did all right. She'd bought this apartment two years ago with a little help from her mom on the down payment, which she'd been paying off ever since.

She owned her car, although it was nothing spectacular. Her bills were always paid on time, and with careful planning, she managed to put a little away each month. There was no man in her life, but she didn't need one, either.

Building the rescue's site was her way of giving back. And honoring Jean-Luc's life.

She emptied the can of vegetable soup into a big bowl with a handle, added a can of water, and stirred. Then she cupped the pottery bowl in her hands and used her unique skills to bring it to temperature. In seconds, it started to boil.

Okay, that was a little *too* hot. Her gifts were tricky things. Difficult to control. Sometimes stronger than she wanted them to be, sometimes much weaker. It was easier just to use them for simple things that didn't matter too much. The idea that she might accidentally hurt someone was enough to quell her desire to practice.

Her grandmother claimed practice would help, but Ephie didn't want to risk it. Besides, she worked constantly. Any free time was spent decompressing in front of the television or going out for walks with Jean-Luc. He loved a good walk. Mostly he loved to roll in the grass or chase a squirrel.

She left the soup to cool down a bit and made her sandwich. Jean-Luc wound around her legs, drawn by the smell of food, no doubt.

He couldn't eat any, but he definitely liked to smell it.

She took her food back to her desk to eat. Jean-Luc joined her, curling up on an empty spot next to her laptop. She checked email to see if her clients had responded. The second one had, giving her the thumbs-up that all was well and he was happy.

She thanked him, then sent that invoice.

There was another email in her inbox to deal with. She clicked on it and found it was from a prospective client. A restaurant in the French Quarter looking to revamp their image to go along with the renovation they were doing with the building and their general direction. They were even changing the restaurant's name.

She loved the idea of a fresh start and was always happy to take on new business. She sent them a note saying she was interested and to see when they could meet. She preferred an in-person meeting at the beginning.

It helped her clients to see her as a real person, not just someone behind a keyboard. It also helped her get a sense of what the business was like. That went a long way toward creating a website that accurately depicted the business. Every place had its own vibe. Cool, hip, trendy, classy, retro—whatever the case, experiencing it firsthand always made a difference.

With all pressing correspondence out of the way, she pulled up the file for the rescue's website and got to work. Doing this kind of thing meant a lot to her. She loved animals, and she loved helping.

People were all right, but there were so many strange ones out there. Living in New Orleans didn't help that, because it was full of odd people, but the city was her home, and, for the most part, it was nice.

She just preferred her own company. And Jean-Luc's, of course.

In a way, she supposed she was the perfect representation of the crazy cat lady. She might only have one, but he was a ghost and she was a witch, so how much crazier could that be?

She preferred to think of Jean-Luc as her familiar. He'd never helped with any of her magic, which would have been nice, but he'd never hindered it, either, and the title felt like a promotion from pet. Not that she'd ever introduced him to anyone other than her mother, and her mother, bless her heart, couldn't see Jean-Luc no matter how hard she tried.

To be honest, she wasn't sure her mother even believed Jean-Luc was real.

But that was all right. He was allowed to show himself or not to whomever he liked. His prerogative. And just another one of his selective abilities, Ephie figured.

She glanced at him. Now deep in sleep, he was barely visible. Sometimes, he disappeared entirely, but she could usually find him by listening for the quiet little snores he made. He was making them now. Dreaming of his former life maybe?

"Such a sweet boy," she whispered.

His whiskers twitched.

With a smile, she typed away, building the pages necessary to make the new website everything it needed to be. And something she could be proud of, too.

Because if she wasn't helping make the world a better place, then what was the point?

Remy reluctantly sat up and yawned. He scratched his scalp. Without checking the time, he could feel that the sun would be fully set in about an hour. More than enough time to pack, take a nice hot shower, and check out. He wasn't looking forward to the drive ahead, but it would be good to get home.

As much as he considered New Orleans his hometown, he had a special affection for Nocturne Falls. At least there, he could be himself. No need to worry who might have seen him when vampire law banned him from returning to New Orleans for more than a few decades. He stretched, releasing the last bonds of sleep from his muscles.

And there was something to be said for sleeping in one's own bed surrounded by the comforts of home. No hotel could ever take the place of his own house, no matter how fancy it was or how good the room service.

He got up, pulled together a clean outfit for the evening ahead, and headed for the bathroom. A hot shower was just what he needed.

He was about to crank on the water when someone knocked on his door.

Frowning, he pulled on a robe and went to see who

it was. He hadn't ordered room service. Maybe they were checking to see if he was leaving today. He'd left things a little open-ended. But the front desk could have called.

He glanced through the peephole, but all he could see was the back of a woman in a dark suit. Housekeeping? He wasn't sure.

He opened the door.

The woman turned. His mouth fell open. Not housekeeping. Not remotely. Instead, he was looking at a woman he never thought he'd see again. The mother of the only woman he'd ever loved. "Leonie."

She nodded. "Remy Lafitte. I didn't think you'd be back in this town again until I was a very old woman. If at all."

He nodded. "I know. But circumstances dictated otherwise. I'm leaving within the hour if that's what you're worried—"

"On the contrary." She tipped her head toward the room behind him. "May I come in? What I need to discuss with you is better done in private." She glanced down the hall like she was checking to see if anyone was watching.

Was she worried about being seen with him? Odd behavior for a woman who'd clearly sought him out.

He was more than a little intrigued. What in the stars could the mother of his ex-girlfriend want from him? It had been years since he'd been in Ephie's life. Since he'd seen her. He stepped back and let Leonie through, closing the door behind her. "You look well. The years have been kind to you."

"You're the best kind of liar." She smiled as she helped herself to a seat at the small table near the windows, still covered with blackout curtains. "And I know you mean well, so I don't mind. You look exactly as I remember you. No surprise there, I suppose."

He sat on the end of the bed, uneasy with her presence and unable to imagine why she was here. "It's the blessing and the curse of my kind."

"Said like a true vampire, but then, that's what you are. Always will be." She smiled at him. She'd never liked him, so the smile wasn't something he was used to seeing. It disappeared quickly. "I know we've never been on the best footing, but I need your help. I wouldn't be here otherwise."

Of that, he had no doubt. "You need *my* help?" He didn't even know how she'd found him, except she was very well-connected.

Worry dimmed her eyes. "Yes. Not for myself. For Ephie."

Now he was listening. "What's going on?"

Leonie held his gaze. "Seventeen years ago, when I was still a lower court judge, I put a man, Abraham Turner, away for manslaughter. It was quite an achievement. He was a real thug, one the police had been trying to nail for some time. He was involved in all sorts of criminal activity. Gambling, prostitution, drugs—you name it."

"A gangster."

"Yes." She dug into her purse. "He's resurfaced in my life by way of these." She pulled three envelopes out and laid them on the table. "All delivered directly to my office without being postmarked."

"Hand-delivered to your chambers?"

"Yes."

He understood how that would worry her. He took the other chair at the table and gestured to the envelopes. "May I?"

"Please."

He read through them one by one. "These are threats, plain and simple, against you and Ephie. Have you gone to the cops?"

"You just read them. Going to the cops will only make things worse."

"You don't know that."

She glared at him. "It's not a chance I'm willing to take."

"Have you told Ephie?"

Leonie gave him a sharp glance. "No. She wouldn't react well to that. It would put her into a panic. She's a little fragile. I need to handle this discreetly. That's where you come in."

He sat back, trying to figure out how she thought he could help. He didn't remember Ephie as fragile. Shy, definitely, but not fragile. Maybe she'd changed since he'd last seen her. "How do I figure into this?"

"I need you to get Ephie out of town without her knowing what's going on."

He laughed, but there was no humor in it. "Ephie isn't going to leave with me. She doesn't want anything to do with me. And you never liked me when we were dating."

"You're a two-hundred-and-some-years-old vampire. She was *nineteen*."

Her implications upset him. "She told me she was twenty-two when we first met, and I believed her. She was mature and sensible and intelligent. And I was turned when I was twenty-nine. Despite the years I've lived, that's about the age I still feel." It was hard to explain to a human how it felt to know you were never going to get any older. How the world around you could change so much while you stayed the same. They never understood, and they rarely had sympathy. Leonie would be no different.

Leonie snorted like his explanation was ludicrous.

He stared at her, feeling a little vindicated that he'd known how she'd react. "Do you feel your age?"

"Right now? Yes. But that's not what I came here to discuss."

He quelled his anger. "I understand you need help, but I'm surprised you thought I could do anything." He got to his feet and walked away a few steps, needing some distance. "You have to go to the police."

"I *can't*. Don't you understand? Whether it's Turner doing this directly or one of his goons, he still has connections on the outside. He says jump, and his crew asks how high. One whiff of police involvement and Ephie will be in the crosshairs. Those letters threaten as much. I can only imagine what they'd do to her."

She looked away for a moment. Her voice seemed thinner when she spoke again. "What would you do if this was your child?"

"I would protect that child myself." He planted his hands on his hips. "But Ephie isn't a child. She's a grown woman who deserves to know she's in danger."

Leonie grabbed her purse and stood up. "I thought you'd care. I thought your past with Ephie meant something. Obviously, I was wrong."

He rolled his eyes. "I do care about her." More than Leonie would ever know. "But you're going about this all wrong."

She gripped her purse against her body like it was a source of strength. "You really think you know better than me? I don't know what you remember of Ephie, but she's not a strong person. She keeps to herself. Works from home, which suits her. The outside world intimidates her. She does best when things are peaceful and calm. She's been like that since school."

What he remembered was Ephie being scared of him as soon as he'd offered to give her the kiss of immortality. Had that fear morphed into something greater? Something that had colored her entire view of life? A sense of guilt crept over him. Along with a sudden swell of responsibility. "But she's got powers of her own. That ought to give her some confidence. She's got a way to protect herself."

Leonie sighed. "Her gifts are simple at best, nothing like her grandmother's power, which is what they should have been. It skips a generation, as you know, leaving me with only the occasional faint hint of foresight and a good idea of when the next rain is coming. Ephie should have been a powerful witch. She isn't. I believe that's part of what bothers her so much. The weight of expectations."

She glanced toward the door. "She's tried to get better, but nothing has worked." Leonie's mouth bent in a sad smile. "She even told me she has a familiar now."

"That's good, isn't it? From what I understand, a familiar can really help a witch focus their powers."

"It's true," Leonie said. "But for that to happen, the familiar would have to be real. Ephie's got herself a *ghost* cat." She shook her head in obvious pity. "I couldn't lie to her and pretend to see it, but she explained it away by saying the cat only shows himself to certain people. I think the cat might just be a defense mechanism."

Remy didn't like any of what he was hearing. His memory of Ephie was of a strong, beautiful woman. Yes, she'd struggled with her gifts, but they'd been brand-new when he'd met her. And, yes, his offer had sent her running. As forcefully as he'd come on, it would have been more surprising if she'd said yes.

Now, however, it seemed Ephie had let her fears get the best of her. That was sad. He had to do something. If she became the victim of this gangster, Abraham Turner, Remy would blame himself until the day he died.

Which would, undoubtedly, be many, *many* years from now. That was a long time to live with a guilty conscience. He groaned softly, his frustrations with himself as much as the woman before him. "So you're asking me, the vampire you wanted to have nothing to do with your daughter, to now come to her aid."

Leonie looked like she'd just swallowed something bitter. "I am."

"If I do this, I do it with your approval? With your trust?"

She hesitated, her jaw muscles working. Finally, she spat out, "Yes."

"What about her husband and her family?" He realized Leonie hadn't mentioned either, but he needed to know exactly what he was getting into.

"She has no husband, no boyfriend, and outside of her grandmother and myself, no other family."

That was interesting. But this was still a terrible idea. He could not believe he was agreeing to this. What else could he do? This was Ephie they were talking about. Ephie who was in danger. *His* Ephie.

He couldn't walk away from her a second time. "How is this supposed to work?"

Ephie didn't love her mother's last-minute invite, but there was no way to graciously turn it down. When Justice Leonie Moreau summoned you, you came. It helped that shrimp and grits were on the menu.

Her mother's cook, Alphonso, made the best shrimp and grits this side of Mr. B's Bistro. Definitely a better offer than the microwave meal Ephie had been planning.

She picked an outfit she knew her mother would approve of: slim black pants and a trim V-neck knit tank top in deep teal. She added the diamond *E* pendant her mother had given her for a birthday some years ago, thin gold hoops, and her most prized possession, an antique diamond and sapphire pansy ring.

Her mother thought Ephie had picked it up at an estate sale for a song. Ephie couldn't tell her where it had really come from or how dear it was to her. Her mother had never cared for vampires. Chief among them was the one Ephie had fallen for in college.

She'd only met him because her mother had insisted she take an elective that had nothing to do with computers.

Ephie stared at the ring. What had ever happened to him? She'd reacted poorly to his proposal. It had been so sudden and so unexpected, she'd been caught off guard. In a big way. She'd made a hasty excuse and gone straight home.

She couldn't marry him. And she couldn't even think about becoming a vampire. Her mother would have died from the very suggestion.

But Ephie had cared about him a great deal. Truthfully, she'd thought of him as her first love. Still did. That night, after she'd gone home and had a long think, she'd promised herself that she would find him the next evening and tell him exactly how she felt.

That never happened. She'd never been able to find him. In fact, after that night, he'd disappeared, at least from her life.

She had looked. All over campus and in the French Quarter at the places vampires were known to frequent. Nothing. Not a hint of his location. It was as if he'd disappeared into thin air. Maybe he had. Vampires were creatures about which she knew less than she should.

Her mother's doing. Not exactly her fault but definitely her influence. Vampires were not a subject for discussion at any time. Her mother's dislike for them bordered on phobic.

Ephie shrugged. She felt the same way about spiders. Terrifying leggy nightmares.

Standing in front of the bathroom mirror, she loosed her hair from the messy bun she'd put it in earlier and revived the mass of curls with a spritz of water and some scrunching. She was due for a trim. Her hair hung past her shoulders and was nearly just as wide. She ran her fingers under the tap water and corkscrewed a few curls at her temples to frame her face.

She did her makeup with a light hand. Too much and her mother would give her the eye. Too little and her mother would say she looked tired.

Being the only child of a prominent woman was tough at times. Ephie loved her mother very much and was inordinately proud of her, but they had different ideas of success. And that was just fine with Ephie.

Not as fine with her mother, but maybe someday her mother would get that what Ephie wanted was a more laid-back kind of life. One not nearly as public but still devoted to helping others. Just in a different way than her mother.

She took a final look at herself, determined it was as good as it was going to get, and went to the bedroom. She put the essentials in a small purse. She wouldn't need much. She made her way to the living room to say goodbye to Jean-Luc.

His translucent form was balanced precariously on the curtain rod, seemingly asleep. Not something any creature but a ghost cat could accomplish. "Jean-Luc *bebe*, I have to go. I'll be home as soon as I can, I promise."

He stretched one paw out in response.

She went up on her tiptoes, reaching to touch it. Her fingertips passed through his paw, and he pulled it back. She blew him a kiss. "See you later."

The drive into the Garden District wasn't bad. Traffic

was light.

Her mother lived in one of the smaller houses. It was still a beautiful place. And not really that small. The house had been divided into two residences well before her mother had purchased it. Both sides had been modestly restored prior to her mother's ownership.

As soon as the contract was signed, her mother had remodeled the side she planned to live in. She went for a much more luxurious style, bringing the home back to its original glory with marble floors and thick crown molding and dark wood polished to a glassy sheen.

The other side she left as it was, and she continued to rent it out.

Ephie pulled into the driveway, her mother's black Mercedes parked under the porte cochere at the side of the house that led to the carriage house. At the time her mother had taken ownership, it had been an apartment, but her mother had turned it into a combination storage space and workout studio.

Ephie parked and went to the front door. As usual when her mother knew she was coming, the door was unlocked. Ephie walked in. The savory aromas of the meal they were soon to eat greeted her, making her mouth water. "Mom? It's me."

"In the sitting room, sweetheart," her mother called out.

Ephie went straight back. Her mother was at the bar cart, making herself a gin and tonic.

Leonie smiled at her. "You look lovely."

"Thanks. So do you." Her mother was in a navy pinstriped suit with a pale blue silk blouse and vintage Chanel earrings. Probably what she'd worn to the office. Ephie set her purse on the couch. "How was your day?"

"Another day of justice done, in the books." Her mother lifted the glass in her hand. "Would you like one?"

"No, I'm all right. I have to drive." Ephie wasn't much of a drinker. There was enough of that in this town, and the results were often reason enough not to drink. She sat by her purse. "Thanks for the invite. What's the occasion?"

"Occasion?" Leonie frowned and moved to the couch as well, where she took a seat at the other end. "Can't I just have my daughter over for dinner? I hardly see you anymore."

They'd seen each other less than a week ago, but Ephie wasn't going to argue. "Well, thanks for the invite. I do enjoy Alphonso's shrimp and grits."

"Best in town," her mother said brightly before taking a sip of her drink. "Do you want anything to drink? Water? Juice? Coffee?"

"Water's fine, but I can wait until we eat. How's work been? Anything new and interesting?"

"Nothing I can talk about, but you know how it is. Always busy. Always another case waiting."

Ephie nodded. Her mother was *always* busy. When she wasn't at work, she was going to some kind of function. Charity benefits, fundraisers, award ceremonies, social events. It was hard to keep up. But then, New Orleans was a very busy town, and her mother was much in demand.

Just thinking about it made Ephie want to go home and get into bed.

Her mother set her glass down on the mahogany and marble coffee table. She seemed unsettled. Not herself somehow. Like she was waiting on something. "How about you? Have you been busy?"

"Very. Just talked to a potential client today. A restaurant in the Quarter. Used to be Tom's Grill but now they're going by Cardinal?" Her mother shook her head. "Anyway, they want to talk to me about giving them a brand-new website. I'm looking forward to working with them. Besides that, it's just been the usual stuff. Updates on existing websites and the pro bono work I do."

"That's wonderful, honey. It's great of you to do that."

Her mother had never actually said that before. Something was definitely up. "Thanks. I like helping."

Leonie studied her flawless manicure. "Listen, I ran into an old friend of yours and invited him for dinner. I hope you don't mind."

Ephie frowned. "Who?" She couldn't think of anyone. No one her mother would invite, anyway. That had to be what this was all about. Was her mother trying to set her up with a guy? Wouldn't be the first time.

"Hello, Ephie."

She turned to see where the voice had come from, and all the breath left her body. A shiver ran through her, raising goosebumps on her skin. She shook her head, her words barely audible. "How ... It can't be."

Looking exactly like he had the last time she'd seen him, Remy Lafitte stood at the entrance to the sitting room in jeans, a T-shirt, and a black leather jacket. An ache she couldn't name filled her chest.

Without realizing she'd moved, she found herself on her feet. "W-what are you doing here?"

His dark brows lifted slightly. "Hello to you, too."

"Sorry, I just—"

"It's all right." He stayed where he was. Like he wasn't sure coming closer was a good idea. "Professor Boudreaux isn't well. He's in hospice, actually. I wanted to see him one last time."

She nodded. "That was ... nice of you. I didn't know he was sick. I always liked him."

"Me, too," Remy said. His gaze lingered on her face a moment longer before taking in the rest of her. "You look ... unbelievable. How have you been?"

"I've been all right. You?" Had he always been that handsome? He hadn't aged, but somehow, he'd changed. He seemed more ... *more*.

"Same, yeah."

"Did you move back? No, you said you were just visiting the professor. Sorry." Her mind was three steps ahead of her mouth. Or maybe it was behind. She couldn't think straight. The very sight of him had befuddled her. She'd never expected to see him again. Certainly not in her mother's house, of all places.

Remy smiled, and her heart broke into little pieces. His smile had always done that to her. "It's really good to see you."

"You, too." Was it, though? She thought she'd broken his heart. He'd broken hers. Why was he here? In her mother's house? There was no way her mother was behind this. Leonie had no love for *any* vampire, even less for this one standing a few feet away from her.

Ephie turned. Her mother was still sitting on the couch. Ephie pinned her mother with a hard stare. "What's going on?"

Leonie shrugged like nothing unusual had occurred. "I found out Remy was in town, and I thought you two might like to catch up."

Maybe Remy had glamoured Leonie into doing this. Ephie was pretty sure vampires could do that. Some vampires anyway. She took a breath and tried to get ahold of what was actually happening, but she couldn't. None of this made sense.

Alphonso appeared at the side door. "Dinner is ready."

Leonie stood and smiled, but her eyes held something darker. "Remy, if you could just give us a moment? There's something I need to speak to Ephie about. Alone."

Remy nodded, glanced at Ephie, then excused himself.

Ephie turned toward her mother, eagerly awaiting an explanation. "Go ahead. I'm listening."

There was no denying the spark between her daughter and the vampire. For once in her life, Leonie was all right with that. It served her purpose. "Ephie, I know what you must be thinking—"

Ephie let out a short little laugh. "I really don't think you do. How is he here? How did you just *happen* to run into him?"

Leonie glanced toward the door, but Remy was gone, no doubt in the dining room already. She lowered her voice anyway. "I have someone who notifies me whenever a new, non-local vampire registers at one of the sanctioned blood banks."

Ephie frowned. "Why?"

Leonie didn't really want to discuss that. She came up with a suitable answer that wasn't a complete lie. "Because I've asked them to. When I saw his name, it got me thinking. I went to see him, and we talked. When he told me he'd come to see the professor, I realized I might have been wrong about him. He's not such a bad guy."

Ephie's eyes narrowed. She wasn't buying this. Yet. Leonie had worried about that, but she really needed her to. "Mom, you hate vampires."

"No, I don't." Except she did.

"Yes, you do. What's really going on?"

Leonie sighed as though her daughter's lack of understanding was hurting her feelings. "I am trying to do something nice for you. I thought you cared about this man and that by inviting him here this evening, you two could get reacquainted and see what happens next. It's not as if you're involved with anyone else. Are you telling me you no longer have feelings for him?"

Ephie edged closer. "Mom, he's a vampire. No matter how softly you speak, he can hear you. He can hear this entire conversation. What I feel is my business. What you did tonight is so ... not you. In my whole life, no man has ever been good enough or *right* for me. Even the ones you've introduced me to. Now, all of a sudden, you've changed your mind?"

Leonie wasn't selling this, and she wasn't sure how to make her daughter believe her. She smiled. "Yes, I have. Am I not allowed to do that? There are far worse people out there you could be involved with. But you aren't. I don't like that you're alone, sweetheart. That you're not happy."

"I am very happy, thank you all the same."

Leonie took a breath, pausing for effect. Then she sighed like she was giving up. "I'm sorry. I clearly made a mistake." She picked up her drink. "I'll ask him to leave."

"Mom, no—"

Leonie raised her brows. "You're all right with him staying?"

"I don't know how I feel about it, but it would be rude

to ask him to leave now. Let's just get through dinner, all right?"

Leonie nodded solemnly. "All right." She took her daughter's hand. "Do you forgive me?"

Ephie made a face. "It's fine. There's nothing to forgive. Which isn't to say that I'm okay with this. I honestly don't know how I feel about it. But I guess your heart was in the right place."

"Where you're concerned? Always." Leonie held on to her. "You know I only want the best things in life for you. You deserve to be loved by someone who's going to treat you like a queen. If Remy's not that someone, so be it. I won't say another word about who you spend time with ever again."

One corner of Ephie's mouth quirked up. "If only that were true, but I don't think either one of us believes that."

"Ephelia." Leonie frowned, taking her hand away from her daughter and placing it on her own chest like Ephie's words had wounded her.

Ephie shook her head. "You know I'm right. Come on, let's go eat. I'm hungry, and we're keeping your guest waiting."

They walked to the dining room together. Leonie felt some relief, but she wasn't convinced Ephie would go along with this plan. Worse still, the real burden now lay on Remy. What had she been thinking to entrust her daughter's well-being to such a creature? How desperate had she become to believe a vampire might actually be the answer?

Perhaps she should come clean to Ephie. Tell her about the letters and the threats. But Leonie worried that Ephie wouldn't be able to deal with it. That she'd retreat further into the safe little world she'd made for herself. That there would be lasting effects.

Leonie didn't want that. She'd meant what she said to Ephie. She truly did want her to be happy and in love with a wonderful man. Not Remy, of course. He was just a means to an end.

But if Ephie knew that a real threat existed to her personal safety, she would shut herself off from the outside world. At least that's what Leonie believed.

After Remy had disappeared from Ephie's life, Ephie had closed down. Neither Leonie nor her grandmother had been able to break her out of the funk she'd been in.

Dealing with a breakup was hard, Leonie knew that. Her own heart bore the scars of love lost. But what Ephie had done was let it change her.

Another incident, another trauma, and Ephie might become a complete recluse. Surely, this *ghost* cat was proof that she was already edging toward that.

Leonie didn't want to be callous, but having a child who was so sensitive was difficult at times. Leonie would have loved to bring Ephie along with her to all the events she attended. There were so many handsome, single men there. Men with purpose and drive. Men who would give Ephie the kind of life she deserved.

The kind of life Leonie had always wanted but had to

make for herself. She didn't want Ephie to face those same struggles.

They walked into the dining room. The lights were dimmed to enhance the mood. Remy stood near the windows, hands clasped behind his back, staring out.

He turned as they entered, his smile and gaze focused on Ephie. "I was beginning to think I'd be eating alone."

Leonie made herself smile like she wasn't bothered by this insolent vampire. She'd already allowed him to enter her home, but only after he'd assured her the invitations had to be granted on a per-vampire basis. Granting him access did not mean any other vampire would be able to enter at will.

She prayed that was true. "I'm sorry we kept you waiting. I'll let Alphonso know we're ready to eat."

She slipped away to the kitchen, leaving her daughter alone with Remy. Hopefully, he'd find a way to convince her to leave with him. That was his part of this plan.

Once in the kitchen, she put a hand on the counter and took a breath, eyes closed. This had to work. She just needed Ephie out of town, then she'd contact the police commissioner. He was an old, dear friend. He would know what she needed to do. And he could look into these threats as well.

"You all right, Ms. Moreau?"

She opened her eyes and nodded. "Just a lot on my mind, Alphonso. I only came in to let you know we're ready for you to serve."

"I'll plate up and be right out."

"Thank you." He was a good man and a talented chef. He only worked for her during the week and only made her dinner. Feeding herself was too much for her to think about after a long day of court.

The minute he'd retired from Brennan's, she'd made him a generous offer. He'd refused once, so she'd increased the offer slightly. He'd agreed after that. She'd have gone higher still, though. She liked getting what she wanted.

She returned to the dining room. Remy and Ephie were standing close, talking softly, their body language open, although Remy looked more relaxed than Ephie did. But then, he had nothing to lose in this.

Unlike Leonie. She fixed a smile on her face once again. "Alphonso will be right out. We should take our seats." She gestured to the head of the table. "Remy, please."

She wanted him close to her but close to Ephie, too.

He pulled Ephie's chair out for her. A good start, Leonie thought. But it was going to take more than manners to get Ephie to leave New Orleans. It might take a genuine miracle. Or magic. What kind of magic did Remy have?

She honestly wasn't sure, but she knew vampires could mesmerize humans into doing their bidding. Would that work on a woman with powers? She hated the idea of him using his abilities on her daughter that way, but needs must.

If Remy couldn't pull this off, Leonie had no use for

him. In fact, she might just report him to the vampire council. They both knew he wasn't supposed to be here. Not for at least another decade or two.

Maybe she should remind him of that.

She sipped her gin and tonic. Or maybe she'd just let him find out the hard way.

Ephie didn't believe for a moment that all her mother wanted was for her to be happy. Not with Remy, anyway. It was far more likely that Remy had come here looking for Ephie, and her mother had decided to try some reverse psychology by inviting him in and then pretending she was fine with the two of them getting back into each other's lives.

It was just like Leonie to try something like that. Just like her to think she could control the outcome by taking charge of the situation and making it seem like her idea.

Ephie knew all of her mother's games. She'd been subjected to them for nearly thirty-two years now. If that didn't make her an expert, nothing would.

Maybe she was wrong. Maybe she had no clue what was actually going on, but Remy was here, Alphonso had made his famous shrimp and grits, and if nothing else, the evening was proving to be very entertaining.

She'd go along and see just how much her mother had actually changed her mind about vampires.

As she took her seat, she smiled at Remy, which wasn't hard to do. "Thank you."

"You're welcome." He moved around the table like he

was going to help Leonie with her chair, but Leonie was already settled.

She spread her napkin over her lap. "This is nice, isn't it? Been a while since I've used this room."

Ephie nodded. "You should have invited Mamere."

Leonie shook her head. "Your grandmother doesn't like eating late."

"It's only eight o'clock," Ephie said. But her grandmother didn't like vampires, either, something Leonie had conspicuously left out.

"She's an old woman, set in her ways." Leonie looked up as Alphonso came in carrying dishes.

He put one in front of Leonie first, then Ephie, before returning to the kitchen for Remy's dish.

Ephie inhaled the delicious scent. "It's been too long since I've had this." The plate was actually a shallow bowl, filled with Alphonso's creamy grits, topped with four fat shrimp that had been sauteed in a blend of seasonings and butter, then drizzled with red-eye gravy flecked with parsley.

Alphonso returned with Remy's dish and a basket of sliced bread. He set Remy's dish before him, then added the basket of bread to the table, setting it right beside the butter that was already there. "Bon appetit."

He looked at Leonie. "Anything else I can get for you, Ms. Moreau?"

She shook her head. "We're good, Alphonso. Thank you for this. It looks wonderful. I'll see you tomorrow."

"Yes, ma'am." He took his leave.

Ephie forked up a taste of the grits and gravy. It was as delicious as she remembered it. Even if tonight went totally bust, the meal was worth the effort of showing up and dealing with her mother's game-playing.

Well, seeing Remy was a pretty sweet reward, too.

"This is amazing," Remy said, food still in his mouth. "It's so good. I literally don't think I've had better anywhere in this city."

Leonie looked genuinely pleased with that. "You won't, either. I hired Alphonso from Brennan's. He is unparalleled when it comes to the classic dishes this town is known for."

"I wish he was still here so I could tell him how great this is," Remy said. "You'll pass on my compliments, won't you?"

"Of course."

Ephie glanced at him. "You make it sound like you're leaving soon."

"I am," Remy answered. "I have to get back to work."

"You work?" He was full of surprises. "What do you do?" She half expected him to say he was just kidding.

"I work for the sheriff's department. I'm a deputy."

She almost dropped her fork. "You're in law enforcement?"

He smiled like he understood her surprise. "I am."

"You wear a uniform and everything?"

He nodded, clearly amused by her reaction. "I even have the power to arrest people."

"Well, I'll be."

Leonie, who'd been quiet, suddenly chimed in. "That's admirable, Remy. A wonderful occupation."

"Thank you, Ms. Moreau."

Ephie couldn't quite get over it, though. "You obviously can't work the day shift. How did you explain that to them?"

A mischievous light twinkled in Remy's eyes. He shrugged as he got another bite of food. "I just told them I was a vampire."

"You did not," Ephie countered.

"I did. The sheriff's a werewolf, so he gets it."

"What?" She frowned at him. "Now you're just teasing me."

"No, I'm not. The whole town is full of shifters, witches, vampires. There are all sorts. In that regard, it's a lot like New Orleans."

"Oh, come on," she said.

"It is. Except in Nocturne Falls, everyone can pretty much be themselves. Within reason," he said. "There's an expectation that no one's going to do anything blatant unless they're on the clock."

"On the clock?" Leonie asked.

He nodded. "The town celebrates Halloween three hundred and sixty-five days a year. They hire supernaturals to play supernaturals. So if you're the vampire on duty and you decide to drink a pint of blood while you're standing around getting your picture taken, the tourists are just going to think it's part of the act."

Ephie sat back. "Why would the town do that?"

"Because it's all part of the shtick. They employ people to be witches, vampires, werewolves, and what have you. There's even a guy who can shift into a unicorn who occasionally gallops through the streets with a Greek goddess on his back. It's something to see."

Ephie really didn't know whether or not to believe him. Remy loved a good joke and had always loved to tease her. "Are you serious?"

"As I live and don't breathe, I swear it to you. Look it up. Nocturne Falls. It's a real place. Created by a vampire family so they could have a safe place to live. The town's water has even been enchanted so that tourists are even more likely to look the other way if they see something a little too hard to believe."

She'd left her phone in her purse, which was still on the couch in the sitting room, but if he'd made a claim that could be that easily verified or disproven, she had to believe him. "That's amazing."

She looked at her mom. "Have you heard of this place?"

"Heard of it but never really knew that much about it. Sounds interesting. Sounds like a great place to visit."

Remy nodded. "Brings in all kinds of human tourists but a lot of the supernatural variety, too. I've always loved New Orleans, but Nocturne Falls is its own kind of special." He shifted his attention back to Ephie. "You should really come see it sometime. I think you'd love it. It's much more of a small town than New Orleans."

"It does make a person curious," Leonie said.

Was her mother actually suggesting that a visit would be a good idea? Ephie couldn't tell if she was trying to get Ephie to go or to stay. Ephie's first reaction was generally to balk at anything her mother thought was a good idea.

So ... Leonie didn't want her there. For whatever reason.

Ephie nodded. "It does. Very curious." She picked up her fork and pierced a shrimp, then held it in place so she could cut it in half. From beneath her lashes, she watched her mother's face. "Maybe I should go back with you. See it for myself."

Leonie gave nothing away.

But Remy grinned. "Yeah? You want to come with me, you're welcome to. I was planning on leaving after dinner. It's a two-day drive, so I really need to get on the road. I'm sure you understand."

Ephie ate the piece of shrimp she'd cut, chewing slowly to give herself time to think and observe. Her mother had suddenly become unreadable. What in the devil was going on? She swallowed and acted like they were all discussing the weather. Not a trip to another state with the vampire who'd broken her heart twelve years ago.

Ephie swallowed. "Of course. You can only travel at night. Do you have an apartment or a house there?"

"House," Remy answered. "With a guest room. You're welcome to it."

Her mother's brows rose the tiniest fraction. Leonie

didn't want her to go. Or she didn't want her to go with Remy. Either way, it was the answer Ephie had been looking for.

She took a sip of her water, then set the glass down and smiled at Remy. "I can pack fast."

Remy honestly didn't know what he'd said or done to make Ephie decide to come back with him to Nocturne Falls. He'd been fully prepared to put on the hard sell, to beg her if he had to, even tell her that he wanted to make things right with her, that this could be their second chance.

None of that had been necessary.

Maybe he'd missed something. Maybe Ephie had read more into something he'd said or something her mother had said … or something her mother hadn't said.

Women were not the easiest beings to understand. Even when you had over two hundred years of experience with them.

He wasn't going to do anything to change her mind about going. Getting Ephie out of New Orleans was all that mattered.

He smiled. "That's great. I welcome the company. And it'll be nice to show you the town. And to catch up."

Ephie was watching Leonie. Looking for her reaction maybe? Ephie nodded. "Yes, it will."

He went back to his food. Shrimp and grits of this magnitude were not to be wasted. But he kept his eyes on Leonie, too.

Her face reflected almost nothing. She had to be pleased. This was what she'd wanted. Ephie away from the possibility of danger. And yet, Leonie seemed impassive. She knew her daughter better than he did. Maybe being happy would cause Ephie to change her mind.

He shook his head and sighed. Women were so complicated.

"What was that for?" Ephie asked.

"What?"

"You just sighed and shook your head."

He thought quickly. "Just thinking about the drive."

Leonie laid her fork across her plate like she was done. "The early start you'd hoped for is gone, I guess. My apologies for that. You'll still leave tonight, though?"

He nodded. She already knew he would. They'd discussed it. "My plans haven't changed." He glanced at Ephie. "As soon as you're done, we should get to your place so you can pack."

She used the edge of her fork to scoop up the remaining grits. "Like I said, it won't take me long. We can go when you're ready."

Leonie finally smiled, but she kept her lips closed, and her eyes held concern. "I hope you have a safe trip. I look forward to hearing about it. You'll call or text, won't you, Ephie? To let me know you're all right?"

Remy wasn't sure that was such a great idea. If Turner was really as connected as Leonie believed him to be, wasn't it possible someone in his organization was tracking Ephie and Leonie through their phones? If so,

Ephie ought to turn hers off or they'd figure out she was leaving.

But how was he going to explain that to her without giving everything away? The answer was, he couldn't. He'd just have to be extra vigilant.

Ephie nodded. "I'll text you. You're really all right with me going?"

Leonie gave her daughter the same tight smile again. "You're a grown woman. You can take a trip if you like. I think it might be good for you. I don't know the last time you got out of the city."

"It's been a while," Ephie said softly.

He ate the last of his food. She wasn't having second thoughts, was she? Time to move, if so. He pushed his chair back. "That was a great meal, Ms. Moreau. Again, please let Alphonso know how much I enjoyed it."

"I will. It was lovely having you both here." Leonie got up.

Ephie stood, too. She spoke to Remy. "I just need to get my purse, then we can go. You can follow me."

"All right."

As she left the room, Leonie glared at him. She kept her voice low. "Anything happens to her and it's your neck, you understand me?"

"Loud and clear," he whispered back.

Ephie returned, purse in hand. Leonie walked them to the door. She kissed Ephie's cheek. "Have fun. Be safe. Love you."

"Love you, too, Mom," Ephie said.

She and Remy went down the steps to their cars. "So weird," Ephie muttered.

"Why?" Remy asked.

She looked at him like he was an imbecile. "My mother is fine with me going away with you and you *don't* think it's weird?"

He shrugged and acted like it wasn't strange at all. "You heard her. She knows you're a grown woman who can do what she likes. Would it have made a difference if she'd told you not to? Would that have changed your mind about coming?"

Ephie put her hand on her car. "It probably would have made me want to go even more."

"So either way, you were going to do what you wanted to do." Best to let Ephie think it was her idea. "Seems like your mother has just decided it's easier to go along. Go along to get along."

"Maybe. But why now after all these years of trying to dictate my life?"

"I can't answer that. I haven't been around."

"Yes, I know." She opened her car door and got in. "My place isn't far."

"I'll be right behind you." He knew they had a lot to talk about. He supposed they'd be doing that on the way to Nocturne Falls. He wasn't sure he was looking forward to that conversation, not after hearing the tone of her voice.

Her apartment building was new, maybe only a few years old. Modern lines but not so modern that it stuck out too much from the buildings around it. They parked and went up in the elevator to the fourth floor.

As they stepped off, she got her keys out. "I have a lot of work to do. I shouldn't be going on this trip."

She was definitely having second thoughts. "You can work while you're there. As much as you need to. I promise, I won't be in your way. I sleep during the day anyway."

"True." She unlocked the door and opened it, going inside. She stopped suddenly. "*Oh*. Jean-Luc." She spun to face Remy. "I can't go. I don't want to leave my cat."

"Bring him along. I like cats." He looked past her but saw nothing. In fact, he saw no sign of a cat anywhere in the apartment. "Are you a big *Star Trek* fan or what?"

"Why would you ask that?"

"Well, you named your cat Jean-Luc."

She shook her head. "His name has nothing to do with *Star Trek*."

Remy still didn't see a cat, although Leonie had mentioned one. A ghost cat that was supposedly pretend. Remy went along with it, not wanting to upset Ephie. "Where is he?"

"Probably sleeping on the bed. You really wouldn't mind if I brought him?" She set her purse on a small table in the tiny foyer.

Remy actually wasn't sure how great it would be to travel with a real cat, but this one was pretend and he had to get her out of the city. If she'd had a ten-foot boa constrictor, he'd have answered the same way. "Not a bit. I think it'll be fun to have him around."

Ephie smiled. "Okay. Thanks." She looked around. "Jean-Luc, where are you? *Bebe*, come here."

A beautiful little white cat came running from the back of the apartment, meowing loudly.

"There you are. Hi, *bebe*."

So the cat was real after all. Remy laughed and crouched down. "Hello there, little man." The cat was handsome. He had one green eye and one blue eye. Remy held his hand out, and the cat sniffed it, then rubbed against Remy's fingers.

"You can ... see him?"

Remy looked up at her. "Of course I can see him and feel him. Why would you think otherwise?"

"Well, because Jean-Luc is a ghost."

Remy picked up the cat, who immediately snuggled against him, butting his head under Remy's chin. The ghost thing made no sense now. The cat was obviously real. "You mean because he's all white? I don't get what you're saying."

"No, I mean because he's a ghost. I found him in a cemetery. Half the time he's invisible or see-through, because I guess materializing takes effort."

"Um ... *okay*." Remy held Jean-Luc out. The cat looked as solid as could be to him. "Does he look transparent to you now?"

"No, but he was when he came running out. It's how he almost always looks to me." She suddenly frowned and put her hands on her hips. "He must be trying to impress you. I don't know why he couldn't do that around my mother."

"I have no idea." Remy hugged the cat to his chest again, scratching his chin and neck. "But he's sweet, and I'd be happy to have him at my place."

Ephie shook her head. "I feel like I'm in some alternate universe."

Remy put the cat down. Jean-Luc hopped up onto the back of the sofa and looked longingly at him, probably hoping for more attention. Remy took Ephie's hand. "Maybe you are."

"I don't think—"

"I noticed you still have the ring I gave you and you're still wearing it." He lifted her hand. Seeing the ring on her finger had touched him deeply. Given him hope.

She nodded. "I couldn't just get rid of it."

It amazed him how her beauty had increased over the years. How she'd grown into it. She was something to look at. The grace with which she moved made it almost impossible to look away. He held her hand in his, lifting his gaze from the ring to look into her eyes. "I'm very happy you didn't. I always wondered what happened to it."

She drew closer to him. "Did you ever wonder what happened to me?"

He couldn't tell her the truth, that he thought about her nearly every day. She'd run again. And he couldn't let that happen when staying here meant putting her in danger. So he nodded and reluctantly let her hand go. "There were definitely times you crossed my mind."

For a long moment, she said nothing. Then she gave him a quick smile. "I should get packed. I'll just be a minute."

"Okay."

"Make yourself comfortable." She turned and went down the hall.

He stayed where he was, looking around the place. It was nice. More modern than he'd expected. A large desk took up the dining area. He scratched Jean-Luc. "Do you need to pack, little cat?"

Jean-Luc closed his eyes and purred.

Remy picked the cat up again, this time cradling him in his arms like a baby. Jean-Luc put one paw on Remy's jaw. Remy smiled. "I already said you could come."

Remy carried the cat with him as he wandered through the space. He checked out the windows for any sign that Ephie was being watched but spotted nothing unusual.

He glanced down the hall. No sign of her yet. He set Jean-Luc down on the sofa and went back to the foyer. He dug her phone out of her purse and turned it off. He would have preferred removing the SIM card, but she'd notice that.

This way, he hoped to buy them some time. Enough to get out of the city undetected. Of course, that advantage would disappear the moment she turned the phone back on.

Maybe he should pull the SIM card, but how would he explain that when she realized what was up? There would be nothing he could tell her but the truth.

And according to Leonie, Ephie would have a meltdown.

He put the phone back in her purse. Jean-Luc chirped at him. "Okay, come on." He picked the cat up again.

There weren't many women who would welcome a death threat, but Ephie didn't seem like the type who'd be left helpless by such news. Nor did she seem fragile. Did Leonie really think that of her daughter? Or had she fed Remy a story to get him to do her bidding?

"All set," Ephie called out. She emerged from the hall with a suitcase in one hand and a large tote bag over the other. She'd changed into flat canvas shoes, jeans, and a striped top with a pale blue, zip-up hoodie. "Just need to pack up my computer and I'm ready."

"Great. I'll take the suitcase down to the car, then come right back up." That would give him another chance to have a better look around outside.

She narrowed her eyes at him, but there was a curious sparkle in her gaze. "Have you been holding Jean-Luc this entire time?"

"Pretty much."

She laughed. "Are you trying to steal my cat?"

Remy shrugged. "He likes it."

"Jean-Luc, you little traitor," she teased.

Remy gave Jean-Luc some extra scratches. "Don't you

need a carrier for him? And what about food and a litter box?"

She shook her head. "He's a ghost. He doesn't need any of those things. At least he hasn't yet."

"Huh." Remy glanced down at Jean-Luc. "You might be just about perfect, little man."

Remy's Ford Bronco easily held Ephie's luggage. She watched him load it into the back, holding on to her computer case. She wasn't going to work in the car, but she felt better having it close by. Her whole life was on this laptop.

She tipped her chin at the large stainless-steel container that spanned the back of the vehicle. "What is that? A cooler?"

"Not exactly. It's more of a self-preservation unit."

"So it's full of … Nope. I don't get it." She'd been about to say protein bars and bottled water, but he was a vampire. He could eat food, but to survive, he needed blood. That much she did know.

"It's not full of anything other than the padded interior lining. It's completely empty in case I can't make it to shelter before the sun comes up."

"Oh," she said softly. She'd forgotten how vulnerable vampires could be. It was a good reminder that the man next to her, for all his strength, speed, and power, had a significant weakness. She was very glad he'd made allowance for that.

Regardless of their past, she didn't want anything bad to happen to him.

Jean-Luc's head popped up over the row of seats. He meowed at them.

Remy laughed. "I think someone's ready to get on the road."

"Then let's do it."

They got into the SUV. He started it up, took a good look around, and got them moving.

She buckled her seatbelt, then decided to adjust the seat. "You don't mind if I move this back a little, do you?"

"Nope. Make yourself comfortable. It's a long drive. Although we'll probably only get about five hours in before we need to stop."

"Or I could drive." She didn't mind. She didn't do a lot of highway driving, but as long as there was navigation telling her where to go, she'd be fine.

"You're sure?" He made a face. "I don't know ..."

She cut her eyes at him. "I'm a good driver. I'm actually a very good driver. I've never had a ticket or been in an accident."

"It's not that."

Sure, she thought. She knew how men were. Or at least, she'd heard enough about them from her mother.

"It's just that my SPU isn't the most comfortable thing in the world."

"SPU?"

"Self-preservation unit."

"Ah, right. The UVPC."

He laughed. "UVPC?"

"Ultraviolet protection chamber."

He was still grinning. "Clever. Might have to change its name. Anyway, it's really for emergencies. Not for long stretches of time. If possible."

"I can understand that. Personally, I don't know how you could get into it at all. I have a little claustrophobia."

"Yeah, I remember that."

"You do? From when?"

"That time we slipped into that janitor's closet in Blessey Hall, for one."

"Oh, *that*." Her cheeks got warm. She'd specifically been trying not to think about what a good kisser he was. Now it was *all* she could think about.

Maybe this trip hadn't been such a good idea. She'd only done it to show her mother she was her own person and could do what she wanted, but now, faced with the reality of it, she was getting a little worried she'd bitten off more than she could chew.

Which sounded like a vampire pun.

"Um, listen," she said. "We should probably establish some ground rules."

"Ground rules?" She could hear the amusement in his voice. He stopped at a red light. "Okay, what are they?"

"I just think you should know I didn't come with you to have some wild fling. You and I are ... Well, we tried being together and it didn't work, so this isn't about that. It's not about rekindling anything. It's just me getting away for a bit and us being friends. And me showing my mother I can do what I want. That's it."

He nodded, but the movement seemed exaggerated to her. Like he was just humoring her.

"I mean it."

"Fine with me. Seriously, no argument. I'm sure that's what your mother would want, too."

Ephie stared at him. Was he messing with her? "If that's supposed to be some kind of reverse psychology, I don't appreciate it. I get that enough from my mother."

"What?" He frowned. "No, I was just— I only meant that I know your mother doesn't like me and I'm sure she thinks I'm going to put the hard press on you. I'm not. That's all."

She suppressed a smile. He was extra cute when he was flustered. "If you know my mother doesn't like you—and you're right, she doesn't. She doesn't like any kind of vampire—why do you think she was okay with me coming on this trip?"

He let out a sigh. "I guess ... she just respects your decision-making skills?"

Ephie snort-laughed. "You clearly don't know my mother."

"No, I don't. Not well. Okay, well enough to be sufficiently intimidated by her, but that's it."

"She doesn't really intimidate you, does she?"

He glanced over. "She could make my life difficult if she wanted to."

"How?" Ephie was genuinely curious. She couldn't imagine how her mother could do anything that would bother Remy. He was a two-hundred-year-old-plus vampire, after all.

"She could report me to the local vampire council in New Orleans. They're stricter than most because of the tourist industry. I shouldn't have been there."

"You just came to visit the professor."

"Not a good enough reason in their eyes. A vampire breaking a rule for a human? Trust me, they wouldn't look kindly on that."

"I don't think my mother has the courage to go before the vampire council. If she could even find them."

"She does and she could. Your family isn't without its own powers. You come from a line of gifted women. Your grandmother is well-known for her love potions, among other things."

"She is, but my mom's powers are pretty minimal. Her real power is in who she knows and who owes her favors."

"What about you?"

"You mean my powers?"

He nodded.

"They're nothing special."

He scoffed at that. "Come on."

"I mean it. They never really turned into anything. I'm okay with it. I don't need the complication. I like my life. It's low-key and simple, and that's just fine."

Jean-Luc appeared between them, standing on the console. He was translucent, but as he leaned toward Ephie, he materialized fully.

"Someone wants attention," Remy said.

She scooped Jean-Luc up, grateful he was solid, and put him on her lap. "How are you doing, *bebe*? What do you think about the car ride, hmm?"

"How did you end up with him?" Remy asked. "I want to hear the story."

Ephie smiled as Jean-Luc curled up in her lap. "I was in the cemetery, laying flowers for my Great-Aunt Hester's birthday, and he came running up to me, crying and pitiful. As soon as I spoke to him, he tried to climb my leg."

"So he was fully materialized?"

"Yep. At first, I had no idea he was a ghost. My guess, and I could be completely wrong about this, is that he'd been trying to get someone to take him home for a long time. I was just the first person who could see him. My mom can't."

"She told me. Pretty sure she thinks Jean-Luc is a figment of your imagination."

"Of course she does." Ephie shook her head. "My grandmother's seen him, though. And you, obviously. But you seem to see him better than even I can."

Remy gave them a quick look. "Well, he was solid just a second ago, but right now, he looks translucent to me. I can see your legs through him. But maybe that's because he's sleeping? I don't have a clue how ghost cats work."

"I didn't either. Still don't, in some ways. It just took living with him to understand what he was capable of."

"And he doesn't eat or drink or need the litter box?"

"Nope. He likes the smell of food, I can tell you that.

He likes to lie in the sun. And I've seen him chase a bug that got in the house. But he couldn't do anything with it." She smoothed her hand over his silky fur. She couldn't feel it at the moment, but she knew how soft it was from memory.

"He seems happy," Remy said.

She nodded. "I hope he is. Even if he's a ghost, he deserves a good life."

"I bet he's going to love Nocturne Falls."

"Yeah? Why's that?"

"For one thing, he won't be the only ghost in town. I know New Orleans doesn't exactly have a shortage, but the ghosts in Nocturne Falls are a lot easier to see. If you want to. And you know the right people."

"Any ghost cats? Or ghost animals of any kind?"

"Not that I know of. But I know someone who might know." He smiled. "I promise I'll ask next time I see her."

"When will that be?"

"Next time I'm at work." He chuckled. "She's the department's receptionist. She's also the sheriff's aunt. You'll like Birdie. She's a real character."

"Didn't you say the sheriff is a werewolf?"

"Yep. And so is his aunt. And his wife. And his sister, who runs the local bar and grill, and his brother, who's the fire chief."

"Whoa. Is the place infested with werewolves?" She wasn't sure she liked the sound of that.

"They're nice people, and you won't be in any danger, I promise. They're wolf shifters, not rougarous."

"If you say so." Once again, she was having second thoughts. But asking him to turn around and take her home would only prove her mother right. Ephie couldn't have that. Her mother would never let her live it down.

She was going to Nocturne Falls, and she was having a good time. Even if that meant being scared out of her mind.

Less than two hours into the trip and Ephie had fallen asleep, despite trying to stay up. Remy didn't mind. They were on different schedules. He'd have been more surprised if she'd stayed awake.

Jean-Luc had slunk across the console and was now snug in Remy's lap, which made him smile. He'd never had a pet before. It was nice. There was something ... special about being the person the animal wanted to spend time with.

He was glad Ephie was asleep, though. She probably wouldn't like Jean-Luc abandoning her for Remy. Seemed like Jean-Luc sensed that, however, as he'd stayed with her until she drifted off.

Occasionally, whenever Jean-Luc looked solid, Remy took his hand off the wheel to pet the little animal. Jean-Luc's purrs rumbled right into Remy's body.

Mostly, though, Remy had been watching the road. The one behind them as well as the one in front. He wanted to be sure they weren't being followed. Once, he thought he'd spotted the same pair of headlights behind them for nearly an hour, but then they'd vanished. So far, nothing else had happened. Which was good.

Even better that Ephie had yet to pull her phone out

and realize it wasn't on. He hoped it stayed that way until they got to Nocturne Falls, but there wasn't much chance of that. They'd have to get a hotel soon, and by morning, she'd want to check something on it. Social media, email, maybe even text her mom. Then she'd know it was off.

Could he power it down before they made the final leg of the journey? He wasn't sure. But he'd try.

As the hours ticked by, he started watching for an exit with food, gas, and lodging. He didn't want to leave things to the last minute. He'd been serious about not having to spend time in the—what had Ephie called it? The UVPC? Yeah, he didn't relish the thought of being cooped up in that until the sun went down again.

An exit sign appeared, showing him everything he needed. With Jean-Luc still on his lap, Remy turned off and spotted a decent hotel that also had a restaurant. He pulled under the hotel's awning and turned off the Bronco.

"Hey, bud," he said softly. He patted the cat's back, but his hand touched nothing. Jean-Luc was in full ghost mode. "Go over to your mama now. I have to get out."

Jean-Luc stretched, then curled up tighter. He showed no signs of moving.

Remy shook his head. "Then I'll move you myself." He tried to slide his hands under the cat to pick him up, but Jean-Luc conveniently remained insubstantial. Remy's hands went right through him.

Remy had no experience with cats and even less with ghosts. Could he just get out? Would Jean-Luc stay on the seat? At the very least, the cat would still be in the car, right? Because if Jean-Luc snuck out and got lost, Remy was pretty sure Ephie would never forgive him.

He didn't have time to think about it. The clock ticked ever closer to dawn. He needed to be safely indoors. Soon. Out of options, he carefully unlatched the door. "Stay in the car, Jean-Luc."

As quickly and as quietly as he could, Remy slipped out and closed the door. He peered in through the window. There was no sign of Jean-Luc. He spun, checking the ground around him. No cat anywhere.

A little panic set in. Ephie would have his head. He never should have agreed to any of this. Not the cat, not the trip, not reuniting with Ephie. What he should have done was insist Leonie call the police. Or maybe called them himself.

Then she would have definitely told the vampire council he'd been in New Orleans before his time. And he'd be in a lot more trouble.

He rolled his eyes as he headed for the lobby. A single employee, a middle-aged man, stood behind the desk as Remy entered through the automatic sliding doors. He got his wallet out and removed a credit card.

The man smiled. His name badge read Jorge. "Evening. Or morning, as the case may be. How can I help you?"

"I'm looking for a room with two beds. We'll be checking out later this evening."

"No problem," Jorge said. "Let me see what I have available."

Jorge bent over his computer.

Remy smelled coffee, no doubt coming from the restaurant, which was probably gearing up for the breakfast crowd. As good as the coffee smelled, he didn't need caffeine. He needed to be able to sleep. But Ephie might want some. She'd definitely want breakfast, too.

Letting her go alone seemed like a bad idea. He didn't think they'd been followed, but that wasn't good enough.

He turned toward the restaurant, pondering if he should get some breakfast to go, and caught sight of himself in the framed mirror near the entrance to the elevators.

Jean-Luc was sitting on Remy's head. Casual as could be.

Remy hadn't felt a thing. "What in the—"

"Sorry, sir, what was that?"

Remy blinked. "Um, nothing. Any luck on that room?"

"Yes, just pulling them up now. Sorry, computer's running a little slow this morning. I have a double queen room available on the third floor and a double full on the fifth. Which would you prefer?"

"I'll take the double queen room, thank you." He put his credit card on the counter. Could Jorge see Jean-Luc? If so, he deserved an Oscar for not reacting.

Remy wasn't sure this hotel even allowed pets. Was a ghost cat technically a pet? He didn't know, but he wasn't about to say anything now. He held still, hoping that would be enough to keep Jean-Luc from materializing. Or doing anything that might get them kicked out.

They needed this room.

Jean-Luc meowed. Remy went still. No one but him had heard that. He hoped.

Jorge looked up.

Remy laughed. "Um, that was my, uh, phone. Silly, I know."

Jorge said nothing. He ran the credit card and soon after presented Remy with his receipt and two keycards. "There you are, sir. There's additional parking around the back. Your key will open the exterior doors. Elevators are just down that hall. The restaurant opens in twenty minutes, and there is a breakfast buffet, if you're interested."

"Great, thanks." Remy grabbed the keys and the paperwork and carefully made his way back to the car.

Ephie was still sleeping when he got in, ducking because of Jean-Luc, which was probably dumb, since the cat wasn't solid.

Trying not to think about what had just happened, Remy drove around to the back of the hotel and parked. He glanced in the rearview mirror. No sign of the cat now. Where was he? "Jean-Luc?"

A little chirp answered him.

He exhaled in relief. As long as the cat was in the car, all was well. Remy touched Ephie's shoulder. "Ephie? We're here."

"Hmm?" Her eyes opened, and she yawned. "What now?"

"We're at a hotel. Sun's coming up soon. I've got us a room. They have a restaurant, too."

"Okay, good." She straightened. "How long was I asleep for?"

Most of the trip, but he didn't mind. "A few hours." He pushed the button to lift the tailgate. "We should get inside. Well, I should."

"Right." She grabbed her purse and got out, getting her computer bag from the backseat. "Aw, look at Jean-Luc. He's the cutest thing."

Remy glanced into the backseat. Jean-Luc was half upside down, tummy on display, and translucent. "Can you get him to be invisible? That would be the best way to get him into the room."

"Sure." She patted the seat closest to her. "Come on, *bebe*. Time to go inside."

He left her to deal with the cat while he gathered their things from the back. Her suitcase, his duffel bag. "Do you need this tote bag?"

"No, I can manage without it for a day. As long as I have my computer, I'm good." She had Jean-Luc tucked into her partially zipped-up hoodie. He looked snug. And smug.

"Okay, let's get inside then. Third floor. Based on where we are, the elevators should be through that door and straight ahead."

He had the duffel shouldered and used the extending

handle on her suitcase to wheel it behind him. The keycard worked on the door as Jorge had said it would, and the elevators were indeed straight ahead.

He glanced at Jean-Luc. He seemed content, but knowing how quickly the little beast could change positions, Remy thought it best to check on him all the same.

He pushed the call button. "Are you going to work while I sleep?"

She nodded. "Not much else to do, is there?"

"Not really, I guess. You can watch TV if you want. I'm a pretty hard sleeper. Won't bother me."

The elevator chimed to announce its arrival. As the doors opened, an exhausted-looking father approached, his toddler daughter holding his hand.

The little girl waved at them. "Hi. We're walking."

"She won't sleep," he explained. "Sorry."

"It's okay," Ephie said. "She's adorable. Go ahead."

The father and daughter got on, then Ephie, leaving Remy to fit himself and the luggage in the remaining space. The father and daughter were on one side, Ephie and Remy on the other. The little girl grinned at Ephie, who responded by wiggling her fingers.

The father and Remy both pushed their floor buttons. The doors closed. Jean-Luc stuck his head out of Ephie's hoodie.

Excited, the little girl pointed. "Kitty! Kitty!

"There's no kitty," the father explained. He gave Ephie a tense smile. "She really needs to sleep."

Ephie zipped her hoodie the rest of the way up, effectively hiding Jean-Luc. "We've all been there."

The doors opened on the third floor, and Remy quickly exited, Ephie behind him.

"Night-night, kitty," the little girl called out.

Jean-Luc meowed. Ephie partially unzipped her hoodie and whispered sternly, "Hush. You're being a stinker."

Remy got the keycard ready. "You have no idea."

Ephie didn't say a word about Remy only getting one room. It didn't matter. He'd be asleep the whole time. And there *were* two beds. Not to mention he hadn't once made her feel like he expected anything in return.

He'd always been that way. Chivalrous, was the old-fashioned term. Around her, he'd never been anything but.

Besides all of that, he'd paid for the room. She certainly could have paid for her own, but he hadn't woken her up to do that. She set her computer bag on the desk. "I'm happy to pay my half. For the room."

He dropped his duffel on one of the beds. "Don't worry about it. We're good. I used points anyway."

She knew he wasn't going to want money. That was just how he was. How he'd always been. "How about I pay for the gas then? We'll have to fill up soon." She unzipped her hoodie all the way. Jean-Luc hopped out onto the bed and started exploring.

He nodded. "Before we leave tonight. If you want to do that, fine with me. You don't have to, though."

"I want to."

"Up to you." He wheeled her suitcase next to the other bed, where a see-through Jean-Luc was still sniffing around. "If you want to use the bathroom or whatever, I was thinking I'd run downstairs and get us some breakfast. Just let me know what you want, and I'll bring it back."

"We could just go down there and eat. That would be easier."

"Not for me. Not if there's daylight coming through those windows."

"Oh, right." She turned to look at the big window on the outside wall. The horizon line was bright with sun. Any minute the whole sky would be ablaze. She pulled the curtains shut, throwing the room into darkness until her eyes adjusted. But she realized why he'd taken the bed closest to the door now. It was also farthest from the windows. "Maybe I should be the one to go get us some breakfast."

"I can manage it. I should be fine by the hostess stand."

"Remy, you've got to be tired. Daylight is coming, and you've been driving all night. I can do it."

He rubbed the back of his neck. "I am tired, but I can stay awake a little longer. How about we go down together then? But bring the food back up here."

"Okay." It wasn't what she wanted to do, but for him, she'd compromise. She got the feeling that he didn't want to be away from her. It was sweet, really. Was he afraid she'd bolt again?

Not very likely, this far from home with no vehicle. She kept her purse with her. He might fuss, but she was buying breakfast, too. Gas and breakfast still probably wouldn't equal her share of the room.

Remy produced a pair of sunglasses from inside his jacket as he looked at Jean-Luc. "Behave yourself, you little monster."

"Hey, he's a good boy."

Remy snorted, stuck the sunglasses on top of his head, and shot her a look. "Oh, he's a very good boy. Other than when he somehow followed me into the lobby when I went to get the room."

"What?"

"Yep. I didn't realize he'd done that, of course, until I caught sight of myself in the mirror and saw him sitting on my head."

"Oh, no!" Ephie slapped her hand over her mouth, unable to suppress her grin.

"Oh, yes."

Ephie burst out laughing. "Jean-Luc, you naughty *bebe*." She laughed some more. "What can I say? He's really taken a shine to you."

Remy was smiling now, too. "I'm glad he likes me. I hate to think of the alternative."

They made sure they each had a room key, then went back downstairs. A young woman in a hotel uniform was just unlocking the accordion gate that separated the restaurant from the rest of the hotel lobby. "Morning, folks. Come on in."

"Any chance you have a table or booth in a dark corner?" Ephie asked.

"Sure. It's way in the back, if that's all right?"

Ephie looked at Remy. If he didn't want to, she'd let it go. "What do you think?"

He nodded, but he was hard to read.

"If you'd rather take the food to go, we can," Ephie said.

He smiled. "I'm sure it'll be fine."

The young woman grabbed two menus and led them back. Dark was a good description. The booth was not only in an interior space but the last in the row. "I'll be right back with coffee."

"None for me," Remy said. "Just water."

They sat. Ephie leaned forward. "You sure this is okay?"

"Yep. It's better than I thought it would be. A lot better."

"Good. Get whatever you want. I'm buying."

"Eph—"

"Hush. I make good money. If I'm going to be along for the ride, you have to let me contribute."

He grinned. "Okay." He glanced at the menu. "But I'm getting steak and eggs."

She laid her menu on the table. "Fine by me. I'm getting the buffet, and I'll be eating my weight in pancakes and bacon."

He laughed. "I've missed you."

She studied his handsome face, the truth as clear as his smile was bright. "I've missed you, too."

By the time they ate and returned to the room, Remy

was obviously flagging. She let him have the bathroom first. He shuffled out in the cloud of steam that lingered after his shower. He was in a T-shirt and boxers, hair damp, the clean scent of soap preceding him.

"Night," he muttered as he pulled back the covers and crawled under them.

"Night."

Jean-Luc jumped from her bed to Remy's, sniffing at Remy for a bit before lying down against his side. Jean-Luc stuck one foot over his head and started licking the back of it.

If Remy noticed, he didn't care. In fact, he was so still she would have thought something was wrong with him if she hadn't known better. Vampires slept like the dead. One of the things she remembered.

She sat at the desk and opened her laptop, ready to get some work done. But it wasn't where her mind was. Remy was all she could think about.

Why, after all these years, had he unexpectedly turned up in her life again? Was it fate? Her grandmother would say so. But then, Mamere was a great believer in such things. She'd probably even say it was auspicious.

Ephie wasn't so sure.

The oddest bit about this whole thing was her mother. What woman who had a deep-seated abhorrence of vampires suddenly decided it was just fine, good, even, for her daughter to take off with the very one who'd broken her heart so many years ago?

Nothing about that smelled right. Ephie would have

been less suspicious if her mother wasn't a known schemer. But what kind of scheme could this be? There was no way Leonie could want Ephie and Remy to end up together.

Was there?

Ephie stared at Remy, watching him, even though he was as still as a statue. Did she still love him?

A part of her had never stopped. But loving the memory of someone and being in love with who they were now ... those were two very different things, weren't they? Just because he hadn't changed physically didn't mean he hadn't changed in other ways. She guessed she'd find out about that soon enough.

Jean-Luc sure seemed to like Remy, but what did a ghost cat know?

Ephie smiled. She should probably text her mom and let her know she was all right. Just in case her mother'd had a change of heart.

She slipped her phone from her purse. The device was off. Maybe it had run out of battery. She got the phone charger from her computer bag and plugged it in, then stuck the end into her phone, expecting the little battery signal to show up. Nothing.

Weird. She pushed the power button, and the phone came right on. She didn't remember turning it off. Maybe a glitch. She had emails, but she'd deal with those on her laptop. There was a text from her mother, too.

No surprise there. She opened the message up.

Just wanted to see how things are going.

Ephie smirked. So typical. She texted back. *Things are going great. This was a fantastic idea you had.*

She turned the phone to silent and set it aside, face down. That ought to give her mother something to think about for a while.

12

Leonie got to work the same time as she usually did, her sense of well-being slightly better than the day before, thanks to Ephie no longer being in town. That felt like a burden lifted, even if her daughter was with Remy.

There were worse choices and definitely worse vampires. It wasn't an ideal situation, but it was still better than having Ephie here where she could easily be targeted.

Leonie planned on reaching out to the police commissioner today. She let herself into her chambers, turning on the lights. She doubted he'd be in his office for another hour or so. She'd call as soon as was feasible.

Her phone chimed. She closed the door behind her and checked the notification. Ephie had responded to her text.

Leonie frowned at the words. It hadn't exactly been her idea for Ephie to leave with Remy, but she supposed there was no point in correcting her daughter's supposition. The end had justified the means, even if Ephie thought it was something else entirely.

Leonie tucked her phone back into her purse and went to her desk. She stopped a foot away, her gaze pinned to the envelope resting on her closed laptop.

How was it possible another letter had arrived so soon? It wasn't with any other mail, just sitting by itself. This was different. This was more direct. She felt sick to her stomach. Only herself, her clerks, and the janitorial staff had a key to her chambers.

Someone was on Turner's payroll.

She looked around the office, wondering if anything else had been touched. Was it possible he'd planted bugs? Could he be listening to what went on in here?

The idea made her feel unsafe. Violated. She couldn't call the commissioner. She'd have to go see him. That was better anyway. She'd take him the letters. If those didn't spur him to action, nothing would.

Darryl Tyson wasn't just the police commissioner. He was also a longtime friend and Ephie's godfather. The man was duty-bound to help.

Leonie didn't care that he probably wasn't in his office yet. She'd sit outside and wait. She couldn't be in this room any longer than she had to. She got a large manila envelope from a drawer in her desk, then used a pen to nudge the new letter into it, careful not to touch it.

She doubted there were prints on it or any of the previous letters, other than her own and Remy's, but if there were, she wasn't taking any chances that she might ruin this one.

The letters she'd already touched went into another large envelope, then she put both into her briefcase and took one more look around. Nothing looked out of place, but then, that would be how they'd want to leave it.

So that she wouldn't suspect a thing.

No one should come into this room. It might be a crime scene. She'd tell Mervin. He'd keep everyone out.

Unless he was part of it.

She shook her head. That wasn't possible. He was a good man, one she'd known for nearly eight years. She'd been to his house and he to hers. She knew his family. They'd been in New Orleans longer than her own.

It wasn't Mervin. She could trust him. She had to believe that. She needed to trust someone. Maybe that person was Darryl.

She left, locking the office door and leaving a note for Mervin that no one was to go in until she got back. Then she drove directly to the commissioner's office.

When she pulled into the parking lot, he was just getting out of his car. She parked and hustled toward him, her heels clicking on the pavement, her briefcase banging against her thigh.

He smiled when he saw her. "Leonie, what a pleasant surprise." He pulled her into a hug. "It's good to see you. Are you here for me?"

"It's good to see you, too." His warm embrace had given her comfort, but she couldn't return his smile. "And, yes, you're the reason I'm here."

As if sensing something was going on, concern took over his face. "What's wrong?"

"Abraham Turner."

Darryl's brows furrowed. "What about him?"

"I need help, Darryl. He's been sending me threatening letters. He's threatened Ephie, too."

"What?" The word exploded out of him in an angry bark. He looked around. "You have the letters?"

"I do."

He put his hand on her shoulder. "Let's go into my office."

Not another word was spoken until they were seated, door closed, in his private space. Him behind his desk, her in one of the chairs before it. "Now," he said, "tell me everything and show me these letters."

She gave him every detail she could remember, including sending Ephie out of town with a friend. That was as much as she was willing to tell Darryl about Remy. Darryl was human, and while he'd lived in New Orleans long enough to have a healthy respect for the supernatural, she doubted he'd understand a real-life vampire.

She finished her story by pulling the two big envelopes from her briefcase. "This one has the letters I've already opened and touched." She placed the second one on top. "And this has the newest letter. I found it on my desk this morning. I got it in the envelope without laying a finger on it. I haven't read it, either."

Darryl nodded. "Let me get some gloves. We'll have a look at it together. While we do that, I'm sending a tech guy to your office to sweep it. If there's a listening device present, he'll pick it up."

"Thank you." She leaned forward. "Wait. If he

removes it, Turner will know I'm on to him. Can he just sweep and tell me where they are, if there are any?"

Darryl narrowed his eyes. "Yes, but don't you discuss sensitive information in your chambers?"

"I do, but there are ways around that. I was thinking maybe we could use the bugs to feed Turner some false information. See if we can draw out whoever's working for him that way."

Darryl frowned. "If you're implying we should use you as bait, I don't like that, Leonie. I won't approve that. A sitting associate justice shouldn't be subject to that kind of danger. Better to pull the bug and let Turner think it malfunctioned."

"Darryl, I love you and I appreciate you, but we've known each other since grade school. Have you ever known me to shy away from hard times?"

He laughed mirthlessly. "No, I haven't. But we're also not talking about hard times, Leonie. This is life or death." He stabbed the desktop with his finger. "Turner blames you for putting him behind bars. He's not a man to be trifled with."

"And I'm not a woman to be trifled with. I've already had to send my daughter away without her knowing anything about this. If I can help you take down some of his crew, I would be glad to." She lifted her chin. "No one threatens me or my family and gets away with it."

"I'm sure he's calling the shots, but his crew is no joke. They are dangerous men. Willing to do whatever he tells them."

"That just means we need to set things up properly. So that I'm protected. I'm not afraid to do this, Darryl. I'm afraid *not* to."

Darryl let out a deep, resigned sigh. "Let's read this letter before we make any decisions, all right?"

She nodded. "All right."

He got up and left, coming back with a pair of latex gloves and an evidence package. "We'll read this letter, then I'm sending all of this to the lab for fingerprints and DNA."

"DNA?" That surprised her.

"If the envelopes were licked, there will be DNA. It's a slim chance, but it's worth checking."

"I'm all for that."

Gloves on, he pulled a penknife from his pocket and used the blade to slit the envelope open. He carefully removed the folded letter from inside and set it on his desk. He looked into the envelope, pushing the ends together to open it.

"Anything?"

He turned the envelope over. A small black feather fell out.

Leonie didn't like that. It felt like a voodoo talisman. "Another threat."

He nodded. "That's how I'd take it, too. Let's see what this says." He unfolded the paper and read. "You think I don't know what you've done. I have eyes and ears everywhere. Nothing escapes me. Your daughter won't either."

Leonie gasped and put her hand to her throat. "He

knows I sent Ephie away."

"Maybe," Darryl said. "But just because he knows she's gone doesn't mean he knows where. This friend she's with, is it someone who can protect her?"

Leonie nodded. "He's a friend of Ephie's from school. He's a cop now."

"Good. He knows what's going on?"

"He does."

"I'd advise you to fill him in on this latest letter."

"Let me take a picture of it to send to him."

Once she'd done that, Darryl refolded the letter and put it back in the envelope along with the feather. "I don't think it's wise for you to be on your own right now, either. You're as much in danger as she is."

"What are you going to do, Darryl? Assign an officer to me twenty-four-seven? That's not practical. And I doubt you have the budget for it."

"When you're at the courthouse, I'm not as concerned about you. There's already a lot of protection there. But when you're home on your own, I'm very concerned. I was thinking you could come and stay with me."

She couldn't keep her surprise from showing on her face. "That's a kind offer, but I cannot imagine the tongue-wagging that might start."

He frowned. "Leonie, we're talking about your life. Who cares what people say?"

She knew he was right. She had an alarm system on her home but no way to actually defend herself if someone broke in. No dog, no gun, no weapon of any kind. "I understand this is a serious situation. But it's Ephie being targeted, not me."

"I don't share your confidence. If you won't stay with me, then I have no choice but to assign you protection."

That would be like walking around with a neon sign announcing her vulnerability. Turner might see it as a challenge. "What if ..." Did she dare? She supposed she had no choice. She liked her privacy. But she liked Darryl, too. Always had.

"What if what?"

"You came to stay with me?"

He smiled. "If that's your compromise, I can live with that." He picked up his phone. "I'm going to get your office swept immediately."

"Thank you." There would still be talk. Darryl's presence at her house would not go unnoticed. But it was a small price to pay to sleep at night.

It might be nice to have the company, too. She and Darryl had always had something between them, a spark of more than just friendship.

But he'd been married until a few years ago, when his wife had tired of her life as a police officer's spouse and left him. Since his divorce, he'd stayed single.

He hung up. "What time do you normally get home? I'd like to be there so I can do a walk-through of your place and assess your current security."

She smiled. "Six. And Alphonso usually has dinner ready by seven. I'll tell him to make it for two this evening."

13

Remy opened his eyes already knowing the sun was soon to set. It was the natural alarm clock built into all vampires. The room was dark except for the flickering blue light of the television, the volume down low.

He pushed up onto his elbows and looked toward Ephie's bed.

She was lying there, eyes closed. He listened and picked up the evenness of her pulse coupled with her soft, rhythmic breathing. She was asleep.

He turned to look the other way and nearly jumped out of his skin.

Jean-Luc sat inches away, staring at him.

"Don't do that," Remy muttered. "It's creepy. And a little rude."

Jean-Luc leaned in and headbutted Remy's chin.

"You're forgiven."

"Hey," Ephie said softly. "You're awake."

"So are you." He sat up.

"I didn't mean to drift off, but to be honest, I got bored."

"Sorry."

She shook her head. "Not your fault. The good news

is, I got a lot of work done. I might actually be a day or two ahead."

"That's fantastic." She looked like she wanted to say more but was reluctant to. "What is it?"

She exhaled. "I'm starving. Breakfast held me for a long time—"

"You did eat your weight in pancakes and bacon, which was seriously impressive."

She laughed. "Thanks. But I'm hungry again. I know you don't need food like I do, but are you hungry at all?"

"I'd be happy to go eat with you." He wasn't hungry for food, but he could get another steak, rare. That would be enough to get him home, where he had his own supply of what he really needed. "Let me get dressed and we'll head down."

"If you're not hungry, which it sounds like you aren't, I can just grab something and eat in the car. You must be anxious to get home. I know we aren't far."

"We're not. Just a little over three hours." Getting home would be good. It would be safer for her than being on the road.

"There's a burger joint next door. I can grab a burger and fries from the drive-through, then we can get going sooner. If that's cool with you. Having food in your car, I mean."

"That's fine with me." He swung his legs onto the floor. "Do you need the bathroom? Otherwise, I'll shower and get ready. We can be out of here in fifteen minutes."

"That fast? Wow, okay. You go ahead. I'll pack up my computer and stuff."

He got up and stretched, glancing at the desk. Her phone was plugged in. "You, uh, charging your phone?"

"Yep."

Which meant her phone was probably on, too. For how long? Since he'd fallen asleep? If she was being tracked, they'd know exactly where she was. They might even be waiting for her outside the hotel.

He hated not being able to tell her the truth. "Listen, don't take anything out to the car, okay? Wait for me. I'll be fast."

She gave him an odd look. "Okay. But I could have my stuff packed if—"

"I'd really rather you waited for me. Please." He smiled to soften the demand.

"Okay, no problem."

"Great." He grabbed his phone and took it into the bathroom with him. He turned on the shower, then checked the screen. An update from Leonie told him another letter had arrived. She'd included a screenshot so he could read it for himself.

Didn't look good. If this Turner and his crew really had eyes and ears everywhere, there was every reason to think they'd show up in Nocturne Falls.

He hated the idea of bringing trouble to his adopted hometown, but that was exactly what he might be doing. The best thing he could do was give the sheriff a heads-up.

He sent Sheriff Merrow a long text, filling him in on the important details and letting the sheriff know their approximate arrival time.

Then Remy took a fast shower. He shaved, got dressed, and came out to find Ephie packed and ready to go. Jean-Luc sat on her suitcase, looking eager for the next leg of their journey.

Keeping the truth from Ephie was getting harder and harder. It would be so much easier if she knew, but Leonie had warned him more than once against it. He didn't see any of the weaknesses that Leonie claimed Ephie had, but then again, he hadn't been around her in a long time.

It was possible finding out she was in danger might cause her to crumble. If that was the case, it would be much better for that to happen at his house than on the road.

For now, he would keep quiet. But once they got to Nocturne Falls, all bets were off. Ephie deserved to know what was going on. And he hated lying to her.

They took everything out to the car, packed it into the back, and got into their seats. He filled up at the gas station on the other side of the burger joint, which she insisted on paying for. Then he went through the drive-through at the fast-food place, getting her fries and a burger along with a diet cola, and a burger and a chocolate milkshake for himself. He wasn't really hungry, but the food wouldn't hurt him, and he didn't want Ephie to feel odd eating alone.

Jean-Luc sniffed at the food and seemed pretty interested in it, but there was no way for him to eat any of it. For that, Remy felt bad for the little creature.

He kept his head on a swivel as they went. The gas station and drive-through were a great opportunity to watch for anyone following them or waiting for them in the surrounding parking lot.

So far, nothing.

Food in hand, he decided to make an executive decision and pulled into a spot that faced the road so they could eat without the distraction of driving. His phone vibrated. He checked the screen and saw his boss had responded.

Merrow had Birdie pulling files on Turner and his crew, and they'd be keeping an eye out, making sure everyone in the department knew to be on the lookout as well.

Remy sent back a note of appreciation. But he hadn't expected anything less from the sheriff. The man hated trouble in his town.

After Remy and Ephie had eaten, they got on the road. Ephie collected the trash and put it all in the burger joint bag to be thrown away at their next stop. That would be his house. He had no plans to stop until they were home.

He kept watch on the traffic behind them, studying headlights and patterns of the drivers around him. Jean-Luc, no longer a stranger to car travel, settled into one of the back seats and went to sleep, becoming nearly invisible.

Remy kept up his surveillance. No one seemed suspicious, but he didn't know how good this crew was. He wasn't going to take any chances.

"What are you looking for?" Ephie asked. She twisted around to peer through the back of the vehicle. "You keep looking in the rearview mirror."

He laughed it off. "Police training. Just a habit." Time to distract her. "How did you never get married? I thought for sure you'd have a husband and a slew of kids."

She faced him again. "A slew?"

He shrugged one shoulder. "Okay, one or two at least."

She shifted all the way back around to face the front of the SUV. "I dated a few guys, but none of them really did it for me. I guess ..." She sighed and studied her hands in her lap. The pansy ring, maybe? "I guess I never got over you."

He sat in shocked silence for nearly a minute. "I didn't know that."

"Of course you didn't. You didn't stick around long enough to find that out."

"I thought, that is, you said you didn't want to marry me." He kept his gaze straight ahead, certain looking at her would be a bad idea. "I'd already overstayed my time in New Orleans. You turning me down felt like the sign I'd been waiting for. It was time to go. So I went."

His peripheral vision told him she wasn't looking at him, either. "You broke my heart."

He sucked in air, not something he was accustomed to doing. "I broke *your* heart? You broke *mine*. You turned me down. You couldn't get away from me fast enough."

"I reacted badly. I accept that. But I never thought that would be the last time I'd see you."

He didn't know quite what to say. "I never thought you'd want to see me again. If I had thought otherwise, I wouldn't have left." He glanced at her. The dim glow from the dashboard made her eyes seem huge and luminous. "I'm really sorry, Ephie. Sorry I broke your heart. Sorry I disappeared on you. I had no idea."

"I never loved anyone the way I loved you." She sniffed and turned her head to gaze out the side window.

If his heart had been working, it would have pounded in his chest.

Before he could respond, she broke the silence with a bitter laugh. "Don't worry. I'm over you. I didn't come on this trip to make some kind of play for you. I'm good being just friends." She wiped the corner of one eye. "It's better that way anyway."

Was it? He sat quietly, trying to process everything she'd just told him. All he could say was, "Okay."

But it didn't feel okay. It felt like the last thread of hope he'd been hanging onto had just unraveled completely, pitching him into an abyss.

The silence spooled out between them. Ephie got her phone out and played some games. He turned the radio on, keeping the volume low just to fill the space with something other than his own thoughts.

He hadn't admitted it to himself until now, but he'd been thinking her visit might be a chance to rekindle things between them. Just to see if the spark that remained was enough to actually light a fire.

His feelings for her had definitely changed over the years, but not because they'd lessened in intensity. If anything, she'd become this kind of bigger-than-life figure. Being with her again after all these years had done nothing to diminish her memory, either.

Ephie was great. Beautiful, funny, sweet, and oddly quirky in a way that he found utterly endearing. Jean-Luc was sort of the icing on the proverbial cake.

But if her feelings for him were gone, then he could only do the honorable thing and pretend his were, too. It was better to be friends than nothing.

He didn't really feel that way, but he was sure he would soon.

They'd have a nice visit, and when it was safe for her to go home, he'd put her on a plane and say goodbye.

Again.

Tired of trying to match up candies to make a bomb that would clear the game screen, Ephie put her phone away.

Remy had gone quiet, but maybe he was just concentrating on driving. She tried to look at him without letting him know she was looking at him. He wasn't mad, was he, about what she'd said?

It had been the truth. Well, mostly. The part about being over him was a lie, but that was for both of their sakes. He had a life in another town. A job that he obviously liked. He didn't need her coming in and upsetting any of that.

The same went for her. Although her job could be done from anywhere.

Didn't matter. If he was still in love with her, he'd have said something. Wouldn't he? Remy wasn't the kind of man to keep anything back. At least he never had been.

The night he'd proposed was proof of that.

She glanced back at Jean-Luc. He was fast asleep and remained nearly invisible, his little snores hard to hear over the sound of the road.

She adjusted her seat, reclining it further.

"Going to sleep?" Remy asked.

"No, just getting comfortable."

"You can sleep if you want. Won't bother me."

"I'm good. Not much longer now, hmm?"

"Nope."

"When do you have to go back to work?"

"Two more nights."

"Are you going to show me around town?"

He smiled. "Yeah, sure. It's a great place. You'll love it. Not as chaotic as New Orleans or as busy but plenty of fun."

"Sounds good." She yawned without meaning to. She was a little tired. If she closed her eyes, she'd probably drift off, but she didn't want to do that to him. It wasn't fair that he did all the driving while she just slept.

"What's Jean-Luc up to?"

"Not a blessed thing." Ephie grinned. "Even for a ghost, he sleeps hard."

"How did you come up with the name Jean-Luc again?"

"I didn't. Not really. His full name is Jean-Luc Beauvoir, and I named him that because that was the name on the tomb he was standing on when I first saw him. Maybe it was his previous owner? I don't really know. I tried researching the name in the census, but I never found him. I know nothing about him. Maybe the tomb he was on had nothing to do with him."

"It's still a good name. It fits him. It's regal. And he clearly thinks he's the boss of everything, so why not?"

She nodded, amused. "He is awfully sweet. Ghost or not."

"You must wish he was real sometimes. Not that he isn't real, but you know what I mean."

"I do." She'd wished a lot of things over the years, but she'd given up on most of those wishes. "Of course, that would mean he'd leave me someday. This way, he'll always be with me." Just like a vampire. The similarities weren't lost on her.

"Good point."

"You seem to like him well enough. Why don't you have a cat? Or a dog?" *Or a girlfriend or a wife*, but she kept those last two to herself.

"Doesn't seem fair to leave an animal home alone so often. I work most nights, and when I'm home, I sleep a lot of those hours."

"Same for most people who have pets. Animals are surprisingly adaptable."

"Says the woman with a ghost for a companion."

"Hey, I've thought about adopting a living pet lots of times. I just don't know what Jean-Luc would think about that, and he was here first. I don't want to upset him. He's a pretty special little guy."

"I would agree with that," Remy said. He put his blinker on, checked the mirror, and got over into the far lane. "Who knows? Maybe someday I'll get a pet. Anything is possible."

Was it though? Ephie wasn't so sure about that.

Remy took the next exit, which took them through some hilly, windy roads. Then a sign appeared.

With great delight, she read it out loud. "Welcome to Nocturne Falls."

It didn't take long for the town to impress her with its dedication to the Halloween theme. All around her, on every side of the street, were signs and motifs that added to the vibe. Even the colors and designs of the buildings added to the feeling. "This place is seriously over the top, but I love it."

"It's definitely got a lot going on." He smiled. "I'm glad you like it."

There was so much to look at that when he turned into a residential area, she was a little disappointed, but she'd see more of the town soon enough.

The neighborhood was nice. Small to medium-size homes, all beautifully kept. All with more land around them than what she was used to seeing in New Orleans. As it was spring, there were lots of flowers, made visible by the exterior lighting on the homes.

He pulled into the driveway of a modest two-story house, the upper level a lot smaller than the main part. The house was dark gray with white trim, black shutters, and a deep purple front door. The front porch had wrought-iron railings, reminding her of the Quarter.

"This is your place?"

He nodded. "Home sweet home."

"I love it. Shades of New Orleans."

He laughed. "Yeah, maybe a few. I've done a few things to it over the years. Some consciously as a nod to

Louisiana, some probably not. You get Jean-Luc, and I'll deal with the luggage."

She grabbed her purse, the bag of trash, then opened the door behind hers. She hoisted her computer bag onto her shoulder. "Jean-Luc, we're here. Time to get up, sleepy head."

The little cat raised his head and meowed at her.

She nodded at him. "That's right. We're at Remy's house. Come on, let's go inside. There will be lots of new exploring for you to do."

Jean-Luc got up, arched his back in a big stretch, then walked over to her, materializing as he did. She gathered him into her arms and headed for the front porch.

Remy had the door open and was carrying their luggage inside. She followed, entering right as he turned the lights on.

"Oh, Remy, this is *nice*."

"What did you expect?"

"I guess something more bachelor-pad-ish?" But his place, while definitely masculine, was gorgeous.

Dark blues and dark purples were paired with deep wood tones, brass fixtures, and touches of tan. Art was framed in gold, and the lighting fixtures were clear glass with Edison-style bulbs. The furniture all had simple, clean lines with a mid-century feel, and books were everywhere.

The vibe was old-school intellectual with money. Almost like an exclusive library had been turned into a home.

He closed the front door. "I'm glad you like it."

"Like it? I love it. Makes me want to redo my whole place."

He laughed. "It's been a work-in-progress for a while."

"Well, you did a great job. I can't wait to see the guest room."

"Don't get too excited. It's pretty simple."

"I'm sure it'll be fine. Can I put Jean-Luc down?"

"Of course. He can have the run of the place. Not like he can get into any trouble, right?"

"Right."

He showed her to the guest room down the hall, opening the door, then reaching in to turn on the light. "Here you go."

The room was decorated in tan and navy with a woven navy and green rug over the hardwood floor. A painting of Jackson Square at night over the headboard picked up all three colors.

The brass bed was covered with a colorful quilt that looked handmade. Crystal lamps sat on the wooden nightstands. There was a dresser, painted navy blue, opposite the bed. A lace runner covered the top, where a small flat-screen television had been set up. A tidy, upholstered chair took up the corner near the window, which was dressed with a simple shade and a lace valance.

She stepped inside. "It's perfect."

He wheeled her suitcase in. "The bathroom is the next door. Across the hall is a small room I haven't really figured out what to do with yet. The upstairs is another room I haven't done much with. The house is really more space than I need, but I like it. My bedroom is at the end of the hall."

"Then I'll know where to find you." She smiled. "Thanks for this. It was really nice of you to let me come stay. I'm sure it wasn't an easy decision for you to make with our history and all."

"Wasn't hard. You wanted to come. I wanted to see you again. Nothing difficult about that. Besides, like your mom was saying, it'll be good for you to get away. Have some fun."

"I'm not sure my mother really meant that, but I agree with her all the same." She was already enjoying herself. Getting to see how Remy lived was pretty interesting. Nothing like what she'd imagined.

A white streak zipped past Remy.

Ephie laughed. "I think Jean-Luc is enjoying himself."

"I'd say so, too." Smiling, Remy glanced in the direction the cat had gone before looking at her again. "You need anything?"

"Nothing I can think of. I guess I'll unpack. What are you going to do?"

"I'll unpack, too. Maybe start a load of laundry. Then ..." He shrugged. "I don't know. Are you going to bed?"

"I feel like I should get on your schedule. At least a little bit. I'm tired, but I can stay up for a while. Do you want to do something?"

He smirked. "I don't think you're going to be interested in what I was going to do."

"Oh?" Curious, she took a few steps toward him. Her mind went in all kinds of dark, vampirey directions. "Are you going to ... drink blood?"

His eyes narrowed in obvious amusement. "No. I was going to get groceries."

Remy really hadn't expected Ephie to want to go grocery shopping with him, but it needed to be done. He didn't have much in the house, since food wasn't a prerequisite for his life. He also hadn't known he was going to have a guest.

It was nice to have her along, though. Much better than doing it himself. And this way, he could get the things she actually liked as opposed to his best guesses.

They grabbed a cart as they headed into the Shop-n-Save. He figured he'd just start at one end of the store and work his way around.

"Nice produce section," Ephie said.

"Get whatever you want."

"I know you eat some food. Do you eat fruits and vegetables?"

"Some fruit. Vegetables don't do a lot for me."

"Spoken like a true man." She grinned. "How about some apples?"

"Whatever you want is fine with me. I mean it. If you want vegetables, get them, too."

She picked out a few things. A bag of apples, some red grapes, a head of lettuce, a cucumber, a pint of cherry tomatoes, and a sweet onion.

They moved on to the meat department.

"Now a good steak I can get behind. I do have a grill. Although fried chicken is always good. Even a nice piece of fish, or pork chops in gravy—"

"You're making me hungry." She put her hand on her stomach. "I guess that burger didn't last as long as I thought it would." She picked up some steaks and then, farther down, a package of pork chops.

"After we get the groceries home, we could go out for something to eat."

"Maybe," she said. "Or I could make something. I mean, we are buying all this food."

"Not much of a vacation if you have to cook."

"I don't mind. I don't do a lot of it at home because it's just me. Cooking for two is different." She turned toward the seafood counter. "You know, I could make jambalaya. Not tonight, but for dinner tomorrow."

Now *he* was starting to get hungry. "Yeah? Is it any good?"

She playfully smacked his arm. "Remy!"

"It's a valid question." He laughed. "You never cooked for me."

"That's not true. I made mac and cheese once."

"Yes, from a box, on a hot plate. That's not really cooking."

"I suppose it's not an accurate representation of my skills. But I make good jambalaya. Alphonso gave me his recipe."

"Get what you need. I'm in."

That required them going back to the produce department for a few more things, then hitting some of the other aisles.

By the time they were done shopping, the cart was about as full as it could get. Ephie had picked out enough for three weeks, but he didn't mind one bit. Maybe she'd stay that long.

Maybe she'd stay forever.

He knew that wasn't going to happen. He was letting his brokenhearted self dream. Nothing wrong with that, was there? Other than the fact he was setting himself up for more disappointment. But that was his business and he'd deal with it.

He couldn't imagine who wouldn't want this beautiful woman at their side. Being with her had definitely reinvigorated all his old feelings.

Her continuing to wear the ring he'd given her only encouraged the small spark of hope flickering inside him. Could he change her feelings toward him? Could he get her to love him again?

Maybe. There was always a chance.

But not if she knew he was hiding something from her.

Right there, in the checkout lane, he resolved to text Leonie and tell her he was done keeping the truth from Ephie. She was a grown woman, and he saw nothing in her that said she wouldn't be able to handle what was going on. In no way did she seem fragile.

He wouldn't let anything happen to her. He put his

life on the line every time he was on duty, and for perfect strangers. As long as he was around, Ephie had nothing to worry about. He'd make sure she knew that.

"Cash or credit?"

He blinked his thoughts away in time to see Ephie getting her credit card out. "Not happening. Put that away."

"Remy—"

"No. You are my guest." He pulled his wallet out.

"But that's a lot of food."

"I couldn't care less if you'd filled the cart with lobsters and caviar." He slid his card through the machine. "Eph, seriously." He lifted his brows, smiling because she was so pretty, he couldn't help himself. "Do you even know what the word 'guest' means?"

She made a face at him. "Yes, I know what it means, but I didn't come here for a free ride. I can pay my own way."

"I know you can. But there's no need. Besides, you're going to do the really hard part of turning all this into a meal." The cashier handed him the receipt as the bagger put their groceries back into their cart.

"Oh, don't think you aren't going to help."

"Nice try, but I don't know how to cook."

She put her hands on the cart to push it to the SUV. "I'm going to teach you."

"That's cute." And so was she. If she thought he was really going to complain about spending more time with her, she'd soon find out how wrong she was.

He got everything loaded into the back. She took the empty cart to the closest corral, and then they got in. He drove back to his place. Between the two of them, they had the SUV unloaded in one trip apiece. Granted, he could carry a lot more than the average man.

Once they were inside and the groceries on the counter, she started unpacking the bags. "Where do you keep the dry goods?"

He looked around the kitchen. "I don't think I have any dry goods. I have coffee in the cabinet over the machine."

She shot him a look of pure disbelief. "Don't you have a pantry? Where do you put your food? I know you're a vampire, but you must have some snacks or something."

"Not really. Just put the stuff where you want it."

She opened the nearest set of cabinets. There was nothing in them. "Remy. How do you live like this?"

He laughed. "Pretty well, I'd say."

She just shook her head at him. "I suppose if you don't eat, you don't need food." She put the bag of rice they'd gotten on the shelf, along with a can of crushed tomatoes, a carton of chicken stock, and the small jars of seasonings she'd needed.

He put the meat into the fridge, pushing aside his personal stock of liquid sustenance to make more room. "Should any of this go into the freezer?"

She looked over and caught sight of the bottles on the top shelf. "Those are what I think they are, aren't they?"

"Yes. Sorry. Does it bother you? I could ... put them in a cooler or something."

"Remy," she said softly. "This is your house. You don't need to apologize, and you don't need to do anything different on my account. I know what they are, and I know you need them to live. They don't bother me. I'm just not used to seeing that sort of thing."

"I don't suppose you are." He closed the fridge. "I want you to be comfortable here."

"I am," she assured him. "You have a lovely home."

"You haven't even seen the backyard yet."

She moved past him to put the fruits and veggies into one of the refrigerator drawers. "I can't wait."

"Do you still feel like going out for something to eat?"

"No, I guess I can manage." She closed the refrigerator. The groceries were all put away. That full cart didn't seem like very much now.

"I don't want you to manage. If you're hungry, let's go get something."

She leaned on the counter, her hands planted on the quartz top behind her. "What are my options?"

"Italian, Thai, pizza, barbecue, burgers, diner food, ice cream, fancy chocolates and desserts, French ..." He shrugged. "If you're in the mood for it, the town probably has it." He caught the time on the microwave. "Although I'm not sure all of that's open now."

"Okay, what is open?"

"I'm pretty sure Mummy's Diner, Howler's bar and

grill, Salvatore's pizza place, and ice cream. Any of those work for you?"

"Probably not the best dietary choice, but ice cream sounds good. Is it good? I'd hate to waste all those calories on something that's just okay."

He grinned. "I don't eat it very often, but people love I Scream's ice cream. Birdie's a big fan, I know that. And she's not one to waste calories, either. I believe they make their ice cream right there at the shop, and they're always changing out flavors for new ones."

"That sounds awesome. Let me check on Jean-Luc and grab a jacket. I didn't think about it being cooler here because of the elevation."

"If you need something warmer, you can borrow something of mine. Help yourself."

"Thanks, but I think I brought a sweater that will work."

As she went off to the guest room, he went to the sliding doors that led out to his back deck and the patio that surrounded it. He'd done most of the work himself, and he was proud of the space. He turned on the lights he'd strung over the patio.

They went from the trees on one side to the trees on the other, casting just enough light to give the space a soft, welcoming glow.

"Oh, that's beautiful," Ephie breathed. She was standing beside him now, wrapped in a long ivory cardigan.

"Thanks. I like my backyard a lot. I spend a lot of time out there."

"I can see why." She turned to him. "Not a major problem, but I can't find Jean-Luc. I'm sure he's around."

"Did you look in my bedroom?"

"No." She chewed the inside of her cheek. "That's your space."

"Let's take a peek."

Together they went back to his room. Jean-Luc was sleeping in the middle of Remy's king-size bed.

"Little traitor," Ephie murmured. "He likes you better than me!"

"I don't think that's true. He probably just didn't know which room was yours." Although Remy couldn't help but think the cat recognized Remy as a similar being, since vampires were technically also dead.

"I'll get him out."

Remy put his hand on her arm. "He's fine. He can sleep anywhere he wants. And I'm sure when you go to bed, he'll come in with you. He's still finding his way around this new space."

"I guess so."

Remy nudged her. "Come on. Let's go eat some ice cream."

16

The I Scream Ice Cream shop was clearly a popular spot, even later at night. Not only were most of the tables inside occupied, but there was a line at the outside service windows. Only three people but still a line at nearly 11 p.m. at night.

Ephie didn't mind a little wait. It was going to take her a second to figure out which flavor she wanted anyway. They had so many, and they all looked good. She pointed at the menu. "Look at that. They have a praline flavor. And bananas foster. Flavors of home. I can see why this place is so busy."

Remy stood beside her, looking up at the menu, too, and nodding. "You see the flavors with the stars by the name? Those have actual alcohol in them. Like the Rummier Rum Raisin. Probably not a lot of alcohol but just thought you should know."

"I see that. Hmm. I'm not much of a drinker, but that Bailey's Chocolate Chip sounds pretty tempting." Her eyes went on to the next flavor. "Oh, hang on. I think I know what I'm getting."

He moved closer to her. Like that might help him see the same thing she was looking at. "Which one?"

She leaned toward him, their shoulders touching, and

pointed. "Right there. The Holy Cannoli flavor. I do love a good cannoli." She read the description. "Creamy cannoli filling ice cream with mini dark chocolate chips and pieces of cannoli shell swirled through."

"I'm leaning toward Big Easy Praline. Brown sugar ice cream with candied pecans and ribbons of salted caramel."

"That does sound good." Was he homesick for New Orleans?

He looked at her. "You can have a bite of mine."

"Yeah? Deal."

They got in line. Only two people ahead of them now and the line was moving pretty fast. Before long, they'd ordered, and Remy had paid.

She didn't love that. It felt wrong to let him pay all the time. They weren't a couple. And cooking dinner wasn't really the same as paying her share. Before she could say anything, a new voice rang out.

"Remy? Hi!"

She turned to see a gorgeous redhead coming toward them with a tall, lanky man in tow. He had dark hair and piercing dark eyes.

Remy smiled. "Hey, Pandora, Cole. How are you guys?"

"Great," the redhead said. She put her hand to her slightly rounded belly. "The baby wants ice cream, so here we are."

The man beside her rolled his dark eyes and laughed. "It seems the baby wants ice cream all the time now."

Remy nodded at Ephie. "This is an old friend of mine, Ephelia Moreau. She's visiting from New Orleans."

Pandora smiled at Ephie. "Nice to meet you, Ephelia. New Orleans is a great town." She touched her hand to the man's arm. "This is my husband, Cole."

"Nice to meet you both," Ephie said. "Please, call me Ephie. And congrats on the baby. That's so exciting."

"Thanks." Pandora was all smiles. "She's not due for a while yet, but we're over the moon."

Remy leaned in toward Ephie and spoke softly. "Pandora's a witch, too."

Pandora sucked in a breath as her brows shot up. "A crafty sister? Nice. We should totally have a secret handshake or something." She laughed, then dropped her voice. "There's a coven meeting this Thursday night. You should come."

"I, um, I don't really practice ..." Ephie didn't want to blurt out that her magical gifts were basically useless.

"No worries. Not everyone does. We have all levels." She dug a business card out of her purse. "My number's on there. Call me if you want a ride. We don't live far from Remy, which I know, because I sold him his house."

"She did," Remy agreed. "Pandora's *the* real estate agent in town. I'll be at work Thursday, so that might be a good thing for you to do."

Ephie took the card. She'd never been to a coven meeting. Her mother had tried to get her to go, but Ephie didn't feel her skills warranted inclusion in a meeting. It would be embarrassing to be the least talented witch there. "Thanks. I'll let you know."

A voice called out, "Remy, order up."

Remy turned toward the pickup window. "That's us. I'd better get that. Enjoy your ice cream."

"Thanks. You, too. We should order or we won't get any," Cole said. "Nice to meet you, Ephie."

"You, too."

He and Pandora moved to get in line. Remy returned with their cups of ice cream. "Want to walk a bit? See some more of the town?"

"I'd love to. They seem nice."

"They're great. He teaches math at the private academy here. He's also her familiar."

Ephie glanced back, more curious now. "He's her familiar? I didn't know that was possible."

Remy nodded, digging out a bite of ice cream with his spoon. "He shifts into a raven." He held out his spoon. "Here. Try this."

She took the bite. "That's amazing. I haven't even tried mine yet. I need to back up a minute. He shifts into a raven, and in that form, he's her familiar?"

Remy nodded. "That's my understanding."

"I might have to go to that coven meeting. I've never heard of such a thing." She tried her own ice cream. It was everything a cannoli was and more, but the straight-up truth was, it was delicious.

"I don't think it's super common. How's your ice cream?"

"This stuff is amazing. I understand the long lines now." She offered him a bite, which he took, nodding. She had another one, the delicious creaminess so good. "Kind of makes me wish I was pregnant so I had an excuse to eat it all the time, too." She caught the odd light in his eyes. "I mean, I don't really wish I was pregnant. I just— Never mind. Just forget I said that."

She shoved another spoonful in her mouth before she embarrassed herself further.

She'd thought about having kids. Probably a standard thought process for most women in her age group. She still had time for that to happen, but if it didn't … it didn't. She'd be sad about it, but— She realized he might think she meant pregnant by him, which would be awesome if that was where their lives led, but he also might think she was implying they do something about it. Mortification set in.

Why had she said that? She really needed to think before she spoke. She quickly pointed to a shop ahead just to change the subject. "That's cute. Hats in the Belfry."

"You want to go in? I don't think they'll care about the ice cream if we're careful."

"Okay." Thankfully, he let her comment go. It had to be awkward for him, having once been romantically involved with her. Could a vampire even have kids? One more thing to add to her list of lacking vampire knowledge.

The shop had all kinds of hats. Fancy ones, silly ones,

practical ones. She left her spoon in her ice cream cup and picked up a black ballcap with the town's pumpkin logo embroidered on it in silver thread. It was adjustable, so no reason to think it wouldn't fit, even over her curls. "I might get this." It would be a nice reminder of her trip.

"Do you want to try it on? I can hold your ice cream."

"Okay." She handed him her cup and tried the hat on, pulling her hair through the back like a ponytail.

Remy smiled. "It looks great on you. But then, you'd look good in anything."

She smiled back. "Thanks." She checked her reflection in a nearby mirror. It was cute. "Sold. Let me go pay, and I'll be right back."

"I'll be here."

She took the hat to the register, paid with her credit card, then rejoined him wearing the hat. That way there was no need for her to carry a bag. She took her ice cream back. "I had no idea the town would be so busy this late or that places would still be open."

They walked outside together. He nodded. "It's a lot like New Orleans in that way."

"Yes, but so far nothing smells like urine, I haven't seen anyone's boobs, and there's been no need to step over vomit."

He laughed hard. "Nothing against New Orleans, but this town is much more family-oriented, and a real emphasis is placed on keeping things neat and orderly."

"I like it." She liked it a lot. Okay, so she'd only been here a couple of hours, but there was a feeling here that had never existed for her in New Orleans. A feeling of being home. That made no sense. None at all. New Orleans actually was her home.

But there was something about this town. A kind of warmth and coziness that she'd never felt in the Big Easy before.

She glanced at Remy. He was eating the last of his ice cream. If things were to somehow rekindle between them, she could see living here. Okay, that was a big if, and she needed to stop thinking like that or she'd end up hurt again. She ate some more of her ice cream.

Actually, even if things didn't rekindle between them, she could see living here. She'd miss her grandmother mostly. That would be hard. But putting some distance between her and her mother might be good for both of them.

What would it be like to live her life without wondering what her mother would think of every decision she made?

"You're quiet all of a sudden," he said.

"Just thinking."

"About?"

About him and what the future might hold. About making a change in her life. About making decisions without caring what her mother might think. But she didn't tell him that. Instead, she just smiled and said, "When I can get more of this ice cream."

He grinned and tossed his empty cup into a nearby trash bin. "We'll come back before you leave, I promise."

She pointed her spoon at him. "I'm going to hold you to that."

He put his hand on his heart. "I'm an officer of the law. My word is good."

"I believe you." Too bad she also believed that all he wanted was to be friends. Could she change his mind?

There was only one way to find out, and it would require courage she wasn't sure she had. Brave was not a word she'd use to describe herself. But what if this time with Remy was her last chance at real happiness?

She took a breath, light from the shops glinting on the diamonds in her pansy ring. She owed it to herself to do what needed to be done.

Alphonso had made chicken cassoulet and corn bread, a meal Darryl seemed eager to dig into. Wasn't like he could do anything else. She'd asked him not to conduct his security check until Alphonso had gone. She didn't want the man worrying unnecessarily.

As soon as they were seated at the table, Alphonso set the dishes in front of them. He went back to the kitchen, returning with a skillet of corn bread sliced into wedges, then paused by Leonie's side. "Anything else I can do for you?"

"No, thank you, Alphonso. This looks perfect. You have a good night."

"You, too, Ms. Moreau. Don't forget, there's vanilla pound cake with bourbon sauce if you get a sweet tooth."

Darryl grinned, knife and fork in his hands already. "I don't think we'll forget that."

Alphonso gave Darryl a happy nod, then went back to the kitchen. He'd leave out the side door, like he usually did.

Leonie picked up her fork but waited until she heard the side door close before she spoke. "Enough suspense. What did your team find out?"

Darryl had already taken a bite of chicken. He swallowed. "One bug in your office."

She stopped eating. "Where?"

"Under one of the bookcase shelves closest to your desk."

"Can you trace where it's sending to?"

"Not without removing the bug, which you asked me not to do."

"You understand why, don't you? Because it'll tip Turner off that I'm on to him. And I don't think that's a good idea. Not yet." Being able to get information to Turner, the information she wanted him to believe, could work in her favor.

Sharing his news hadn't done anything to lessen Darryl's appetite, apparently. He kept eating. "I understand that, but if you forget it's there and slip up, if you say something he shouldn't know about, then what?"

"I'll be careful. I'm thinking about faking a phone call to Ephie and leading him to believe she's in Mississippi." She shrugged. "We have some distant family there. It would be plausible."

"You going to give that family a heads-up? Let them know what's going on? What if Turner sends men out there?"

She didn't like the idea of doing that. "Don't you think he's already stretched thin if he's surveilling me?"

Darryl dabbed his mouth with the napkin next to his plate. "Leonie, the man has more resources and more people than we've been able to count. Don't underestimate him. He wouldn't even necessarily need humans to do his surveilling."

She knew that, but she hadn't seen any strange animals around, either. "I'm not underestimating him. But I refuse to live my life like he's got me scared." To her, that would be giving him a victory, albeit a small one.

"Nothing wrong with being scared. Fear serves a purpose. Keeps us sharp. Makes us alert. Don't be worried about being scared. Be worried about being dumb."

She frowned at him. "Darryl Jerome Tyson. Did you just call me dumb?"

He laughed. "Wouldn't dream of it. But you've got to be smart about this. Turner is crafty. And he's done things we can't explain."

"You telling me you believe in his voodoo powers now?" Darryl had long maintained that Tyson's special abilities were nonsense. That voodoo was just another tool he used to intimidate those around him into doing his will. Another way he frightened people into obedience. Real or not, it worked.

Darryl also had no real idea what the women of her family were capable of. Sure, he knew her mother made love potions and other assorted spells, but so did most of the women in the bayous.

"You know that feather in the letter?"

She nodded.

"One of the techs in the lab, a young man who specializes in the occult, had a hunch about it. He ran a few tests and found it was coated with a powdery substance that contained several toxins, including one from a plant called datura. Do you know what they call datura in Haiti?"

She shook her head, almost afraid to find out.

"Zombie cucumber. They dry the plant and use the powder for zombie rituals." His eyes burned with a hard, angry light. "The powder on that feather also contained tetrodotoxin. Puffer fish venom. It's a paralytic that can lead to death."

Her food forgotten, she stared at him in horror.

"Turner meant for you to touch that feather and for harm to come to you. This isn't something you can brush off, Leonie. If you don't testify on his behalf at the parole hearing, he's going to attempt to kill you and your daughter. Have no doubt."

She swallowed, her stomach churning. "I don't doubt it," she said softly. "But you know I cannot allow him to go free."

Darryl's voice softened. "I know you can't. I wouldn't expect that of you. But we have to protect you and Ephie. You need to let the friend she's with know about all of this. They need to keep their eyes open." He sighed. "Truth is, she's probably in more danger than you are. Killing her would be a good way for Turner to prove how serious he is."

A sob escaped Leonie's throat before she could stop it. "That cannot happen, Darryl."

He reached across the table and took her hand.

"Nothing's going to happen to you, Leonie. Not as long as I have anything to do with it."

She nodded. The feeling of his big strong hand gave her some comfort. "What about Ephie?"

"You said the friend she's with is in law enforcement?"

"Yes. He's a deputy for the sheriff's department."

"Then he's armed. That's a good thing. But you need to let him know everything you can about Turner. That he might be using unexpected means to get to Ephie."

"You really think he knows where she is?"

Darryl shook his head. "I don't know, but just like I told you, I don't want to underestimate him. Better to be overprepared and have nothing happen than ... you know."

"Yes." She let go of his hand and pushed her chair back, making herself give him a quick, reassuring smile. "Excuse me a moment. I won't be long. You eat while your food's still hot. And then, before dessert, you can do your security check, all right?"

He nodded and made a face, but she wasn't in the mood for more explanation. She dashed upstairs to her bedroom and went to the jewelry box on her dresser. She opened one of the small drawers along the bottom and lifted out a necklace her mother had given her years ago, when she'd first become a judge.

It was a long, thin silver chain with a pierced dime dangling from it. The dime had been spelled with rites of protection and blessed by the local priest. Leonie had never put much stock in such things, despite the powers that ran in her maternal bloodline.

She slipped the chain over her head, tucking it and the dime under her clothing. The cool metal warmed quickly against her skin. Now was not the time for skepticism. Any advantage was a good one.

She would text Remy later and tell him they needed to talk privately. There was too much to explain by text. Besides that, she needed to hear his voice so she knew he was taking this seriously.

If anything happened to Ephie, she would hold Remy responsible. And if it came to that, the vampire council would be the least of his worries.

They'd walked long enough that Ephie had finished her ice cream and thrown the cup away. Remy wondered if she was tired by now. As much as he wanted to show her the town, he didn't want to wear her out, either. "Ready to head back? We can cross the street and come up on the other side so you can see what's over there. Or we can stay on this side. Whatever you want to do."

"Let's cross over," she said.

They waited for the light and crossed when it turned. They hit the opposite side, and she hugged her arms around herself like she was cold.

"Chilly?" he asked. It did get cooler in the evenings here because they were higher up. New Orleans was about as low as you could go without actually being underwater.

"A little. Probably from the ice cream. I'll be all right."

He slipped off his leather jacket and put it around her shoulders. "Here. Temperature doesn't bother me that much."

"You're sure?"

He nodded.

She pulled it closer around her. "Thanks."

They walked in silence the rest of the way back to the

car, mostly just taking in the sights and sounds. People-watching was really something special in a place like this.

At the car, he got her door, then went around and took his seat behind the wheel. She seemed to be drifting off as he drove. Understandable. It had been a long day.

He parked in the driveway. She stayed asleep, buckled into her seat. He went around to her side, opened her door, unlatched her seatbelt, then carefully picked her up and carried her to the door.

The sweet scent of her perfume enveloped him. He bent his face into her hair and inhaled. He'd missed that. She'd always smelled good to him.

Holding her with one arm, the warmth of her body seeping into his, he unlocked the door and took her straight to the guest room. He laid her on the bed, still wrapped in his jacket. He slipped off her shoes, then shook out the throw from across the foot of the bed and covered her with it.

He backed away, thinking he could leave without waking her, but then Jean-Luc trotted in and meowed.

Ephie blinked her eyes open and let out a big yawn. She smiled at him as she realized where she was. "Did you carry me in here from the car?"

"I did. I hated to wake you."

Jean-Luc jumped up on the bed, going right to Ephie as he materialized. She scratched his head. "Hey, buddy." She looked at Remy. "I guess I was sleepier than I realized. I'm too tired to stay up any longer. I realize you probably aren't going to bed yet. Sorry."

"You have nothing to apologize for, and you don't need to keep the same hours as me. You're here to enjoy yourself and have a nice break. Not to entertain me."

"Thanks for tonight. That was fun."

"You're welcome. I'll see you tomorrow, okay?"

She nodded, still petting Jean-Luc. "Okay. Good night."

He left her and went to his room. There were plenty of hours before the sun rose. There were a few things he'd been meaning to do around the house, but those things would make noise, and Ephie would be sleeping.

He'd also planned on telling Ephie about why she was really here, but that wasn't going to happen, either. Not now, anyway. Better to let her sleep, but he'd do it first thing when he woke up tomorrow.

He checked his phone, which he'd put on silent earlier, just to see if he'd missed anything important. He found he had. A call from Leonie and a text a few minutes after that telling him to call her as soon as possible.

She probably hadn't meant at one in the morning, but she'd said as soon as possible. He didn't want to wake Ephie up, so he went outside to sit on the front steps. He preferred the backyard, but that would put him closer to the guest room window.

He dialed, expecting to get Leonie's voicemail. After three rings, he got her instead.

"Hello," she mumbled.

"Sorry to wake you, Leonie, but I just saw the text. What's going on?"

She sighed into the phone. "You had me worried when you didn't answer. I don't like that, Lafitte."

"Ephie wanted ice cream. We were busy."

"She's safe then?"

"Perfectly." He frowned. Like he'd let anything happen to her. "What was so urgent?"

"Turner tried to kill me. Or at least incapacitate me."

Remy's mouth fell open. "What? How?"

"He sent me another letter, the one I sent you the picture of. In the envelope was a black feather laced with a variety of toxins. He meant for me to touch it. If I had, I would at least be in the hospital."

Where she'd be more vulnerable.

"Worst-case scenario, we wouldn't be having this conversation."

"But you're all right?" He didn't like the woman, but he didn't want her dead, either.

"Yes, I'm fine. The police commissioner is an old friend. He did a security check on my house and chambers. My chambers were bugged, by the way."

That caught him off guard but made him think, too. "Turner's really serious about this."

"You think?" She made a noise like she was sucking her teeth. "You need to take this seriously. It's very possible they tracked Ephie to your town. They could be there now."

He scanned the street before him, paying close attention to the few cars parked along it. Most people parked in their garages or driveways, but now and then there were cars on the street. He couldn't see anyone in the cars currently parked on the curb. "They won't get past me. Nothing is going to happen to her."

"That's easy for you to say. You don't know what this Turner is like. He's ruthless. Vicious. He'll do anything he thinks necessary. And Darryl believes he'll hurt Ephie first just to show me what he's capable of and to scare me into testifying on his behalf so that he can get parole."

Remy scrubbed his hand across his chin. "I've made the sheriff aware of the threat and the possibility that Turner could send goons here. Extra precautions are being taken. I promise I'm doing everything I can."

"Where is Ephie now?"

"Asleep in the guest room."

"Do you have an alarm system? Is it on?"

"I don't have one. I'm a vampire. I'm my own alarm system."

"Not good enough, Lafitte. That is my only child."

He frowned. "What do you want me to do? Sleep on her floor? She's safe, I promise."

"Sleeping on her floor isn't a bad idea."

"You have to be kidding. If you want her to really be safe, she needs to know what's going on."

"*No*. Ephie won't be able to handle it. She'll want to come home immediately, and that will only put her in more danger."

The Vampire's Former Flame

He sighed just to let her know he didn't approve. "I don't like lying to her, Leonie."

"You're not lying to her. You're protecting her."

He didn't like Leonie's opinion of her daughter. "You don't give her enough credit. She's not this fragile flower you make her out to be."

"Oh, and you know this because after twelve years away, you've spent a couple days with her and suddenly you're an expert? I've known her her whole life. I'm the one who put her back together when you disappeared and left her a broken mess. Don't pretend you know her, because you don't."

That hurt. He'd loved Ephie deeply. Probably more than she'd loved him. He'd been prepared to spend eternity with her. He wanted to hang up on Leonie, but he didn't need her running to the vampire council and turning him in. "She will be safe here. You can count on that."

"I hope so. You realize things are only going to get worse once his parole hearing happens and I don't do as he wants."

"Ephie can stay here as long as she needs to. You just worry about yourself."

"I have a lot of people looking out for me."

"Does that mean the entire force knows and not just the commissioner?"

"A select few know, yes. Enough to provide me with the protection I need."

"Good. I should go."

"Fine. But listen—I want daily texts from you letting me know things are all right. You understand?"

"I do. Good night." He hung up. He sat a moment, unhappy with everything that was going on. Ephie being threatened, most of all. But her not knowing about it really upset him, too. He was being forced to lie by omission.

He hated that. If things were ever going to work out for the two of them, this was not a good start.

He got up, keeping his phone in his hand, and walked to the sidewalk. He looked in both directions. There were two cars to the right and one to the left. The vehicle on the left-hand side was an SUV with tinted glass. The two cars on the right were sedans, no tint. He could see right through them.

Didn't mean there wasn't someone crouched down inside them. He went to the right first, strolling toward the sedans with purpose. He stopped at each one, using the flashlight on his phone to illuminate the interiors.

Both were empty.

As he turned to head toward the SUV, it started up and drove off. He quickly took a snap of the license plate, but when he looked at the photo, it was dark, blurry, and hard to make out.

He stared after the vehicle. It was too far away and too dark for even his eyes to read more than the first few digits on the plate. What bothered him more was that he hadn't heard anyone get in it, which had to mean someone had already been inside.

Wasn't any kind of proof where Ephie was concerned, but it didn't sit well with him. He had the make, model, and the first three numbers of the plate. He'd see what Birdie could do with that tomorrow.

He went back inside and found Ephie standing in the foyer, visibly upset. "What's wrong? Are you okay? Is Jean-Luc okay?"

Her fists clenched. "What were you doing out there? And why were you talking to my mother? What do I need to be protected from? More importantly, what are you lying to me about?"

Confronting Remy made Ephie felt sick to her stomach. She didn't like confrontation. It made her want to run away. It had ever since the night he'd proposed.

Flashbacks of that night filled her head.

He opened his mouth, then closed it and shook his head. "Let's sit down and discuss this."

She was too upset to move. "What are you lying to me about? Just tell me. Then I'm packing my bag and leaving."

"You don't have a car."

"I'll rent one. Stop changing the subject and answer me."

He raked his hand through his hair and closed the door behind him, locking it. "A man named Abraham Turner has threatened you and your mother. It was her idea that you come back here with me so that you'd be out of town and away from the danger, but I'm not so sure it worked out that way. I really do *not* want you to leave."

"Why? What do you care?"

He took a step toward her, his brows bent in concern. "Ephie, I know you're mad at me right now, and I don't blame you for that, but I do care about you. I always have. I can absolutely protect you."

"I can protect myself." Even as she said it, she knew it wasn't true, but she had some pride. She wasn't completely helpless.

"Maybe you can, but Turner is a voodoo practitioner. One of the letters he sent your mother contained a feather laced with toxin. He meant to do her serious harm."

"Why?"

"Because she put him in jail and he believes that if she testifies on his behalf at his next parole hearing, it will be enough to sway the parole board into granting it."

"My mother will never do that."

"I know. Which is why you both need protection. She's spoken to the police commissioner and assures me steps are being taken."

"What did Turner do? I don't remember him, but then she's never told me much in the way of specifics. How bad is he?"

"Pretty bad. He's a gangster that runs crews throughout the city. Gambling, drugs, women—he's into all sorts of things. Your mother put him away for manslaughter, but it was just a scratch on the surface of the things he was truly guilty of."

Some of the wind left her sails. "How much trouble am I in? And don't sugarcoat it. I want to know the truth."

He came closer. "I believe you're in serious trouble. I also believe Turner would hurt you, and probably even kidnap you, in order to get your mother to do his bidding. Are you in trouble? Yes, I think you are."

She shivered involuntarily.

Remy put his arms around her. She didn't resist. He held her, speaking softly. "I will not let anyone hurt you, Eph. I swear it on my life. Please, don't go. Stay with me."

There was no fight left in her now that the weight of the truth had been laid upon her. "I don't like that you were keeping all of this from me."

"I didn't like it, either. I was going to tell you tonight, but you were too tired for a big conversation. I figured I'd do it first thing tomorrow. Please believe me, I hated keeping this from you. But your mother was against you knowing. She didn't think you could handle it."

Ephie scoffed as she pulled out of his embrace. "Of course she didn't. She barely trusts me to cross the street on my own."

She folded her arms over her chest and stared toward the backyard. She was still mad, but she knew how her mother operated. Ephie had every reason to believe her mother had found a way to threaten Remy into doing what she wanted.

"I'm sorry, Ephelia. I really am."

His use of her full name and the sincere tone of his voice got her attention. She turned toward him. "I know you are. I know how my mother works. What did she threaten you with? Or don't you want to tell me?"

He laughed humorlessly before answering her. "You really do know your mother, don't you? Better, I'd say, than she knows you." He frowned. "She threatened to turn me in to the local vampire council for being in New

Orleans. No exceptions, not even for emergencies. Certainly not one related to a human. According to the council, I cannot be within city limits for more than twenty-four hours for another sixty-eight years."

She blinked in astonishment. "Sixty-eight years? What did you do to deserve that?"

"Nothing. It's just a precaution applied to all vampires so that no one notices we don't age. We can't reside in the city for longer than forty years at a time, either. Once we do, we have to leave for eighty years. A generation must pass before we take up residence again."

She had no idea such things existed. "What about this place? How long can you be in Nocturne Falls?"

"For as long as I like. There is no local vampire council here. This town is owned by a family of vampires, and they never set one up. I guess they were tired of those kinds of rules, too. But this town is also magically protected so that humans won't notice if someone doesn't seem to age."

"So you can live here for the rest of your life, if you like?"

He nodded. "I can."

She liked the town even more now. It seemed so unfair that New Orleans had forced Remy out. And that he might be penalized for returning to see a dying friend. She went toward the front windows, reaching to pull the drapes back so she could look out.

"Don't do that."

She stopped where she was. "Don't do what?"

"Don't go by the windows."

"Are you trying to frighten me on purpose?"

"No, not at all. But there was a car out there earlier ..." He chewed the inside of his cheek. "Might not have been anything, but I can't be sure. It took off before I could get a better look."

She backed away, a new fear welling up inside her. "You really think Turner's got men here? Looking for me?"

"I don't know. They could be tracking your phone."

Her phone. Which had somehow gotten turned off when they'd been driving. "You turned my phone off before we left New Orleans, didn't you?"

He nodded. "I did. Just in case."

"You know I've had it on since we left the hotel."

"I know. I couldn't very well ask you to shut it down without explaining what was going on, and your mother had forbidden that."

"My mother." Ephie rolled her eyes. "I'm going to turn it off right now, then you and I are going to deal with this. Does this town have a twenty-four-hour drugstore?"

"It does. What do you need?"

"A pay-as-you-go phone, since mine's about to be unavailable. I also need a box and, as soon as possible, a visit to the post office. If they want to track my phone, I'm going to use that to my advantage. I'm going to mail my phone back to my apartment. Let them think I changed my mind about getting out of town."

He smiled. "I had no idea you could be so cunning." He nodded. "I like it."

She flipped her hair over her shoulder. "Thanks. First, though, I'm going to see if they really are tracking my phone. If they are, I might be able to get some information on them."

"How?"

She arched her brows. "You know I graduated with a degree in computer science, right? Magna cum laude, too, by the way."

"I knew that was what you were studying, but I didn't know about the magna cum laude part. Smart and beautiful. Impressive."

If he was trying to get back on her good side, it was working. With a smile, she rubbed her hands together and wiggled her brows at him. "Watch and learn, my vampire friend. Watch and learn."

She headed to the guest room with him following close behind. She had to fire up her computer, then connect her phone and run a few tests, but she'd make sure she was protected first so anyone monitoring the phone wouldn't detect her activities.

"So," Remy said. "Does this mean you're not mad at me?"

She abruptly stopped, almost causing him to run into her. "I'm not mad at you. Like I said, I know how my mother works. How she manipulates situations and people. You're a victim in this, too."

"I wouldn't say I was a victim, but I'm glad you aren't mad at me. I felt terrible about not telling you the truth."

He was only a few inches away, the woodsy-clean scent of him filling her senses. She was reminded of her earlier resolution, one she'd forgotten about because she'd fallen asleep. But she was awake now.

And what better time than the present to see how he actually felt about her?

She leaned in, laced her arms around his neck, and kissed him full on the mouth.

For a split second, Remy froze, immobilized by the very act he'd believed would never happen again.

Ephie.

Was.

Kissing.

Him.

Then he snapped out of his disbelief and kissed her back. He slipped his arms around her waist and tugged her against him. The warmth of her spread through him, urging him on. He deepened the kiss. She didn't resist. In fact, she leaned closer. Curious, for a woman who claimed she was over him.

So curious, he almost laughed. He managed to stifle it at the last moment but apparently not well enough.

She pulled back. "What was that?"

"A kiss." He gave her a skeptical look. "Odd you wouldn't know that, considering you started it."

She playfully smacked his arm. "I meant that little noise you made."

"I made a noise?"

She rolled her eyes. "It sounded like you were about to laugh." She backed away. "I know I shouldn't have done that. I just wanted to see if ... you know."

He genuinely didn't know. "To see if what?" Then it dawned on him. "If you still had feelings for me?" He grinned. That kiss had definitely felt like feelings. Serious ones. "So? Do ya?"

She opened her mouth to reply, but his impulses took over. He grabbed her and pulled her close again, kissing her a second time. This time, he put more effort into it, holding her near, hands on her hips, and when he let her go, her eyes stayed closed for a few seconds longer than necessary.

"Oh," she breathed.

"Oh, indeed. You, Ephelia Moreau, most certainly still have feelings for me."

Her eyes were wide open now. "No, I don't."

"Yes, you do."

She frowned again. "And you don't for me?"

"Did I say that?"

"No, but—"

"Because I am nuts about you." If she needed him to say it first, so be it. He had no problem doing that. Although his ring still being on her finger gave him a fair idea of where she stood. "In fact, I've never stopped being nuts about you."

She seemed to melt slightly. "Are you being totally honest with me? Don't play with me, Remy. It won't go well."

"I wouldn't play with you. And I wouldn't lie to you, especially not about something like this." He would have asked her to marry him again right then and there, but he sensed that, much like the first time, it wouldn't be well received.

"I thought ..." She shook her head as if completing the sentence would open an old wound.

He understood. If there was anything keeping them from each other, it was emotional scar tissue. "Twelve years ago, we both screwed up. I was too impulsive. I wanted too much too soon. I scared you away, I know that. I'm sorry. But my intentions were pure. I only wanted to give you the best possible life. To protect you in the only way I knew how. To make forever with you a reality."

She gazed into his face, her own unreadable. She reached for him, putting her hands on his shoulders and tucking her head under his chin as she settled against him and exhaled. "I should have told you then that I wasn't ready. I shouldn't have run away. But you did scare me coming on so strong."

He wrapped his arms around her, his hold on her loose and easy. He reveled in having her so close again. He could have stayed that way for hours. Her presence in his arms filled gaps he hadn't realized existed. He felt complete. "I know."

She stayed there, sighing softly. "My mother put such a fear of vampires into me that I didn't know what to think at that moment. At least not until I got home and really examined what I was feeling. I did love you. But I was afraid of that love. Of what my mother would do if I told her the truth. Of what being with you would mean. I wasn't brave enough to accept the changes loving you would bring. But I didn't want to lose you, either."

She lifted her head to look at him. Tears shone in her eyes. "I was going to tell you all of that the very next day. I looked for you everywhere. On campus. Places where I knew vampires hung out. Clubs. Cemeteries. Anywhere I could think of. But you were gone."

"I had no idea." He'd already been on his way to Nocturne Falls.

"I know." She blinked the tears away before they fell. "Funny how life works sometimes."

"Do you ... think you could love me again?"

She hesitated. Choosing her words, maybe. "Remy, there's a part of me that never stopped."

"But?"

She smiled. "We're different people now. Which is a good thing. We need to get to know each other again. I've changed a lot in the last twelve years."

He nodded. "You're somehow more beautiful, I know that."

Her smile widened. "You always were a sweet-talker." But the smile didn't last. "Do you really think I'm in danger?"

"I do." He watched her carefully for any sign she might not be able to handle the truth, as her mother thought. Any sign she might crumble. "Doesn't mean anything is going to happen to you. Not while I'm here. And I'm not going to leave you, so while you need to be cautious, there's nothing to lose your head over."

"What about when you have to go to work?"

That was a problem. "We'll figure something out. A different place for you to stay, someone to stay with you, something."

"I don't want to put anyone out."

"Eph, please." He grabbed her hand. It felt so good to hold it again. "This is your life we're talking about. And the safety of the townspeople and visitors, too, for that matter. Being proactive about this isn't putting anyone out."

She took a deep breath. "Then let me get my phone sorted out and we can go to the drugstore for a burner phone."

"How long do you need?"

She looked toward the guest room. "Ten minutes, maybe twenty. I'm not sure until I get in there and see how deeply embedded the tracking info is. All depends on how sophisticated their tech person is."

"Okay. I have a few things I can do until you're ready to go."

"Can you do them in the same room as me? I don't want to be alone right now."

"I'm all yours." He followed her into the guest room, where Jean-Luc sat on the window ledge, looking out.

She set herself up on the bed with her laptop, phone, and a connector cable and went to work.

While she did that, he texted Birdie the photo of the SUV he'd taken along with a message. *Possible suspicious vehicle. GA plate. First three digits X45. Black Lincoln Navigator probably less than five years old.*

He knew Birdie would be asleep, but this way she'd get the text first thing.

"Unbelievable," Ephie muttered.

He looked up. "What?"

Irritation masked her pretty face. Angry sparks gleamed in her eyes. "I've only had this phone for about a month. I got a notice about a free upgrade recently, and who wouldn't take that, right?"

"Right."

"Yeah, well, there's a tracking program on it. One I did *not* install," she fumed. "The absolute nerve."

"Turner."

"Has to be. But now that I've confirmed its existence, we can go. There's nothing I can do to find out who installed it, because it'll just show that I did it. Which I didn't, obviously."

He nodded.

She smiled at him. "Let's go get me a new phone and a box to mail this one back in. And then I really need some sleep."

He got to his feet, putting his phone in his pocket. "Just let me get my keys."

Ephie woke up in a dark room, forgetting for a moment where she was. Remy's house. Nocturne Falls. She blinked, but it was so dark from the blackout shades that she couldn't make out more than shapes.

It had to be daylight, though. She grabbed her new phone to check the time. Nearly 10 a.m., so she'd slept longer than she'd expected, even with not going to sleep until two in the morning.

After going to the drugstore for the phone, she'd crashed. She'd left her old phone, the one Turner was using to keep tabs on her, with Remy. He'd promised to package it up and get it ready to mail.

She stretched and used the dim light of the phone to look around the room. "Jean-Luc? Where are you?"

Not in the room. Not where she could see, anyway.

She got up, pulled on some leggings over the underwear and T-shirt she'd slept in, and went out to start some coffee and, hopefully, find her cat.

The hall was as dark as her room. So was the whole house. But Remy needed it that way. Curiosity got the best of her, and she peeked into his room.

He was on his side in his big king bed, facing the outside wall.

Jean-Luc, traitor of all traitors, was tucked into the bend of Remy's knees.

She shook her head. "I see how it is," she whispered.

Jean-Luc's eyes came open to slits, then closed again. A single flick of his tail was his only response. She closed Remy's door, which wouldn't impede Jean-Luc's access, since he could walk through it, and went on to the kitchen.

The light was on over the stove. It was enough to see by, so she left the blinds down.

She peered through the ones that covered the window over the sink just to see what kind of day it was. The backyard really was charming. He'd done beautiful work out there. From the steps of the deck to about ten or twelve feet out was a patio paved with big pieces of flagstone.

A table with an umbrella and two chairs sat on the patio, beckoning her. A citronella candle in a squat glass jar sat in the center. The underside of the umbrella was dotted with LED lights.

Maybe she'd have her coffee out there. She'd promised Remy she wouldn't go anywhere without him, but this was just the backyard.

It was so inviting. Especially with the sun shining. The day was too nice to be ignored.

Sad Remy couldn't enjoy it with her.

She found the coffee and the filters and got a pot going, doing her best to keep quiet, although from what she understood, vampires slept very solidly. She still didn't want to be the reason he woke up before he was ready.

Jean-Luc suddenly appeared by her feet, fully materialized. He wound around her ankles and rubbed against them like he loved her more than anything in the world.

Despite how much favoritism the little cat had shown for Remy, Ephie scooped him up and kissed his face. "You little stinker. You're kind of a user, you know that? I see how much you like Remy. Is it because he's ... not ... that is ..." She didn't like to say the word "dead" in front of Jean-Luc. It sounded so final. He was anything but dead.

"You know, you're both unalive. Is that why you like him so much?"

Jean-Luc snuggled up to her, extending one paw to touch her face.

She smiled. "I can't stay mad at you when you're this cute. Want to go outside with me while I have some coffee? There's all sorts of things to investigate out there."

The backyard was fully fenced in, too. Not that a fence would keep Jean-Luc contained, but then, neither would the walls of the house, so attempting to keep him in was pointless. If he wanted to go, he would. Whenever and wherever.

She took a quick shower, then came out to find the coffee had finished brewing, so she found a big mug and fixed a cup. Quietly, she went to the sliders, unlocked them, and slipped out. She left them open a few inches just in case she needed to get back inside quickly.

She stood on the deck and took her first sip. The

coffee was good. Not her usual brand. In fact, it was nicer. Remy had good taste.

Jean-Luc came outside and sat next to her.

"What do you think? Nice, huh?" There was no outside for him at home unless she took him for a walk. There was no yard when you lived in an apartment. The best she could do was open a window for him on nice days. He might be a ghost, but he loved sniffing the fresh air.

She didn't know if he could truly smell things. Seemed like he could, the way he reacted to food. Maybe a sense of smell was one of the senses a ghost retained. She'd never know for sure unless Jean-Luc suddenly developed the ability to talk.

"Let's go down to the patio." She walked down the steps, and he followed.

She took a seat at the table. Jean-Luc went beyond the patio to the grass. He rolled around in it as if he could actually feel it. A little white butterfly flitted past, catching his attention.

The hunt was on. He crouched low, wriggling his butt and making Ephie laugh. He was so cute.

"Hello?"

Ephie jumped, nearly spilling her coffee. She glanced toward the voice and saw an older woman had come through the gate that opened onto the front yard. The woman had short blue hair, a few extra pounds, and a bright smile. She held a piece of folded paper in one hand. A fringed and bedazzled purse swung from her shoulder.

Ephie grabbed for her phone and realized she'd left it inside. Dumb move. Although the woman didn't look very dangerous. "Hello."

"Didn't mean to startle you. I know Remy's still asleep." The woman smiled as she walked over. "I was going to stick this in his front door, but then I smelled the coffee and thought I'd take a chance he was out here in the shade. You're awfully pretty. You must be Ephelia."

Ephie had several questions. "You smelled the coffee from the front yard? How do you know my name? And sorry, I don't mean to be impolite, but who are you?"

The woman laughed. "I'm the one who should apologize. I'm Birdie Caruthers. I run the sheriff's department. My nephew, Hank Merrow, is the sheriff. He'll tell you he runs it, but everyone knows that's not true. I know your name because Remy filled us in on what was going on. I mean about you-know-who threatening you and your mom. And I smelled the coffee because I have especially acute senses."

Birdie tapped the side of her nose, and her eyes flashed blue.

Ephie's mouth came open. "What was that?"

"Oh, honey. I'm a werewolf. Didn't Remy tell you?"

"I—maybe. No, he did. You just startled me. So you're Birdie?" Remy had mentioned her. And Ephie had no reason to doubt her. Although he could have said something about the blue hair.

Birdie nodded. "Any chance I could wrangle a cup of that coffee? Smells great."

"Oh, sure, yes. Please, have a seat. I'll go get you a cup and be right back. Cream and sugar?"

Birdie helped herself to the other chair. "Sweet and light, that's how I like it."

"I'm on it." Ephie went in, made the cup of coffee with a big splash of cream and two and a half teaspoons of sugar, hoping that would be enough. She gave it a good stir, then carried it back out.

"Here you go. I hope it's sweet enough." Ephie sat. "It's nice to meet you, by the way. Remy talks about you like you can pretty much do anything."

Birdie grinned. "That's because I can." She laughed at her own joke. "Within reason, of course." She sipped the coffee. "It's perfect. Thank you." She pointed toward Jean-Luc. "That little nugget yours, or did Remy get a cat?"

"He's mine. That's Jean-Luc. You can see him, huh?" He did seem to be fully materialized as he continued to stalk the butterfly.

Birdie frowned. "I'm old. I'm not blind."

Ephie snorted. "I didn't mean it that way. Jean-Luc is a ghost." Maybe he thought being fully materialized would give him a better shot at catching his prey. Hard to tell what went through that little head.

Birdie stared harder. "Is he? Well, I'll be. I never would have guessed. Looks real to me."

"So, um, what's on the paper? Or is it top-secret sheriff's department stuff?"

"Not all that top secret. I just wanted to show him the report on the plate he called in."

"Plate?"

"As in license plate. It came back registered to a 2019 Kia Sorento and was listed as stolen."

"That's not good." Ephie stared out at the yard. Jean-Luc had given up on the butterfly and was now lounging, eyes closed, belly up, in a pool of sun. He'd gone translucent again.

"With what I understand is going on, I'd say it's not. Have you seen anything to indicate that Turner's men are here in town?"

"I haven't, no. But if that vehicle had stolen plates, that could mean something. Remy said something about a car, but that was all."

"Probably didn't want to worry you."

"Probably. Or it just slipped his mind." They'd been a little busy kissing. Ephie smiled. Then she remembered about her phone. "Could I ask you for a favor? I know you don't know me, so that's a bit bold, but—"

"Nonsense. What can I do for you?"

"I have a package that needs to be mailed. Could you drop it off at the post office for me? I'll give you some money. Turner's got a tracker on my phone, so I'm going to mail it back to New Orleans and let him think I've changed my mind about staying here."

Birdie grinned. "I like that. I'd be happy to mail it for you, and Remy can settle up with me when I see him next. I'll do it soon as I finish this coffee. Anything else you need?"

"Nope. I have work to keep me busy until Remy wakes up."

Birdie's eyes narrowed. "Uh-oh. I think your cat just disappeared."

Ephie glanced at him. He was right where she'd last seen him, translucent in a puddle of sun. "He's still there, but he's back to being all ghosty." Curious that Birdie could only see him when he was solid.

"How'd you figure out about the tracker on your phone?"

Ephie shrugged one shoulder. "I ran a systems check for hidden apps, anything running in the background. I'm fairly computer-savvy. I've got a degree in computer science. I'm a web designer by trade. It's what I do."

Birde's brows lifted. "You don't say? I do a little dabbling myself on the interwebs." She wiggled her fingers. "Comes in handy at the sheriff's department."

"I'm sure it does."

"What are you going to do when he goes back to work? Doesn't seem to me like you should be alone."

"I don't know yet. He said we'd figure it out."

"Well, if you don't mind the company of a more seasoned woman, I'd be happy to come over and spend the night. My boyfriend's out of town. He went out to visit his granddaughter at college for a few days. So I'm free."

"That seems like an awful imposition. You still have work during the day."

"It's all right. I can get ready and go from here. Remy and I will overlap, meaning you won't be by yourself. And while I might not be a vampire, I can be pretty formidable when necessary."

"I have no doubt." Ephie smiled, trying to imagine Birdie in her werewolf form. Would the wolf have blue hair, too? "I think I'd like your company very much."

Leonie felt the weight of the world upon her shoulders, but she had to do what was right. Abraham Turner could not be allowed back out into the world. He belonged in prison, and she was going to do everything in her power to keep him there.

If something happened to her because of her convictions, so be it. If something happened to Ephie, God forbid, she'd find a way to make Turner pay. He wasn't the only one with friends and connections.

He had to understand that. He had children of his own. Even if he wasn't active in their lives like she was in Ephie's, he must understand that coming between a mother and child would have repercussions.

She tugged at her jacket, waiting to be called in before the parole board. Turner would be in there, so she'd have to see him. Not something she was looking forward to, but it couldn't be helped.

She touched the spot on her chest where the dime pendant rested on its chain, feeling the metal under the silk of her blouse.

The chamber doors opened, and the bailiff came out. "They're ready for you, Your Honor."

The Vampire's Former Flame

She gave him a nod and strode through, chin lifted, a practiced look of seriousness on her face.

Turner sat in handcuffs and shackles, his prison orange jumpsuit a glaringly bright spot amidst the dark business tones everyone else had on.

He grinned at her, causing the tiny cross tattooed next to his right eye to crinkle into a lopsided X.

She ignored him and took her seat. She might have to be in the same room as him, but she did not have to acknowledge his presence. But that grin told her he was fully aware of the letters and threats she'd been subjected to.

Her blood boiled. She wanted to strangle him.

Instead, she smiled politely at the parole board hearing panel. "Good morning."

The head of the panel was a man Leonie recognized from previous hearings. She believed he was a deputy commissioner with the parole board. William something. He nodded at her. "Thank you for attending, Your Honor. We're ready to hear your statement. Begin when you like."

"My statement is a simple one because the facts speak for themselves. Abraham Turner is a violent man with ties to a long list of crimes that include felony theft, illegal gambling, prostitution, human trafficking, the sale and distribution of narcotics, and the one that finally incarcerated him, murder."

"Manslaughter," Turner spat out.

"*Mr. Turner.*" The head of the panel glared at him.

Turner clucked his tongue and leaned back like everything she'd just said was nonsense.

She went on. "As you know, I presided over the trial at which he was declared, by a jury of his peers, guilty of first-degree manslaughter. I saw the crime scene photos, heard the testimony of his surviving victim and those of the deceased victim's family."

Turner coughed, using the sound to cover a derogatory curse word clearly aimed at her.

The head of the panel glared at him. He held Turner's gaze. "Mr. Turner, you aren't doing anything to help yourself. Another outburst of any kind and we will end this hearing early."

Turner held up his hands in a pretense of innocence, his expression smug and not at all repentant. "My apologies. The damp conditions of the prison have left me with a cough I can't shake."

The head of the panel nodded to Leonie. "Please continue, Your Honor."

"I will conclude by saying that if Mr. Turner is released, it will only be a matter of time before he commits another criminal act or, worse, takes another innocent life. I will not have that on my conscience. I hope you will feel the same way and refuse to grant him parole. I also believe his admission of remorse was a falsehood for the sole purpose of being eligible for parole. He'll do anything to get out, but prison is the only place he belongs. Thank you for allowing me to speak."

"We appreciate your time, Your Honor. You're excused."

Without another glance at Turner, she got up and left, the bailiff holding the door for her. When she stepped out into the hall, she noticed two men who hadn't been there before. Thick, muscled men in black jogging suits, wearing gris-gris bags on leather cords around their necks.

Without a doubt, Turner's men.

They eyeballed her with menace, eyes narrowed, mouths bent in hard scowls.

She snorted. Like mean mugging was going to bother her. She gave them her best deprecating frown, pulled out her phone and snapped a picture of each one. Couldn't hurt. Darryl might know who they were.

"You can't do that," one of them snarled, his Haitian accent thick.

"It's a public place. It's perfectly legal. But if you have a problem with it, I'd be happy to call the police on your behalf."

He glared at her and sucked his teeth. The second man bumped the other man's shoulder and pushed his hand toward the floor like he was telling the first man to calm down.

She tucked her phone back into her purse and strode toward the exit.

She'd done her part. Now it was up to the parole panel to do the rest. She kept a careful eye on her surroundings until she was back in her car, doors locked.

She drove straight to the courthouse, parking in her reserved spot, but before she got out, she called Darryl.

He picked up right away. "Leonie?"

"Yes, it's me."

"How did it go?"

"I don't know yet. I just left. I'm at the courthouse now. Hopefully, we'll hear something soon."

"How did Turner seem?"

"Same as he always does. Arrogant. Like the law shouldn't apply to him. He tried to intimidate me. In fact, he had men outside, and they tried to intimidate me, too. I took pictures of them."

"You did what?" Darryl laughed. "You are something else, Leonie. Text them to me, and I'll tell you if I know them."

She took the phone from her ear and sent him the two photos. "Just sent."

"Let me put you on speaker and have a look at them." A moment passed with just the ambient noise of his office filling the space. "I know them all right. Phillippe and Francois Charles. Brothers who work for Turner. I'm sure Phillippe didn't like you taking his picture. He's got at least three outstanding warrants. Just a moment."

She heard him pick up his office phone and dispatch officers to the parole board to pick Phillippe up. Then Darryl returned to her. "Are you okay after that? It had to be unsettling to be in the same room as him, knowing he wants to hurt you and your daughter."

"It wasn't great fun, but I'd do it again. It needed to be

done. And he needed to see that he can't intimidate me into doing his will."

"You're a brave woman. Be extra careful today. If that hearing goes the way I think it's going to, Turner isn't going to be happy. And he's going to want to take it out on you."

She sighed and stared through her windshield, watching for anyone she didn't recognize. "I know. You sent an officer to the courthouse?"

"I did. He should already be there. Have him clear your chambers, if you want."

"You think Turner could have something waiting for me there?" She'd almost said bomb, but she couldn't bring herself to say the word. There was no good reason to put such a thing into the universe.

"The man is capable of things he shouldn't be capable of. Why take a chance you don't have to? I'll be there to follow you home."

That brought her some relief. "Alphonso's making fried chicken tonight with greens and macaroni and cheese."

"Mm-*mmm*." He laughed. "You keep feeding me like this and I might never leave."

She smiled. There were worse things that could happen. He was a good man. And great company. "See you soon, Darryl."

"You be careful, Leonie."

"I will. I promise I'll call at the slightest hint of trouble."

"You do that. Bye now."

She hung up and tipped her head back for a moment. She was very ready for this all to be over. At least Ephie was far away and safe.

Remy would protect her. Leonie felt certain of that. Didn't mean she wasn't still worried about her daughter. She was.

But some of that worry was that Ephie might fall for that blood-sucking scoundrel again. Ephie could *not* be with a vampire. It would ruin her. It would change her. In ways her daughter didn't even realize.

Leonie sighed. Life never seemed to get less complicated, did it?

Tantalizing aromas that took him back to a different time and place drifted into Remy's dreams, pulling him out of sleep and opening his eyes. He lay in bed for a moment, coming awake with the realization of what he was smelling. "Jambalaya," he whispered, smiling.

That got him up and moving. He went straight into a hot shower, then dressed in jeans and a T-shirt before heading into the kitchen. Hair still damp, he stopped at the entrance to take in the sight before him.

Ephie was at the stove, a dish towel over one shoulder, her curls knotted up on top of her head in a messy bun, her feet bare, showing off candy-pink toenails. She stirred a pot, sending more delicious scents into the air. Spices and meat and veggies and all manner of good things. A translucent Jean-Luc was perched on the counter nearby, looking very curious at everything that was going on.

Remy inhaled. "It smells so good in here."

She turned, saw him, and smiled. "Yeah?"

He nodded and leaned against the wall. "It smells like my memories in the best possible way. And as much as I want to hang out, I'm going to run to the post office and get that package mailed for you."

"No need," Ephie said with a coy smile.

He straightened. "Why's that?"

"Birdie already did it for me."

"Birdie was here?" He hadn't heard a thing.

"Yep. She dropped off some paperwork for you. Info on the plate you had her run. It's on the table there. We sat and chatted over coffee for a while. She's really nice. I like her a lot. She's volunteered to spend the night with me when you have to go to work."

He let that all process for a second. "How long was she here?"

Ephie shrugged. "Maybe an hour or so?"

"How did I not hear any of that? I'm pretty sure talking would have woken me up."

"We sat outside. On the patio. Jean-Luc really enjoyed the yard. He chased a butterfly and everything." She leaned toward the cat. "Didn't you, *bebe*?"

He meowed confirmation of his enjoyment.

"You were outside?" Remy didn't care for that.

"Yes. With Birdie." She shot him a look. "It was perfectly safe. She's a werewolf, you know."

"I'm aware. I still don't like the idea that you were out there. Visible to anyone who might have been around."

"Your yard is fenced. Not easy to see into. I was fine, I promise."

"Obviously, because you're still here. But I don't think we can be too careful."

"I understand that. But do you really think your own backyard isn't safe?"

"I'd rather err on the side of caution." What bothered him was there was no way he could have done anything about her safety if she'd been in the yard and someone had tried something.

The daylight would have turned him into a walking smoke bomb, and not long after that, he would have gone up in flames, leaving Ephie to the mercy of Turner's men.

She nodded. "I don't want you to worry. I won't do it again."

He shook his head, hating this for her. "It's not fair to you. I know that. But it won't be forever."

"About that ..." She put the lid on the pot and set the wooden spoon down on a folded piece of paper towel. "I texted my mom my new phone number, and she texted back to say the parole board denied Turner parole."

"As they should have."

"I agree. Except she and Darryl—he's the police commissioner—believe Turner will now try to exact his revenge, since he's got nothing to lose."

"I thought as much. Not good." Remy sighed and reached into the fridge for a bottle of blood.

She glanced at it, then quickly looked away.

"Sorry. I can take this out to the deck now that the sun is down." He held the bottle by his side and slightly behind his leg, hiding it from her.

"It's fine," she said, offering him a tight smile.

"I know you don't like it."

She quickly shook her head. "It's not that. It's just ... it's nothing. Never mind. It's fine. Your house. Drink it wherever you want to. I have biscuits to make." She headed for the counter, where a large bowl and a bag of flour sat waiting.

"Jambalaya and biscuits? You're spoiling me."

She smiled. "I could say the same about you paying for everything. Works both ways, you know."

He'd been about to leave. He lingered a moment longer. "I know. But I like taking care of you. It's in my blood."

She was measuring flour but stopped to look at him. "That's because you're a man of a different time."

"Anything wrong with that?" He took a few steps toward the sliding doors that led out to the deck, but only because those steps took him closer to her.

"No." She was still smiling. "I like the man you are. Always have. Doesn't it bother you that I'm not of that age?"

"Not a bit. You might be a modern woman, but you definitely have an old soul. I mean that as a compliment. You're perfect just the way you are."

"You're sweet."

"So are you." He leaned in and kissed her cheek, then went over to Jean-Luc and held his hand out. The cat materialized so Remy could pet him. After a quick scratch under Jean-Luc's chin, Remy took the bottle outside, swiping the paper Birdie had brought off the table on his way.

He stood on the back deck, drinking his first dinner

and reading the report on the plate. Stolen. His gut told him that Turner's men had been in that SUV. Seemed the most likely explanation. He didn't like that one bit.

He stared into the growing darkness, studying the houses around them. There was no sign of anything unusual. No strange noises, no new smells, nothing that seemed out of place. He'd check the street out front in a bit, too.

He emptied the bottle and went back inside. He rinsed it and set it aside with the others for recycling. "Weren't you going to make me help cook?"

"I was. But I thought it might be nicer if you woke up to dinner being ready."

He wasn't going to argue. His cooking skills were not great. "What can I do to help?"

"Set the table?"

"I can do that." His phone vibrated with an incoming call. Probably Leonie, he figured. Then he checked the screen and saw it was his boss. "Right after I take this call." He answered, walking out to the living room. "Sheriff."

"Lafitte. How was your trip?"

"More complicated than I expected."

"So I understand. Birdie's been doing some digging on this Abraham Turner. Bad news."

"Yes, sir, he is."

"I don't want that kind of trouble in my town."

"Neither do I, sir."

"You need a few more days off?"

Remy sighed and ran his hand through his still-damp hair. "I do and I don't. Your aunt volunteered to stay here with Ephie while I'm at work. If she does that, I wouldn't mind being on patrol, looking for signs of Turner's men. I have a feeling they might already be here."

"I'll expect you at work tomorrow night, then. Anything happens in the meantime, let me know. This needs to end before it starts."

"Agreed. Thank you."

With a grunt, Merrow disconnected.

Remy stuck his phone back into his pocket, then went to the front windows and parted the blinds enough to see out.

He could just see the back end of a silver SUV parked on his side of the street about two blocks down. "Eph?"

"Yeah?"

"I'm going to grab the mail. I'll set the table when I get back in."

"Okay. There's time. I'm just putting the biscuits in the oven now."

"Great." Turner's men were probably watching the front door.

Remy went out to the back deck again, leaped over the fence that divided his backyard from his neighbor's, went through their yard, then leaped over the wooden fence that separated their yard from the next one. He skirted around a swing set and used the gate to exit toward the street.

He kept the neighbor's car between him and the street, inching slowing around while he surveyed the SUV. It was right in front of him now. Driver and front passenger seat were empty, but the rear windows were tinted too darkly for him to see the vehicle's interior without a flashlight.

Vampire eyes were good, but even they had limitations.

Suddenly, he saw a faint spot of light in the back of the car. Like the screen of a cell phone.

He rushed forward, using his supernatural speed to cover the ten yards or so in a second. He knocked on the rear passenger door, wishing he had his badge on him. "Nocturne Falls Sheriff's Department. Open up."

It was a risky move, but Ephie's safety was worth the gamble. And even if whoever was inside was armed, he could move faster than them, and while bullets would hurt, they wouldn't do fatal damage.

The door opened to reveal a light-skinned black woman in jeans and sneakers clutching a T-shirt in front of her to cover her bra. She looked to be about Ephie's age. Most likely younger. "I'm sorry, officer. Am I in trouble? I just stopped to change my shirt. I swear, I'm not loitering."

Not what or who he'd been expecting. Wrappers from fast food and protein bars littered the floor, along with an empty bottle of Coke. Part of a hardshell suitcase was visible behind the seat. The faint aroma of stale food and pine air freshener drifted out. "No, no trouble, ma'am. That's fine. Sorry to disturb you. Have a good night."

"Thank you. You, too."

He nodded and headed toward his house.

Behind him, the SUV's door closed.

He'd been a cop too long and a vampire for longer. Something about the woman didn't sit right with him. He pulled his phone out, fired up the camera, and snapped the plate. Just like he'd told Ephie, he'd rather err on the side of caution.

But at least for tonight, everything was safe.

The SUV pulled away.

He texted the photo to Birdie with a simple message. *Another one to check.*

He put his phone away and looked back at the vehicle. It was nearly out of sight.

He smiled. It was a beautiful night. Cool but not cold. Ephie said she liked the backyard. Maybe they would eat out there tonight. The patio was very romantic with the strings of lights on. And Jean-Luc could do some more exploring.

He grabbed the mail from the box and went through the gate and inside via the sliding doors on the back deck, since the front door was locked and he didn't have his key. He called to her as he went toward the kitchen. "Eph? How'd you like to eat outside on the patio?"

As he entered, she was adding shrimp to the jambalaya. "I'd like that very much. Might need to put a jacket on, but I'm game."

"You know you can borrow anything of mine you want. I'll get that table set." He collected the silverware and napkins, figuring they'd fill their plates and then bring them out.

He turned on the string lights before stepping outside, the soft glow bringing a sweet warmth to the entire area. With the sliders still open, he leaned back. "Jean-Luc? Door is open if you want to come out. I'll watch him, Ephie."

"Thanks."

Remy took the napkins and silverware to the table. Jean-Luc zipped past him, a luminous white blur. Remy laughed at the cat's antics as he arranged things under the glow of the umbrella's LED lights. When he was done, he turned to watch Jean-Luc chase a bug through the grass.

"This is so pretty." Ephie stood in the doorway with two steaming plates. She had one of his jackets on. It hung to her hips.

"I'm glad you like it."

She brought the plates over.

"I forgot to light the candle."

"I've got it," Ephie said. She narrowed her gaze at the glass jar holding the citronella candle, and a second later, it sparked to life.

"Nicely done."

"Thanks." She smiled.

He smiled, too. Hard not to. If this was a taste of domesticity, he wanted more. More of this happiness.

More of this easy banter. More time with this amazing woman. More time kissing her and holding her hand.

But Ephie's life was in New Orleans. What would it take to convince her to give Nocturne Falls a more permanent try?

Once again, Ephie had drifted off before Remy and, once again, she'd woken up before him. She'd made coffee, and as much as she wanted to sit outside on that gorgeous patio, she wasn't going to.

She'd told him she wouldn't go out alone, and she was going to stick to that, even if he wouldn't know the difference.

It was a little like being under house arrest, but she understood the reasoning. Over dinner last night, Remy had told her about the SUV with stolen plates. There was a good chance Turner's men had tracked her here. All the way to Remy's house.

That stupid phone.

Taking chances might be fine for someone like Remy, who had the benefit of his vampire powers to give him an edge in dangerous situations, but her skills were ... meh, at best.

Even so, there was a part of her that really wanted to go to the coven meeting tonight to see what it was like. A big part of her. She'd never been to one, and she *had* been invited.

Remy would be at work. Maybe if he drove her and picked her up and she promised never to be alone, he'd think it was safe enough. Birdie had promised to stay with her, too. Although Birdie probably couldn't go to the coven meeting, seeing as she was a werewolf and not a witch. Ephie knew a little more about witches than she did vampires, and that seemed like a given.

She carried her coffee cup to the front windows. Being stuck inside on such a pretty day felt like punishment, even knowing the reason for it.

Not even Jean-Luc wanted to hang out. He was sleeping with Remy. She'd checked.

She sighed and peeked through the blinds. A car had pulled into the driveway behind Remy's SUV.

Ephie smiled as a blue-haired woman got out. She was carrying a cloth shopping tote that looked full. Ephie went to the front door, unlocked it, and swung it open. "Hi, Birdie," she whispered as loudly as she dared.

Birdie came up the front porch steps. "Hi, Ephie. I hope you don't mind the visit, but I had an idea, and I thought you might be bored with Remy sleeping."

"A little. I have work I could do, but it's hard to be inside on a day like this."

"Should we go out to the back again like yesterday then? I don't want to wake Remy."

Ephie made a judgment call. "Okay, let's do that." She wasn't going out there by herself. She was going with a werewolf. Remy could fuss about it all he wanted, but a werewolf was pretty good protection. "You go on through, and I'll fix you a cup of coffee."

"Perfect," Birdie said.

When Ephie brought the coffee out, her own cup refilled, Birdie was at the table, her shopping bag by her feet. She put the cup in front of Birdie. "Here you go."

"Thank you." Birdie left the cup on the table and reached into her bag. "I have just the thing to go with this coffee."

"You do?"

"Yep." She set three boxes of various sizes on the table. "I figured since you can't really go out, I'd bring some of our town's best treats to you."

"And you're not going to get into trouble because you aren't at work?" Ephie liked Birdie a lot. She didn't want to be the reason the woman's responsibilities were ignored at the sheriff's department.

"I promised I'd be back in an hour." Birdie winked. "Or two. Now, first we have doughnuts from Zombie Donuts. They're just the best. They used to be made by a necromancer, but now they're made by a winter elf. I got an assortment, since I didn't know what you liked."

Ephie didn't quite know what to say.

Birdie opened the first box, revealing a dozen delicious doughnuts with everything from chocolate to sprinkles to colorful icing on top.

The smell made Ephie's mouth water. "Those all look amazing."

Birdie grinned and added a stack of paper napkins next to the box. "Of course, if you're in the mood for something different than doughnuts, we have one of Mummy's Diner's famous cinnamon buns."

"Just one?" That surprised Ephie. After all, the first box had a dozen doughnuts. One cinnamon bun seemed a little lacking by comparison.

Birdie snorted. "One is plenty." She opened the second box, proving her point.

"That's one?" Thick white frosting enrobed a massive swirl of pastry dough that had been generously spread with cinnamon. The aroma of pastry and butter mixed with the cinnamon nearly had Ephie drooling.

"Yep." Birdie brought out more paper napkins along with two packages of plastic utensils.

"Wow."

"This last box isn't really breakfast food, but I had to bring you some anyway. These are all handmade chocolates from Delaney's Delectables. She's a vampire. The flavor combinations will knock you out. I got the spring sampler. There are strawberry and basil creams, agave pear jellies, salted raspberry dark chocolate truffles, peach and ginger bombs in white chocolate, and these new lemongrass creams that I am currently crazy about."

Ephie sat in amazement. "You have all of this here, in this town? Not to mention that ice cream we had the first night. And I thought New Orleans had some good food."

Birdie looked pleased with herself and rightly so. "What should we start with?"

"How about a doughnut? They're the easiest to eat and the most like breakfast food. Although that cinnamon bun is a very close second."

The Vampire's Former Flame

"You pick a doughnut, and I'll cut us each a wedge of cinnamon bun."

"Deal." Ephie picked a chocolate glazed doughnut that had been filled with something. The glaze was sprinkled with chopped peanuts, which made sense as soon as she took a bite. The filling was peanut butter whipped cream. "Oh, man. I love chocolate and peanut butter together. That combo of salt and sweet is so good."

"I'm glad you like it." Birdie put a slice of cinnamon bun on a napkin for Ephie. "Here you go." She handed her a plastic fork, too.

"I'm going to be in sugar overload."

Birdie grabbed a doughnut slathered with hot-pink frosting and pink, white, and green sprinkles. "You say that like it's a bad thing."

Ephie laughed. "What flavor is that?"

"Snozzberry. It's a combination of strawberry and lime. It's delicious."

"This town is so cool." Ephie took another bite of her doughnut.

"You haven't even scratched the surface. Maybe you should stick around a while."

Ephie nodded. "It's already occurred to me that moving here could be good in all kinds of ways. That would mean moving away from my mother, which wouldn't be the worst thing, but I'd be moving away from my grandmother, too. And that I'd be less happy about. A lot less happy."

Birdie nodded thoughtfully. "I can understand how

that would be tough." She sipped her coffee. "Are you going to the coven meeting tonight?"

"I don't know. I'd like to, but I think Remy would feel better if I stayed home."

"You'd be surrounded by women more than capable of protecting you."

"I'm guessing that wouldn't include you?"

Birdie shook her head before picking up her piece of cinnamon bun. "No, but they aren't allowed to come to pack meetings, either."

"Makes sense. I'll talk to him. See what he thinks. I was hoping if he drove me and picked me up, and you were here at the house to hang out with me while he's at work, he might be all right with that."

"Whatever you need. Let me know." She wiped her mouth, then opened her purse. "That reminded me that this is another reason I came. The report on the plate he sent me last night."

Ephie frowned. "He didn't mention that to me."

"Probably didn't want to worry you. And I can see why. It wasn't anything. Just a rental car rented locally. Town's full of those."

"No big deal then."

"Not that I can see."

"Did you happen to see who it was rented to?"

Birdie opened the paper. "It was reserved with a credit card in the name Dee Mills. Mean anything to you?"

"Nothing. I'll be sure to give it to Remy, though."

"Thanks. Listen, if you want to go tonight, I'm sure

Pandora would pick you up and drop you off again. And I'll be here whenever you want me to be."

"I really appreciate it. I'll talk to Remy and let you know."

"Sounds good."

They ate some more of the treats she'd brought, finishing up the coffee, too. Jean-Luc appeared in the yard, having apparently walked through the wall that separated Remy's bedroom from the backyard.

Birdie still couldn't see him unless he was fully materialized.

After a little more small-talk, Birdie sighed. "I hate to run, but I should get back. You wouldn't believe how cranky my nephew can get."

"A cranky werewolf doesn't sound like a good thing."

Birdie grinned as she got to her feet. "I can handle him. But it's not good for his blood pressure. You enjoy the rest of these goodies, and I'll talk to you soon. I can see myself out through the side gate."

Ephie jumped up. "Thank you so much for coming by. I really enjoyed talking to you. And everything you brought was just great. As soon as all this nonsense is over, I would love to take you to lunch."

"Well, we'd better get this nonsense over with, then." Birdie hugged her, then headed for the gate. "Bye, Ephie."

"Bye, Birdie."

As soon as the gate closed, Ephie closed all the boxes, stacked them up, and took them, the report Birdie had brought for Remy, and the two coffee cups back inside.

Jean-Luc, evidently bored with the hunting of insects, came in with her.

She set the boxes on the kitchen counter before putting the coffee cups in the sink. She left the report on the table. Then she went back to the guest room and fired up her laptop. Might as well get some work done.

As she was getting ready to check her email, she got a text from her mom.

How are things? All's gone quiet here. Not sure if I should be more worried about that or less. Tell me you're all right.

I'm fine, Ephie texted back. *All quiet here too. Glad you're good.*

So am I. Still not sure it's safe for you to come home. Are you going to be all right there for a few more days?

Ephie smiled as she thought about the man sleeping in the room next door. *I'll be just fine.*

Remy put his uniform on, ready to get back to work but not at all ready to leave Ephie. And not just because he felt duty-bound to protect her. He liked spending time with her. Loved hanging out and talking and laughing.

He stood before his dresser mirror, making sure he was squared up. Jean-Luc sat on the dresser's top, watching.

Things were better between him and Ephie now than they had been in college. For one thing, Ephie had matured and was more self-assured. More confident. That shy girl was mostly gone, replaced by a poised young woman who took his breath away. Or would have, if he'd had breath.

He was more in love with her than ever. He knew that as much as he knew anything. What he wanted was for her to stay. That would take some convincing, but one thing he could do was make sure she fell in love with the town.

His phone vibrated with an incoming call. Leonie.

He answered. "Hello?'

"I wasn't sure you'd be up."

He stared at the ceiling. "Yep. About to head to work, but don't worry, someone else will be with Ephie. A very capable woman who also works for the sheriff's department."

"That's good to hear. I'm not sure how important it is now, though."

He frowned. "Why? What's happened?"

"Turner was wounded in a prison riot. He didn't make it. Not a great way to go, but I can't say I'm broken up about it."

"You sure about that? With his voodoo connections—"

"He was stabbed in the neck. No one loses that much blood and survives, even with supernatural help."

Remy sat on the bed, relieved. "So it's over then?"

"I should think so. Darryl isn't quite so certain. He thinks there could be repercussions or possibly revenge for Turner's death, but that would be focused on me, not Ephie."

Remy nodded. "Thanks for letting me know. Do you have protection then?"

"I'm surprised you care. I do. Besides Darryl, I have a rotation of officers at the courthouse."

"Good. I'll give Ephie the news. Darryl's probably right about this. I think it's still wise for us to be cautious. Be safe, Leonie."

"Thank you." She hung up.

Remy stuck his phone into the holder on his belt, and with Jean-Luc trotting along beside him, Remy walked out to the kitchen, ready for a little sustenance before he clocked in. "Eph? Ephie?"

"Out in a minute," she called from the guest room.

He got a bottle out of the fridge, noticing a piece of paper on the table. He read it as he drank his dinner and waited on her. Jean-Luc milled about, probably wanting attention. The report didn't really give him any new information, other than the name of the woman who'd been inside the car.

Ephie appeared right after he'd set the empty with the others for recycling and picked up Jean-Luc. She had on jeans, a silky white and pink printed top, and a rose-colored cardigan, all paired with crisp white low-top sneakers.

"You look very pretty," Remy said. Jean-Luc jumped out of his arms to rub against Ephie's legs.

"Thanks." Her smile seemed tentative. "I was hoping you'd be all right with me going to that coven meeting tonight."

"That's tonight? I guess it had slipped my mind."

"Pandora said she'd pick me up and bring me home and Birdie will meet me here. I'll text her as soon as we leave the meeting. I won't be alone for a second."

He nodded. "You really want to go?"

"I do."

He kept a poker face, but the truth was, he wanted her to go probably more than she did. If she enjoyed herself and made some friends, it could only work in his favor. "You promise to keep your eyes open? Not take any chances?"

"I swear it."

"Text me when you leave and when you get home."

"I will." She smiled. "Thanks. I thought I was going to have a much bigger argument on my hands."

He shrugged. "You're a grown woman. You're in charge of your own decisions. And I can be here in a matter of minutes should something arise. Also, your mother just called to say Turner is no longer an issue. He was killed in a prison riot."

"I'd say I was sorry, but that would be a lie."

"We should still be careful for a few days in case any of his crew decide to take revenge, but Darryl thinks that will be aimed at your mother, not you. And she's being protected."

"I'm glad for that. And Birdie will still be here this evening." Ephie came over to him, smoothing her fingers down the line of buttons on the front of his shirt. "You look very handsome in your uniform."

He lifted his chin, enjoying her attention. The tension created by Turner's threats had evaporated, and that was a good feeling. Mercy, she was pretty. And she smelled good enough to eat. "The uniform is a popular look with a lot of women."

"A lot of women?" She narrowed her eyes, but her smile remained. "Who exactly are these women?"

He laughed and shook his head. "You have a jealous streak. Good to know."

"Just curious, is all. Hey, you want a doughnut to take with you?"

He gave her a look. "Is that a cop joke?"

"No!" She laughed. "Birdie brought some by earlier. Along with a cinnamon bun and some chocolates. Everything she brought was so good, I can't even tell you. I've already eaten more sugar today than I should have, but it was worth it."

He wasn't even paying Birdie and the woman was helping him out. He put his hands on Ephie's waist. "This town has some good eats."

"I'll say." She rested her arms on his shoulders and smiled up at him. "When will you be home?"

"About forty-five minutes before dawn. I won't wake you, and please don't worry about trying to stay up. You and Birdie just get some sleep. There will be patrols by the house at random intervals, so there's nothing to worry about."

"I'm not worried. Especially with Turner out of the picture. Birdie's good company, too. But if you want to wake me up when you get in, it won't bother me."

He wouldn't, but it was sweet of her to say. He leaned in and kissed her. "I'll keep that in mind. Now, as much as I hate to leave you, I should go soon. Do you know when Pandora will be here?"

Two quick beeps of a car horn answered that question.

"She's here." Ephie grabbed her purse off the table. "Perfect timing."

"Hang on." He opened the drawer that held odds and ends and took out a spare house key on a Nocturne Falls pumpkin keychain. "You'll need this to get back in."

"Good thinking." She tucked the key into her purse, gave Jean-Luc a quick scratch on the head, and then they walked out together. Remy hung back to turn on the porch light and lock the door, then went down the steps to greet Pandora.

Pandora rolled her window down as he walked toward her. "Hi."

"Hi. Thanks for the taxi service. Very nice of you." He rested his hands on the edge of the open window.

"Glad to help."

He smiled at Ephie, now in the front passenger seat. "Have fun. And keep your eyes open."

"I will," Ephie assured him.

He patted the roof of the car before stepping back. "Go ahead and go. I have a few things to do before I leave."

"See you later," Ephie called out.

He waved again. He didn't have anything he needed to do before he left, but he wanted to be sure Pandora's car wasn't being followed. Just because Turner was gone didn't mean his men knew they could back off. Remy watched Pandora's vehicle until it turned the corner. All clear.

He got into his own SUV and headed for the station. Hopefully, it would be a slow night. One that left him some time to drive by the house and check on things.

Ready to back out, he checked the rearview mirror and saw Jean-Luc sitting in the backseat. He laughed but shook his head and turned to face the cat, deciding to talk to him sweetly in the hopes it would get his attention. "Now listen here, *mon petit*. You cannot come to work with me. You need to get back in that house and wait for your mama. She'll be very upset if she can't find you."

Jean-Luc meowed, a long, plaintive, argumentative sound.

"No fussing. I'm very serious. Out you go." Remy pointed to the house.

Jean-Luc's second meow was softer, more resigned but also a little grumpy.

"I know," Remy said. "Life is unfair at the best of times."

With a flick of his tail, Jean-Luc slipped through the side of the SUV and trotted toward the house, where he disappeared through the front door.

Despite Pandora telling Ephie on the ride over what to expect from the coven meeting, Ephie was still nervous. These were powerful, accomplished witches. At her best, she could heat up soup and light the odd candle. Sometimes, if she really focused, she could conjure a small ball of fire, but that wasn't something she had a lot of call for.

Not only was she not in the same league, she also occasionally felt like she wasn't even playing the same sport.

But she was looking forward to the experience of a real coven meeting all the same. She'd long ago accepted that her skills weren't worth worrying about, and she'd made peace with that reality. So long as this group was okay with her presence, she'd enjoy the opportunity to be here.

Walking in, Ephie saw more women than she'd expected. Maybe twenty or twenty-five women of all ages. Clearly, Nocturne Falls was the place to be if you were a witch.

Or any kind of supernatural, she supposed.

They got coffee from the refreshments table that had been set up. Ephie skipped the plate of cookies. She'd had enough sweets already.

Pandora introduced Ephie to her mother, Corette, who owned the bridal boutique in town, and her sister, Marigold, who owned the florist shop. They were both lovely people, and Ephie lost track of time chatting with them until someone rang a bell.

"Ladies, if you could take your seats."

Everyone found a chair. They'd been set up in the meeting room in rows before a long folding table. The woman standing in front of the table gave them a nod. "Welcome, all. We have a visitor with us this evening."

The woman smiled at Ephie. "Always nice to have a sister join us."

Ephie smiled and nodded back.

Pandora leaned over and whispered, "That's Dominique. She helps run things."

Dominique continued. "As you know, we have a special presentation tonight by Maude Adams. Maude's new to town and has just opened a gem and crystal shop. She's going to show us some of her more interesting acquisitions and help us better understand how crystals and gemstones can be used in our magic."

Dominique glanced at the newcomer, an older woman with wild gray curls and round, red-framed glasses. "Maude has also promised me that this is not a commercial for her shop, but she did bring a selection of things for purchase, which she'll be offering to us at a twenty percent discount. Maude, the floor is yours."

Ephie was fascinated by the woman's talk. The very idea that her meager powers might be amplified by something as simple as wearing a pendant of the right stone really appealed to her.

When the talk concluded, Ephie put her hand on Pandora's arm. "Are you in a rush? I'd like to speak to Maude for a minute. I might buy something."

"Go ahead," Pandora said. "I'm curious about a few pieces myself. Let's go have a look."

They went up to the table where Maude had laid her wares out. She smiled at them. "I hope you enjoyed the presentation."

"I did," Ephie said. "Very much. What would you suggest for someone whose gifts lean toward fire?"

"You?"

Ephie nodded. "Fire seems to be my skill, although it's not as … strong as I'd like it to be."

"What gift is?" Maude laughed. "I would suggest carnelian or sunstone. Both can help focus your powers in a way I believe you'll like."

"Can you show me what those look like?"

"I have wearable pieces in each one, bracelets, necklaces, earrings, but my personal favorites are the simple wire-wrapped polished drops. They're unobtrusive and less in-your-face witchy than, say, an actual shard of crystal on a chain."

Maude selected one from the table and held it up. "This is sunstone. What do you think?"

It was really pretty. The peachy-colored polished teardrop, about the size of a chickpea, was shot through with ripples of tangerine and darker orange. As Maude turned the necklace, it caught the light, and the colors within seemed to glow and sparkle.

Ephie nodded. "I love it. It looks like there's fire inside it." She glanced at Pandora. "What do you think?"

"It's beautiful," Pandora said. "And if it helps amp up the magic, why not?"

Maude leaned in. "Between us, I think it's a lot prettier than carnelian."

"How much?" Ephie asked.

"Chain, too?"

"Yes, please."

"With the discount for coven members, fifty-seven."

"Oh," Ephie said. "I'm not a member. I'm just visiting."

"All the same to me," Maude said.

"In that case, I'll take it. I'll wear it right now, if that's all right."

"Sure, here you go." Maude handed it over.

Ephie took the necklace, giving Maude her credit card in exchange. While Maude ran the card, Ephie slipped the chain over her neck.

"Good choice," Pandora said.

"Do you really think the sunstone will give my powers a boost?"

"I've seen stranger things happen. But even if it doesn't, it's still really pretty."

Maude returned Ephie's card along with the receipt. "Wear it in good health."

"Thank you."

Pandora was still looking, so Ephie stepped back from the table to give her more room. Maude was busy. Ephie studied the pendant on the end of her chain. She was interested to see if it would do anything for her abilities. Maybe when she got home—

"Pretty."

"Thanks." Ephie looked up into the kind eyes of an older woman. She was shorter than Ephie and a bit wider, but she had the look of ancient wisdom about her. Ephie couldn't quite explain it, but there was something about her that reminded Ephie of her grandmother.

"You're visiting from New Orleans?"

Ephie nodded, not sure how the woman knew that. "I am. I take it you live here."

"I do. Alice Bishop. Nice to meet you ..." Her brows lifted.

"Ephelia Moreau." Ephie stuck her hand out. "Everyone just calls me Ephie."

"Welcome to Nocturne Falls, Ephie." Alice took her hand but didn't shake it. She held it between both of hers, eyes narrowing slightly. "Interesting. There's more to you than meets the eye. More than you even understand yourself. A darkness at play with the light."

Ephie didn't know what to say to that. Or what it meant. Or who this woman was, other than another member of the group. Thankfully, Pandora returned.

"I see you've met our illustrious coven leader." Pandora smiled at Alice. "How are you this evening, Alice?"

"Fine. You?" She let go of Ephie's hand as she spoke to Pandora. "How's the little one doing?"

Pandora rested her hand on her belly. "She's doing great. We both are."

"Wonderful to hear." Alice gave them a nod, but her gaze lingered on Ephie. "Nice to meet you, Ephie. Have a good evening. Both of you."

As soon as she was out of earshot, Ephie turned to Pandora. "Okay, that was interesting."

"I'm sure it was. Alice is the most powerful witch I've ever met. I'm not certain there are many who are more capable. She's a force of nature. Whatever she said to you, take it to heart."

Ephie wasn't sure how to do that, but it was something to think about. "That powerful, huh? She looks like a grandmother."

"Looks can be deceiving."

"I guess. Did you buy anything?"

Pandora held up a small shopping bag. "A rose quartz heart for the nursery. We can go if you're ready."

Ephie nodded. "Great. Let me just text Birdie." She sent Birdie a quick note to let her know they were headed back to the house, then they went out to Pandora's car.

As soon as Ephie was buckled in, she got her phone out again. Birdie had texted that she was on her way. Ephie sent a thumbs-up back to her, then sent a new message to Remy.

Headed to the house. Had the best time. So glad I went. Hope you're having a good night.

His response came quickly. *So far so good. I'm glad you went too. Tell Pandora and Birdie I said thanks.*

Will do. Ephie put her phone away. "Thanks again for driving."

Pandora nodded as she turned onto Main Street. "Did you have a good time?"

"I had a great time. I'm so glad you invited me."

"I'm glad you came. Always good to have new people, even if they're just visiting." Pandora smiled.

"There were more people there than I expected."

"It's a good group. Very supportive. No judgment. All-around awesome folks." Pandora hesitated. "You know, if you somehow end up staying in Nocturne Falls, you could become a member. I'd sponsor you."

Ephie smiled. "Yeah? Thank you for that. I'll keep that in mind."

"I'd tell you I could find you a house, too, but Remy's got a pretty nice place. I can't see why either of you would want anything different."

"He does," Ephie agreed. "That backyard is so pretty."

"He did a nice job on it, that's for sure. If he ever decides to hang up his badge, he could start his own landscaping company. Provided people didn't mind the work being done in the middle of the night."

They both laughed.

Some minutes later, Pandora pulled into Remy's driveway. The house was dark. The front porch light must have burned out. Maybe Ephie could find a bulb and replace it before Remy got home.

Birdie hopped out of her car, which was parked on one side so that Remy would still have space when he got home. She had a bulging tote bag in one hand, her purse in the other.

"Did you have fun?" Birdie asked.

Ephie nodded as she got out. "I did." She looked back at Pandora before shutting the door. "Thanks again. That was awesome."

"You're welcome. Have a good night."

"You, too." Ephie closed the door and walked toward Birdie. She lifted the sunstone pendant. "I bought this at the meeting. It's a sunstone. It's supposed to help focus and enhance my natural abilities."

"I love it. Very pretty." Birdie hefted her purse strap higher on her shoulder. "Did they have anything for sale that helps burn excess calories?"

Ephie laughed as she dropped the pendant under her shirt so it would be out of the way when she changed. "Not that I'm aware of. You want help with your bag?"

"Nope, all good."

"All right." Ephie got the key out that Remy had given her and went to the door. "I really appreciate you coming over."

"Happy to do it. Although I don't know how long I'll be able to stay awake."

Ephie pushed the door open. "That's all right. I'm not on Remy's schedule yet, so I don't plan on being up too late myself. Maybe we can watch a little TV or something? Fair warning, I don't watch much television, so you'll have to pick."

"Sure. I'm always up for a good show. And maybe one of the truffles from Delaney's, if you have any left."

"I do." Ephie stood at the door, holding it open to let Birdie go in ahead of her, planning on closing the door and locking it once they were both inside. She'd explain about Turner and all of that as soon as they got settled.

Birdie walked in. "He really has a nice place for a single guy."

Ephie nodded. "He does."

Birdie's nose wrinkled. "Is that your perfume?"

Ephie shrugged. "Maybe. I don't smell anything." She walked in behind Birdie and was about to turn to close the door when something crashed into her, shoving her forward into Birdie.

They both crashed to the floor as the door slammed shut. Birdie's bag went flying, her purse skittering across the hardwood in the other direction. Ephie gasped, unable to breathe for a moment, the impact knocking the air from her lungs.

"What the—" Birdie growled, a low guttural sound that raised the hairs on the back of Ephie's neck. The snap and crackle of what sounded like live electricity filled her ears as a long black metal rod reached past her and zapped Birdie on the back of the neck.

The older woman stiffened, crying out before she slumped flat. Ephie tried to roll over to see their attacker, but before she could move, the stun gun was at her back.

A violent jolt went through her, pain shooting into every muscle, tensing them against her will.

She caught sight of Jean-Luc in the doorway of the kitchen. He was solid, back arched, ears flattened, teeth bared. With a blood-curdling yowl, Jean-Luc launched himself into the air.

Then everything went black.

Remy knew he was being ridiculous, but Ephie had only texted to say she was leaving the meeting, not when she'd gotten home. A small thing, but it was bothering him. He was sure everything was fine. Turner wasn't even a threat anymore. It wasn't hard to figure out what had happened.

Ephie had gotten back to his house, where Birdie had been waiting, and now the two of them were hanging out, probably eating chocolate or some other goodies while Birdie regaled Ephie with story after crazy story about her life in Nocturne Falls.

They were most likely laughing themselves silly and having a great time. He smiled just thinking about it. Texting him that she'd arrived had just been forgotten. He understood.

But he still wanted to be sure she was okay. Maybe it was the cop in him, maybe it was some protective instinct that had kicked in when she'd reentered his life, but a drive-by couldn't hurt.

He drove down Main Street, headed for his house, but stayed on patrol all along the way, watching for suspicious activity or anyone in trouble. It was a quiet night, which was always a good thing, but then, the full moon wasn't for another three weeks.

Full moon evenings tended to be crazy. Probably crazier than in most towns. He didn't mind. The occasional hectic night kept the job interesting and made him appreciate his nights off even more.

Not that he needed any help with that now that Ephie was here. She was more than enough reason to appreciate time off.

He turned onto his street, slowing in the residential area. Everything was as it should be as he checked on his neighbors. Cars in their driveways, lights on inside the homes, and some exterior illumination giving him more than enough light to see by.

He slowed further as he approached his own house. Birdie's car was in the driveway, and everything looked fine. Except there were no lights on inside that he could see. Not even the flicker of the television. There were no lights on outside, either, and he was certain he'd turned on the porch light before going to work. He usually kept that on when he was gone.

The entire house was dark. Oddly so.

His personal internal alarm system began pinging softly. Nothing jumped out at him as being obviously wrong, but where were they? Out on the back patio? Maybe, but they'd have lights on out there, and he saw no telltale glow. It was also possible they'd both gone to bed already, but it wasn't quite nine thirty yet.

That was early for both of them. Even a woman Birdie's age.

It was enough to warrant an investigation, even

though the shadow of Turner's threats no longer loomed over them. Remy wouldn't be satisfied until he'd seen both women and knew they were all right.

He parked across the driveway, blocking Birdie's car in, then called in his location to dispatch before exiting his vehicle.

He rested his hand loosely on the grip of his service pistol. A bullet might not affect him, but it would make a pretty good impact on a human. Even one who practiced voodoo. He'd only shoot if absolutely necessary, and then it would be to injure and immobilize, not kill.

Probably overreacting, but so what. This was Ephie and Birdie. They were worth a little overreacting.

He stayed in the shadows as he approached, doing everything according to his training, even though what he wanted to do was rush into the house and see that Ephie was all right as fast as possible. She had to be. There was no other option he would accept.

He went up the front porch steps, keeping to the edges where the wood was firmly supported and wouldn't creak. With his side to the front of the house so that he was a smaller target, he carefully inched toward the windows. The drapes were open.

His exceptional vision allowed him to clearly see a good portion of the living room. No movement. No signs that anything had been disturbed. He crept forward a little more, opening up the field of view.

There was something on the floor in the living room. A lump of some kind. What was that? Suddenly, the shape made sense. It was a woman's purse. Not Ephie's, though. Her purse was a simple leather rectangle. This one had fringe.

Had to be Birdie's. So where was she? And where was Ephie?

He left the porch, went around the back of the house and up onto the rear deck. The drapes covering the sliding doors were open as well, giving him a clear view inside. Beyond the dining area, he could see the purse better. He could also make out that the foyer was empty.

A frantic meow was followed by the weight of Jean-Luc's materialized form on Remy's shoulder. He picked up the cat, looking him over for signs of injury before cradling him. "Hey, buddy. You okay? Where's your mama?"

Jean-Luc pushed his head against Remy's chest, pawing at him. The cat seemed needier than usual. Almost anxiously so.

"It's all right, *mon petit*." Remy petted the animal, attempting to soothe him. "Let's go inside."

He used his key to open the lock and slowly slide the door back. If there was anyone in the house, they'd undoubtedly heard him already, but caution was still good.

As he'd learned from one of his colleagues who was a former Navy SEAL, slow was smooth and smooth was fast.

He stepped inside, hand once again on the grip of his pistol. He set Jean-Luc down. The cat hung close but returned to his usual transparent state. Remy scanned the space. No one in the kitchen, dining room or living room, but Remy smelled something that sent chills down his spine.

Blood. It was faint, but it grew stronger as he moved toward the front of the house. Not good. Not good at all. He cleared the rest of the house without finding a sign of either woman or any intruder, then went back to the front.

He flipped the lights on. Three small spots of blood dotted the hardwood approximately seven feet in from the door.

Jean-Luc went right to it, standing next to it and staring up at Remy. The cat was solid again. He trilled out a little meow, lifting one foot, then the other in a nervous little dance.

Remy crouched down. "What are you trying to tell me?"

Jean-Luc lifted his foot again, pawing at Remy's knee. That's when Remy saw the tiniest bit of crusted blood stuck to the fur on Jean-Luc's toes.

"Someone was here, weren't they? And you scratched them? You attacked whoever took Ephie and Birdie?" Just saying the words made Remy's throat constrict, but he was sure that's what had happened. They'd been taken. What other explanation was there? "Good boy," he managed to get out.

He stood and squeezed the radio on his shoulder. "Dispatch, I need backup at my house. Suspected abduction."

Next, he texted the sheriff. It wasn't a text he wanted to send, but Merrow needed to know his aunt had been taken. *My house asap. Birdie and Ephie gone.*

To preserve the scene, Remy went back out through the sliders and around to the front of the house. Jean-Luc was nowhere to be seen.

Dispatch responded as he was rounding Birdie's car, his radio crackling with the incoming message. "Backup is three minutes out."

"Roger," he responded as he stood in the middle of the driveway looking for any other clues he might have missed. Tire marks, an oil spot, a footprint. Anything.

A soft, muffled moaning came from the trunk of Birdie's car. Without hesitation, Remy gripped the edge of the trunk and pulled. Metal screeched as it gave way, the lock popping free with a tinny clunk.

Birdie was inside, duct tape binding her wrists and ankles and covering her mouth. There was a bruise on her cheek. Her eyes were closed. She moaned again.

"Hang on, Birdie, help is on the way." He carefully removed the duct tape from her mouth, then tore the pieces off her wrists and ankles. She remained lethargic. He picked her up and lifted her out as gently as he could.

He carried her to his SUV and tried to stand her up beside him, but her legs gave out when he tried to put her on her feet. He put his arm around her waist and held her upright while he got the back door open.

"Drugged," she mumbled as he helped her onto the seat.

He held on to her wrist and squeezed his radio again. "Dispatch, send an ambulance to my house. Female in need of medical attention." Her pulse was slow.

"Birdie, can you hear me? What happened? Who did this to you?"

She groaned and moved her head a fraction of an inch. In the light of his vehicle's interior, he could see a red mark on her neck. He peered closer. There was also grayish powder on her face. He brushed at it.

A moment later, his fingers began to tingle. Numbness spread through them. It only lasted a few seconds, but it was enough to indicate whatever was in the powder was the agent that had immobilized Birdie.

He grabbed the handkerchief he kept in his pocket and used it to wipe the rest of the powder off her face, gathering it carefully so the powder could be analyzed.

Her lids flickered, and she opened her mouth to speak, her voice hoarse. "I'm not ... really sure. We were ... attacked as we ... came in. Stun gun ... I think." A shudder ran through her. "I tried to fight but ... something overwhelmed me ... drugs ..."

"It knocked you out. What happened to Ephie?"

Birdie shook her head, eyes now fully opened. A tear slipped down her cheek as she gazed at Remy. "I don't know."

Remy greeted Merrow as he jumped out of his car. "Sheriff."

"What's going on?"

"Birdie isn't gone, just Ephie. I found Birdie tied up, drugged, and locked in her own trunk, but she's doing better now. She's sitting in the back of my patrol car." Remy had given her a bottle of water from the supply in his trunk. "Thanks to her exceptional metabolism, the drug wore off pretty quickly once I got the rest of it off her face."

Merrow frowned as he walked toward Remy's vehicle. He crouched down by the open door and took her hand. "Aunt Birdie, are you all right?"

She nodded and looked up at Remy. "Thanks to that young man, I am."

Even at two hundred years old, it was sweet to be called a young man. Remy shook his head. "I just did what anyone would have done."

"Aunt Birdie, I want you to go with the paramedics and get checked out. Especially that burn mark on your neck. And I'd like them to do a tox screen so we can get more intel on what was used to drug you."

She nodded. "Whatever you need." She glanced at

Remy again. "I'm sorry I couldn't help Ephie. That was the whole reason I was here, and I failed."

Remy quickly shook his head. "I'm sure you did what you could." This shouldn't have happened. Turner was dead. Had one of his crew decided to carry out his boss's wishes anyway?

The sheriff cleared his throat. "Why don't you tell us what happened from the beginning? If you can remember."

She stared at the back of the seat in front of her like she was remembering. "I think I can."

"Take your time," the sheriff said.

"Pandora dropped Ephie off. I was already here, in my car. I got out when they pulled up. We talked for a minute in the driveway. Ephie showed me a necklace she'd bought at the coven meeting. A special stone that was supposed to enhance her powers. Then she got her key out, unlocked the door, and we went in."

Remy gestured toward the front of the house. "Was the porch light out when you got here?"

Birdie narrowed her eyes. "Yes. I believe it was."

The ambulance arrived. Merrow held his hand up to let them know to hold back a moment. "What then, Aunt Birdie? After you went inside?"

"It all happened so fast. I went in first, Ephie behind me. The next thing I knew she hit me, like she'd been shoved into me. We both fell to the ground." Her hands went to her face. "I hit my cheek."

"You have a bruise," Merrow said softly. "Then what?"

"I tried to get up, even though Ephie was on top of me. But something bit me on the back of the neck. It hurt for a second, then I passed out. When I started to come around again, I got powder blown into my face and almost instantly, I went numb. Paralyzed head to toe. Then I passed out again."

Remy nodded. "That's the powder I wiped off of you. There could be more stuck to the duct tape that was on your mouth, but I saved as much as I could in the handkerchief." He flexed his hand. "My fingers went numb when I touched it, but that didn't last long."

Merrow looked up at him. "Vampire metabolism probably works a little faster than werewolf. Or maybe it didn't affect you the same way, seeing as how you're technically dead."

"Could be," Remy answered. "It was still potent stuff. Probably voodoo-related."

Merrow patted his aunt's hand, then stood. "Turner."

"I'm sure," Remy responded. "Don't know if you heard, but he was killed in a prison riot."

Merrow frowned. "Then this shouldn't have happened."

"Could be one of his men trying to make a name for himself. Or exacting revenge."

"Possibly." Merrow beckoned the paramedics forward. "You did a great job telling us what you remember, Aunt Birdie. Now let's make sure you're all right. You remember anything else, you call me."

Birdie sighed. "I will."

Remy had never heard Birdie sound so deflated or defeated. She didn't seem like herself at all, but he understood she was in shock and obviously feeling bad because of Ephie.

He wasn't doing so great in that department, either. He was equal parts sick to his stomach and filled with rage, but acting without a plan wasn't going to help. "We need to set up roadblocks on both sides of town in case they try to run with her." He thought for a second. "They might be planning on using Ephie to draw her mother out. Leonie is most likely their true target."

Merrow pinched the radio on his shoulder and called the roadblocks in, then put his hands on his hips. "We should talk to Pandora, see if she saw anything unusual and find out what other vehicles were on the street."

"There's blood in the house, too," Remy said, just remembering. "I'm pretty sure Ephie's cat scratched the attacker."

Merrow's eyes narrowed. "You sure it's not Ephie's blood?"

"No. Doesn't smell like it, but it's only three drops. Also, there's blood on the cat's foot. He wouldn't scratch Ephie. For one thing, making that kind of contact would take serious effort on his part. For another, he loves her too much to hurt her."

Merrow made a face. "Why would it take effort for a cat to scratch someone?"

"He's a ghost," Birdie murmured from the stretcher

the paramedics had her on. "I can't even see him unless he materializes."

Merrow glanced at his aunt, then back at Remy. He tipped his head toward the house. "Show me the blood."

He walked with Remy toward the house, not saying another word until they were on the porch.

Remy stopped to put gloves on before opening the door.

As he did that, Merrow spoke. "Tell me now about why it would take effort for the cat to scratch someone."

"What Birdie said. The cat's a ghost." On a hunch, Remy reached up to the porch light and turned the bulb. It came on the moment it was tightened.

"So that wasn't the drugs talking?"

"No. He can materialize into a solid being, but it's not his usual state. That light bulb might have prints on it."

Merrow wiped a hand over his face. "A ghost cat. Okay."

Remy opened the door and reached in to flip the lights on. He checked the area immediately inside for any evidence. Footprints, scuff marks, debris. Anything that hadn't been there when he'd left. He found nothing.

He stepped inside and pointed. "Blood's right there."

Merrow stood beside him. "Get your evidence kit. The sooner we can run this down, the better."

"Agreed. I'm sure I can collect a strand of hair from Ephie's brush to compare the DNA against."

"Good. I'll lean on the lab to rush it."

"Thanks." Remy stared at the blood. He hadn't really

considered until now that it might be Ephie's. That it might be indicative of something more. Jean-Luc could have scratched the attacker, but Ephie could have been hurt, too.

Merrow frowned. "I'm sorry about this."

"Me, too."

"We'll find her."

"We have to." Remy refused to think about the alternative.

"You going to contact her mother?"

Remy grimaced. "That won't go well."

"You want to wait until morning, fine by me."

"Maybe we'll have her back by then." That was something to shoot for. But they were going to need all the help they could get. "Any chance you're picking up the attacker's scent? Enough that you could track them?"

Merrow's nostrils flared. "Nothing's standing out to me. I smell the blood, the presence of vampire, werewolf, food odors, the sort of general scents of male and female bodies. Nothing I can pinpoint. Maybe Birdie could, though. She had contact with the attackers. Might be worth giving her a crack at it."

The fact that the sheriff was willing to offer up his aunt's help after everything she'd been through spoke to how desperate he knew this situation was.

Remy looked outside. Birdie was in the back of the ambulance now, being tended to by the paramedics. He turned back to the scene. "If you want to ask her, that would be great. I'll start collecting evidence."

The Vampire's Former Flame

"Roger that." Merrow clapped him on the shoulder before leaving.

Remy snapped pictures of the scene, getting different angles of the blood, before going to his trunk to get the evidence-gathering equipment he needed, the sense of urgency pushing at him. The sooner this could be processed, the better.

He needed a lead. Something to go on. A direction. With that in mind, he called Pandora.

She answered, sounding a little sleepy. "Hey, Remy. What's up?"

"I'm sorry to bother you, but there was an incident at my house after you dropped Ephie off. Long story short, Birdie was hurt and Ephie was taken."

"Hurt? Taken?" Pandora sounded completely awake now.

"Yes. Birdie's going to be fine, but Ephie's gone. Did you see anything in the neighborhood that looked out of place or unusual when you were driving in?" He took the evidence kit back into the house.

"No, nothing that stuck out to me."

"What about cars on the street?"

"Um ... let me think. There were some, but I didn't really pay attention to them."

"Think hard, Pandora. We don't have a lot to go on right now."

She blew out a breath. "There was some kind of silver sedan, at least I think it was a sedan, but it might have been one of those crossovers, and two SUVs. A white one for sure. The other was either black, dark blue, or dark green."

His grip on the phone tightened. "Where was the dark SUV in relation to my house?"

"Down the street a bit. Two houses down, same side. I think it was a Tahoe. I actually remember it better because I drove past it on my way home."

"Do you remember anything about the license plate? What state it was from? Any of the numbers? Did it look like there was anyone inside?"

"I don't remember any of that. I'm sorry. Do you have something that's near and dear to Ephie? I could cast a location spell. I can come over immediately."

He glanced at the blood. "What if you had a blood sample from one of the attackers? Could you do anything with that?"

"Blood magic is not my specialty. Besides that, it's a gray area. Not white magic but not exactly black magic, either. I know in this context, it would be used for good, obviously, but …"

"But what?" He wasn't going to ask her to do something she was uncomfortable with, but he still wanted to know more.

"Doing that kind of magic while pregnant isn't a good idea."

"Oh. I didn't realize."

"It's okay. Look, I'll call Alice. I'm sure she'll help. She met Ephie tonight. They talked, just briefly, but Alice knows who she is. Give me a couple minutes."

"Okay. Thank you."

"You got it."

As he hung up, Merrow yelled for him. "Lafitte."

Remy jogged outside. "What's up?"

Birdie was sitting up on the stretcher in the back of the ambulance, paramedics on either side of her. She reached her hand toward Remy, an IV line dangling from it. "I remembered something. Hank asked me about what I smelled, and after that powder, I don't recall anything, but before that? Something came to me."

Remy took her hand. "What was it?"

Birdie gazed up at him, her eyes red-rimmed and weary. "Based on what I picked up, I feel very strongly that the person who attacked us was female."

Little sounds filtered through the fog surrounding Ephie. Muted voices. Canned laughter. A soundtrack.

Television.

She kept her eyes closed and did her best not to move. Although she wasn't sure she could anyway. She felt disconnected from her body. Almost like she couldn't feel it anymore. It had to be there, though.

Was she hurt? She had no idea, since she had no sensations anywhere. Just like she had no clue about where she was or how she was positioned. Her head felt thick with ... something.

She thought hard, trying to recall what Darryl had told her once. Advice if she was ever knocked out and kidnapped. What was it now? Do your best not to let your kidnapper know when you return to consciousness. Use that to your advantage for as long as you can, unless you know you're alone.

He'd given her tips about being shot at, being mugged, being chased in a car or on foot, and if she felt threatened in a public area. Even how to win if she had to fight a gator, something you just never knew about when you lived in Louisiana.

Darryl was a nice man. Her mother liked him but had

never really given him a chance since his divorce. She ought to date him. She could certainly do worse.

Ephie almost smiled at that thought, then realized it would be a sign that she was coming out of the fog she was in. If she could smile.

Was she coming out of it, though? She tried to move her toes, but it didn't seem like she'd succeeded. She really hoped she still had toes. They were so cute when they were painted for the summer.

Where was she? Why did she feel like her brain was the only living part of her?

A chilling thought occurred to her. Maybe she was dead. Maybe this was what death felt like. A sense of being detached from everything else. Did Jean-Luc feel like this?

Oh, her poor, sweet *bebe*. Was she never going to see him again? A feeling of utter despair tore through her.

Her eyes went hot with building tears. That would not do. Neither would this pitiful attitude. Whatever had happened to her, she would figure it out, make a plan, and act on it. Even though she was scared, she would not go down without a fight. Not just for herself but for Jean-Luc. And Remy.

She loved both of them so much it hurt.

So what had happened to her? Turner wasn't supposed to be a threat anymore. He was dead. Had he ordered his men to come after her no matter what happened to him?

She thought hard, trying to figure out who had done this to her.

She remembered going into Remy's house after Birdie, then getting hit and knocked down. Birdie had gotten zapped with something that looked like a stun gun or a cattle prod. Jean-Luc had been there, obviously frightened by what was going on.

Whoever had scared her cat was going to pay. That made Ephie angrier than what had been done to her.

She focused again on remembering.

He'd jumped, she thought. She seemed to remember that. But then everything had gone dark. No, first there'd been pain. It had followed the same buzzing sound she'd heard right before Birdie had gotten zapped.

Which had to mean Ephie had been zapped, too. That had to be what had knocked her out.

But that didn't explain why she couldn't feel her body. Unless she'd been injured in some way and that had left her paralyzed?

She prayed that wasn't what had happened. That would make it very difficult for her to get out of this situation.

The fog in her head seemed to be lessening a bit, but her body was just as distant as it had been. Or was it? She had a sudden awareness that she was upright. Was she in a chair? On a couch? She couldn't tell.

She listened closely, trying to hear past the sound of the television, trying to determine if there was anyone else with her.

She couldn't tell. Didn't seem like it but if someone was purposefully being quiet, she'd have no way of knowing.

Cautiously, she opened one eye a tiny bit. It took her a second to figure out what she was looking at, then it dawned on her. Motel carpeting. That was the only thing that explained the patterned ugliness she could see. Didn't look very clean, either.

That wasn't all that was visible in her small field of vision, though.

She could make out the lower half of her body and part of a wooden chair. But not her arms. They seemed to be behind her. Tied behind her, maybe?

She learned something else. From the angles, her head was down, her chin nearly to her chest. She was in the same clothes she'd gone to the coven meeting in. The room was dim. The little flickering blue light near the edge of her vision came from the television.

She opened the other eye with the same cautious approach. She could see more now. The side of a bed and the cheap, tacky-looking bedspread that covered it. The corner of a dark wood dresser, the veneer on the one visible leg chipped.

Final assessment: she was in a budget motel tied to a chair. Felt pretty accurate but did nothing to help her situation. She didn't know where she was or who was holding her. An educated guess said it was Turner's men, but again, that wasn't a great help.

Nothing would help until she was able to move. And she wasn't sure that was ever going to happen again.

She didn't feel injured, but she couldn't feel anything. She took the risk of trying to move her head. Her view didn't change, telling her she hadn't succeeded, but she could have sworn it felt like she'd almost done it. Whatever drug she'd been given was like alcohol but not.

That was helpful.

She focused on what was around her again, looking for anything she'd missed. There wasn't much light, other than what the television was giving off. Was it still nighttime then? Maybe she'd only just gotten here. Or could it already be the next day?

More importantly, was Remy looking for her?

He had to be. Maybe he was about to burst in and rescue her. Maybe Turner's men had already been taken into custody and Remy was torturing them to find out her location. Baring his fangs at them and threatening to rip out their throats if they didn't come clean. He could be crazy scary when he wanted to be. She imagined, anyway. She'd never seen him like that, but she'd seen vampire movies.

Him torturing Turner's men was a nice thought.

She smiled.

Whoa. Had she actually smiled? She pursed her lips. They felt heavy, but at least she could move them. As much as she wanted to test her voice, there was no point in screaming until she could make a run for it or react in some way to whatever reaction that scream caused.

A door opened, bringing in the sounds of traffic, a little cool air, and human movement.

She closed her eyes. One of her captors had come into the room. That had to be it. The sound of traffic beyond the door meant the motel was near the highway, she assumed.

So she probably wasn't in Nocturne Falls anymore. Just a guess. She didn't know the town well, obviously, but she hadn't seen any cheapie motels in the areas Remy had taken her. Didn't look like the kind of town where those sorts of places would exist.

On the outskirts of town then? That made more sense. Would Remy know how to find her? She hoped so. He was a deputy. He'd been trained for this.

Suddenly a new thought struck her. Birdie. Ephie hadn't seen any sign of her. Had Birdie gotten away? Or was she being held somewhere else?

If Turner's men had hurt her or worse ... Once again, Ephie felt the threat of tears. But she was more than sad. She was angry.

So angry she wished she could set on fire whoever had done this. Birdie did *not* deserve to be caught up in this.

Ephie heard movement, footsteps and rustling coming closer. She risked opening one eye. No one would be able to see that with her head hanging down, not unless they were crouched low and looking up at her.

Legs went by, clad in sneakers and jeans. The

sneakers had tacky pink sparkly trim on them. The jeans were acid-washed.

She'd been kidnapped by a woman stuck in the '80s.

The smell of French fries and meat drifted over. The rustling she'd heard had to have been a fast-food bag.

So she was in a cheap motel near the highway with a fast-food place nearby and her kidnapper was fashion-challenged. If only Ephie had her phone. And wasn't tied to a chair. And could move her fingers.

She ground her teeth together, which made her realize she could move her jaw now, too.

Was the rest of her coming back? That would be super helpful if so. Because at some point, her kidnapper had to sleep, didn't she?

Ephie's best hope was that she was fully operational when that happened. Or that Remy found her before her kidnapper decided to move her.

Either one would be good. But she was holding out for Remy.

Standing in the foyer of Elenora Ellingham's mansion, Alice looked at the sample Remy had given her. She turned the tiny plastic vial in her hands. The single drop of blood inside barely moved. "This isn't very much to work with."

Remy glanced at his boss. Merrow shrugged. Remy sighed. "There wasn't much to begin with. Can you make it work? What about the strands of Ephie's hair I gave you?"

Alice raised her gaze to Remy, although for a moment, it seemed like she was looking over him and not at him. "You don't *make* magic work. It decides that. So I can't answer your question except to say, we'll see."

He ignored the fact that she'd said nothing about the strands of hair. "Then you'll do the spell? Or cast the—whatever it is—you'll do it?"

"I will. Tell me what you know about this abductor."

"She's female," Remy answered. "That's as far as we've gotten. DNA is still processing, but the blood type is different than Ephie's, so we know the sample didn't come from her."

"This woman who took Ephie ... she won't want to be

found. That will make it harder. Does she have magic of her own?"

Merrow chimed in. "We don't know that, but we believe she's doing the bidding of a voodoo practitioner, who is now deceased. Birdie was drugged with something that paralyzed her."

"And," Remy added, "Ephie's mother was sent a black feather that had been coated with paralytic toxins."

"Zombie dust." Alice's brows went up. "Curious. Do you have a sample of that?"

"No," Merrow said. "But I can get you one. Do you need it for the spell?"

"No. Just something I'd like to have." Her eyes narrowed as her focus returned to Remy. "You love Ephie."

It wasn't a question, but he answered anyway. "I do. Yes. Very much. And I want her back as soon as possible."

Alice smiled. "Good. You can stay. That energy matters." She looked at the sheriff. "You, I don't need." She started down the hall. "Come along."

Remy turned toward his boss.

Sheriff Merrow shook his head. "I'll be in the car."

Remy went after Alice, catching up to her in a few long strides. "How long will this take?"

"As long as it needs to."

He rolled his eyes. Thankfully, she couldn't see him.

She snorted softly. "For a vampire, you're rather skeptical."

"I know you're a powerful witch. I understand that.

But time is ticking. I need to find Ephie before it's too late. And you're not exactly giving me a lot of reassurances."

They came to a nondescript door. She stopped and put her hand on the knob. Once again, her gaze seemed to drift past him for a moment. "Magic isn't science. I can only do what it will allow me to do."

She opened the door. "This way. Touch nothing."

She went down a short hall that bent left and dead-ended at a pair of impressive double doors. She opened one and went through. He followed, still frustrated, but knowing there wasn't much he could do except have patience. Much harder than it sounded.

They walked into a room that had the feel of a medieval chamber to it. At least to him. Walls of shelves filled with books, boxes of various sizes, and small, curious objects. Bottles, little carved figures, bowls, a crystal bell, a polished, spiraling shell. A blackbird's wing.

An enormous fieldstone fireplace took up most of one wall. It had embers in it, glowing red, but no flames. A chair was positioned by the fireplace. It was upholstered in worn tapestry fabric. Next to it was a small stand holding a couple of narrow books and a cup of tea.

But the centerpiece of the room was a large, plain wood table, scarred and stained with ages of use. Behind it was one of several tall, gothic-arched windows that gave a brief glimpse of the night beyond.

An intricately woven rug of many colors covered the floor. It showed signs of age, but the threads were still glossy. Silk, he thought. It would have been a comfortable room to spend time in if not for the acrid scent of magic.

"What is this room?"

"My practice. A sacred place where magic is performed."

He stuck his hands in his pockets, careful not to touch anything. Something about the place unsettled him.

"There are elements here that can be used against vampires. That's what's prickling your skin and raising your hackles."

He shot her a serious look. "You work for a vampire. You live in a vampire's house."

Alice went to her shelves, opened a large wooden box, and took out a large beeswax candle. "I am beholden to Elenora for many reasons. She's not just a vampire but a dear friend. That has nothing to do with anything in this room. I would never do her harm, nor would I do harm to anyone who meant no harm toward me."

She set the candle on the worktable, then went back for another box, this one smaller and carved from translucent stone. She brought it to the table.

She took the lid off. Inside was either salt or sugar. He guessed salt. She used it to make a circle around the candle, about six inches out from it. Then she removed a long, narrow glass rod from a cup on the table. There were other glass rods in the cup along with different kinds of feathers, some metal rods, and a few writing implements.

"Pay attention to the flame. Any information I can

gather will be there in the flame. There isn't much blood, so the image, if it appears, won't last long."

"But then you can use Ephie's hair?"

"No. That's for something else."

He didn't understand why she'd needed it then. "What will we see in the flame?"

"Whatever the owner of the blood is looking at during the brief moments the blood burns."

Remy shook his head. "What if she's sleeping? It's nighttime."

"Then we'll see nothing." Alice raised her eyes to him. "Would you rather I wait?"

He tried not to let his frustration show, but that was hard. "No."

"I know you're concerned," Alice said softly. "If this doesn't work, we can try again, but this time we will attempt to locate Ephie."

"I don't have any of her blood."

"No, but you have her familiar."

Remy frowned. "You mean her cat?"

"Yes." Alice waved her hand over the candle. The wick sputtered with fire.

"I know you talked to Ephie at the coven meeting. Is that how you know about Jean-Luc?"

"No." Alice twisted the stopper off the plastic vial. "I know about him because he's been sitting on your shoulder since you arrived."

"What?" Remy felt both shoulders, but there was nothing there. "Jean-Luc, where are you?"

The cat appeared midway through his leap to the floor. He landed, chirped at Remy, then hopped up onto Alice's table.

"Sorry." Remy reached for him.

"Let him stay," Alice said. "There is more pure magic in that creature than either of us has. And he loves Ephie, too. His presence is a good thing."

Jean-Luc stared at the flame, his tail swishing slowly.

"How did you know he was there when he wasn't visible?"

Alice's coy smile was her only answer to that question. "Hush, now. I need to open the spell."

He had no idea what that meant, but he went quiet.

"Let what is hidden be shown. Give us sight through the eyes of the one who possesses the blood." Alice dipped the end of the glass rod into the vial and turned it, collecting the blood on the end.

She carefully lifted it out, turning the rod continuously so none of the blood dropped off. Then she passed that end into the flame.

It flared and shot up, then leveled off.

The flame widened about a half-inch from where it danced on the wick. Then it widened a little more.

Remy leaned in as a picture appeared inside the flame. It wasn't much. A small flat-screen TV on a dresser displayed an unrecognizable show.

But next to the television was a mirror. And in that mirror, Remy caught a glimpse of a woman in a chair. *Tied* to the chair. He recognized the hair and the outfit.

The image disappeared as the last of the blood burned away.

He straightened. "You saw that, right? The woman in the chair?"

Alice nodded.

"That was Ephie."

31

Inch by inch, Ephie's awareness of her body returned. Sitting still was hard. She had pins and needles itching at her skin. She wanted to move in the worst way, to stretch and feel each muscle so that she'd know she was in full control again.

But she couldn't. Not with her captor just on the bed. The woman would see, and Ephie didn't want to risk losing her advantage.

Her plan remained a simple one. Wait until her captor fell asleep, then free herself from the chair and get out of the room.

It had to be soon.

As best Ephie could tell, the woman, who'd finished her fast-food meal, had to be getting tired. After eating, she'd approached Ephie, who'd quickly closed her eyes and relied on her other senses to tell her what was happening.

The woman had poked Ephie in the shoulder. Ephie, of course, hadn't responded.

"Dang," the woman had muttered, her accent rounded with the smoothness of the bayou. "Maybe I gave you too much of that dust. Well, you're bound to wake up sooner or later. Hope it's sooner, cuz I don't wanna carry you back to the car."

Then she'd left Ephie alone, gone into the bathroom and, judging by what Ephie had heard, had taken a shower.

During that time, Ephie had studied her restraints as much as was possible. That had been her one good shot at moving. She'd rolled her head around and shrugged her shoulders a few times, trying to get the blood flowing where she could. Her legs still weren't cooperating, but her upper torso was nearly a hundred percent.

The restraints felt like standard zip ties. That was good, Ephie thought. Her idea was to use her minimal abilities to melt them to the point that she could either stretch them wide enough to free her hands or just break them.

She couldn't test out her plan, however, because she was pretty sure the smell of melting plastic would tip her captor off that Ephie was up to something. If the smoke didn't set off the alarm. Although in this motel, maybe it wouldn't.

Either way, Ephie was not-so-patiently waiting for the woman to fall asleep. That seemed like Ephie's best shot at getting free. What the woman had planned, Ephie had no idea. Maybe not knowing was better. Knowing might only make Ephie panic, and it was easiest to work her tiny bit of magic when she was calm.

Right now, the woman was reclining on the bed, still watching television. Like she was waiting for something.

Ephie got that impression, because every so often, the woman would sigh or mutter something. So far, she'd said, "Come on, already," and ,"What's taking so long," along with a few more choice words.

Whatever was happening, or wasn't happening, the woman didn't like it.

She was growing impatient.

Ephie didn't quite know what that meant for her personally. All she could do was hope the woman would drift off and give Ephie the chance to get free. And soon.

Ephie had no way of telling the time, but she knew that once the sun was up, Remy would have to end his search for her.

She didn't want to think about that. She wanted him here, with her, just like she wanted out of this room and away from this woman. She had no doubt that the search for her would continue, but she wanted Remy more than anything else.

A soft buzzing sound interrupted Ephie's thoughts. Had to be the woman's phone vibrating with a call.

She answered. "Yeah, what's up? You took long enough to call." There was a brief pause. "Well, I couldn't answer then, could I? I was in the middle of taking care of *her,* and my phone was on silent."

A much longer pause, then the woman sucked in a ragged breath. Ephie heard movement, too. Like she'd sat up on the bed. "What?" A ragged sob escaped her. "He's dead? My daddy's *dead*?"

Ephie steeled herself not to react, but all the pieces

The Vampire's Former Flame

fell into place. Turner had been killed in a prison riot. Did that mean Turner was this woman's father? It seemed that way. If so, what would happen now? Ephie didn't want to answer that question, but it felt obvious there were two possible ways this could go.

Either this woman would immediately leave to go home, forgetting all about Ephie. Or Ephie was about to become the focus of this woman's wrath.

The woman let out a howl that was full of anguish and rage. As she wept loudly, something hit the mirror with a hard *thunk*, shattering it into pieces. Shards of glass and the woman's phone fell to the floor.

Ephie barely managed not to jerk back in response to the frightening sound. The question had been answered.

The woman's feet appeared before Ephie, facing her. "This is your fault," she snarled through sobs. Her fists ground against her sides, knuckles white. "Your mother did this. She put him in there. She testified against him so he didn't get parole. He coulda been *out*. Now you gonna pay."

With that, the woman stormed out of the room, slamming the door behind her.

Terror flooded Ephie, the rush of adrenaline helping her shed the remaining numbness. This was her chance. She couldn't wait any longer. She had to do something. And she had to do it now.

She shifted slightly, centering herself, and focused on the sunstone that rested against her chest. For once in her life, her abilities had to work better than they ever had before. Not only did she need to free herself, but she needed a diversion.

Something sizable enough that her captor would be distracted by it and forget about Ephie.

First, she worked on the restraints on her wrists. That was hard to do without seeing them. She'd never used her magic blind that way. She pictured the zip tie in her mind, how it might appear around her wrists.

As she did that, she put tension on the zip tie, pulling her wrists apart as far as they would go, and tried to send her magic to the part of the zip tie that wasn't touching her wrists.

She swore the sunstone felt warmer.

Then heat seared her wrists. She sucked in air, grimacing. Her magic was definitely working. Just a little bit more ... Pain darted across her skin, and her wrists came free, flying apart. The zip tie shot onto the bed next to her.

She carefully rubbed at her wrists. A blister was already forming on her skin from where the melted plastic had touched her, but it was a small price to pay for being free. She bent over as much as she was able to see the ties securing her ankles to the chair. Her body still didn't seem to be cooperating completely, because she couldn't lean as much as she wanted to.

Seeing the zip ties made a huge difference, though. Using her magic again, she got her right foot free just as the door flew open again.

"What are you doing?" the woman screeched. She

had a tripod in one hand and a ring light in the other. She tossed them on the bed and came at Ephie, shards of broken mirror crunching underfoot.

Ephie tried to stand even though one ankle remained attached to the chair, but she couldn't get up. Instantly, she realized the back of her jeans was connected to the chair. No wonder she hadn't been able to bend all the way forward. A zip tie through one of her belt loops? It had to be. Explained why she hadn't fallen out of the chair when she'd been passed out.

She sat down hard, panic flushing through her system. Then instinct and the self-preservation drive took over. She shoved her hands out in front of her and called every shred of power she could muster. The sunstone pulsed with warmth.

A large bubble of fire burst forth from her palms. The woman swerved in time to avoid it, but it hit the wall and exploded in all directions, spreading heat and flames like a gob of jelly. Fire raced over the wall, down to the floor, up to the ceiling.

The woman screamed and started batting at the flames with the closest thing to her, a magazine off the dresser. Her efforts only fanned the flames higher.

Ephie cringed at the heat. She hadn't meant to produce *anything* like that, but she'd gotten the distraction she'd wanted. She reached behind her, found the zip tie holding her to the chair and used more power to melt through it, then removed the last one off her ankle. She got up, her body stiff and prickly from sitting so long.

She hobbled around the bed, trying to get to the door as she cringed against the heat. The fire was spreading rapidly. A large portion of the ceiling had caught, and the flames were licking their way across it to the other wall.

An alarm went off. Sprinklers in the ceiling activated, but only one of them shot any water out, and it was basically turning to steam as it hit the fire.

Ephie's captor was frantically gathering her things. She caught sight of Ephie and turned on her. "Witch," she spat. She lunged at Ephie, tackling her to the floor.

Ephie, weak from being drugged and tied up, collapsed beneath the woman. She mustered enough energy to fight, shoving at the woman to get free of her. "We need to get out of here."

"Your mother killed my father. You're not going anywhere." The woman reared back, haloed by the flames above her, and punched Ephie across the jaw.

Pain radiated through her face. She threw her hands up to protect herself but shifted tactics mid-movement and sent both fists into the woman's stomach.

Ephie's captor doubled over, coughing and taking in smoke as she rolled to the side.

There was no avoiding the smoke. It billowed through the room. Ephie used the side of the dresser to pull herself up. Her head swirled with dizziness that had nothing to do with the drugs she'd been dosed with.

She tried holding the edge of her cardigan over her mouth and nose. She had to get out of the room, but the door seemed so far away.

The curtains burst into flames, the fabric dripping away like lava. The alarm continued to peal, but the fire seemed to grow louder.

Ephie's vision wavered. She forced herself to take a step toward the door.

A hand wrapped around her ankle, tugging her back. Her grip on the dresser was the only thing that kept her from stumbling to the floor.

She tried to get free, but the woman's grasp was too strong.

Then the woman grabbed a fistful of Ephie's jeans in her other hand and pulled.

Ephie held on to the dresser for dear life, but what strength she had left was fading fast. The heat was almost unbearable. It was getting harder to breathe. Harder to see. She kicked out her leg, trying to shake the woman off. "Let me go! We need to get out!"

Fire dropped from the ceiling, some of it clumps of building material, some of it just free-falling flames.

The woman yanked on Ephie's jeans, finally pulling her to the ground. Ephie landed half on the woman, who cried out as Ephie made contact.

Ephie dug her elbows into the woman and shoved. Her will to live was the single thing driving her now. Her body was only barely responding.

At least being low meant the air was a little easier to breathe. She inhaled, trying to fill her lungs for one last attempt at freedom.

She had to get up. She had to get to her feet and make

it to the door. She needed to get outside, to get free. Maybe she could crawl.

She started forward, but the woman had hold of Ephie's hair. Ephie would have screamed at her, but her throat was already raw from the smoke. Ephie shoved at the woman again, who seemed to finally be weakening. Ephie managed to get free, roll off and onto her back.

One of the windows shattered. The fresh influx of air turned the existing flames into a raging inferno.

Ephie lay there, trying to breathe, knowing she had to get up. The heat was intense. The room was an oven. The rivets on her jeans burned into her skin.

Darkness beckoned. Sweet, cool darkness.

Ephie fought a moment longer, struggling to get up. She fell back, her strength gone, her will to live no longer enough.

She tucked her thumb over the stones on her pansy ring, needing to touch them, her mind on Remy. She hoped he had a good life.

Then she closed her eyes.

32

The Peach Tree Motel was in chaos, the parking lot crowded with firetrucks, ambulances, first responders, and onlookers. The flames billowing off the building were so bright, they lit the night sky like it was day.

Remy knew without a doubt that this was where Ephie was being held. He had a pretty good hunch that she'd started the fire, too.

He'd arrived just ahead of the Nocturne Falls Fire Department, having heard the call come in over the radio. He'd sped here straight from the station, where he and the sheriff had been trying to determine which motel Remy had seen in Alice's spell.

Then the call had come through, and they'd both known.

The sheriff arrived after him. The flames were coming from a block of rooms near the end of the motel. At least three were engulfed with a fourth about to be.

He was headed for the second room when one of the plate-glass windows shattered from the heat.

Air rushed in, pushing the fire out of the way for a split second. That was all the time he needed to see two bodies on the floor.

Ephie.

Personal safety was no longer an issue. He leaped through the broken window, ignoring the shard that sliced his right biceps, ignoring the searing heat that had already begun to blister his skin. Ephie and another woman who looked vaguely familiar lay motionless on the melting carpet.

"Ephie." He scooped them both up, kicked down the burning door and carried them out.

Paramedics met him, taking the women from him as he sagged under the pain of the injuries he'd sustained.

Merrow grabbed him up with an arm under his shoulders. "Stupid thing to do. Damn brave, though."

"I'll heal," Remy groaned. His skin felt like it was still on fire. He would heal with some time. He just needed blood. And rest. And to know that the woman he loved was going to be all right. "Is Ephie ... alive?"

"Don't know, son. Let's get you seen."

Remy struggled to turn, trying to see her. "I need to know."

"I'll check soon as you're getting looked at."

"Now." Remy softened his tone. "Please."

Merrow tightened his grip on Remy, moving him toward one of the waiting ambulances. "There's nothing more you can do for her except look after yourself. I promise I'll see to her once I get you help."

Remy hurt too much to argue anymore. Behind them, firefighters battled the blaze. Merrow handed Remy off to a pair of medics. "Vampire," he said softly.

With matched nods, they got Remy onto a stretcher.

The woman put an oxygen mask over Remy's face. "It's just for looks, but if you want to breathe it in, it won't hurt you."

Remy didn't fight it. He was straining to see through the crowd, to find Ephie. The other paramedic was cutting Remy's charred clothing off his body.

The woman got an IV into Remy's arm and started a solution dripping into him. "Plasma. It'll help." Then she prepped a syringe and slid it into the port, depressing the plunger.

"What was that?" Remy asked through the mask.

She smiled. "You need to rest. I promise we'll take care of you." Her eyes glowed blue momentarily. "Your boss is my pack leader, and I have no intention of upsetting him."

Remy opened his mouth to ask about Ephie again, but the words wouldn't form. His eyes went back in his head, and his pain was forgotten as everything went black.

He woke up in his own bed.

He had no idea how that had happened. Had he dreamed the fire? No. The acrid stink of smoke clung to his skin and hair.

The sun was down. Still down? Or newly down? Time didn't exist. He could have been in that bed for a day or a week or a month.

Carefully, he tossed the covers back and eased out of bed. He felt ... better than he'd expected. Not a hundred percent but not awful, either. Someone had undressed him. He wore a pair of boxers and nothing else.

He stood in front of the mirror, studying what he saw. Patches of new pink skin covered most of his arms, chest, and neck. There was a wide swath of pink across his forehead as well as the right side of his face. He was missing a lot of hair on that side of his head, as well.

He touched the stubble that had already started to regrow. Maybe he'd only been in that bed a day or two. It didn't matter. None of it mattered.

What mattered was Ephie. He had no idea what had happened to her. If she was even still alive. He trusted she was. He wanted to believe that he'd know if she'd left this plane. That he'd feel it somehow.

His bedroom door was closed. He grabbed the knob, opened it, and walked out into the hall, realizing a moment later that he wasn't alone.

"No fussing now. I've already brushed you twice. Do you want to play with your catnip mouse again? Here, go fetch."

A furry purple mouse came flying out of the kitchen, a solid Jean-Luc hot on its trail.

Birdie followed the scampering feline, a cup of tea in her hand.

"Hey," Remy said.

Birdie jumped, spilling the tea and yelping as her hand went to her chest. "Stars in heaven, I didn't know you were awake." She looked at him, then quickly turned away. "And naked."

Boxers weren't exactly naked. He shrugged. "Sorry. I didn't know anyone was here."

"Sergeant Cruz will be by shortly. It's nearly the end of my shift." Birdie went back into the kitchen, reappearing without the cup of tea. She'd swapped it out for a towel, which she used to clean up the spill. "I think Jean-Luc likes him better anyway. They have more in common, you know, what with him being a big cat shifter."

"I don't need anyone. I'm fine. How's Ephie? Tell me the truth. Did she make it?"

Birdie straightened, twisting the towel in her hands. "She's in the hospital. They have her in a coma." Her chin quavered. "She's badly burned. She's in critical condition."

He felt sick. "I need to see her."

Birdie nodded. "I know you do. But you should feed first. There's plenty in your fridge. You mind if I go with you to the hospital?"

"Okay. How long have I been asleep?"

"Not long. A day."

"I'll feed and shower, then we'll go." He went into the kitchen, grabbed two bottles from the fridge and took them back to his room. He paused at the door. The bruise on her cheek was nearly gone. "How are you? Are you okay?"

She smiled. "I'm just fine. You get ready."

He drank one bottle waiting for the water to warm up. He drank the second when he got out. He pulled on jeans and a soft, long-sleeved shirt that covered most of his burns. He put on his Nocturne Falls Sheriff's Department hat to hide the missing hair and pink scalp.

The shower and the feed helped. He felt better physically than when he'd first woken up. Emotionally and mentally, he was hanging by a thread. The news about Ephie wasn't good.

He grabbed his wallet, his keys, and his badge, then took the empty bottles back to the kitchen.

Birdie was sitting at the kitchen table with her tea. She had Jean-Luc in her arms like a baby and was singing softly to him. She looked up at Remy. "That was fast."

"I want to go."

"Right." She stood. "Sorry, little cat. Aunt Birdie has to leave you."

"Bring him."

"What?"

Remy patted his shoulder. "Put him here." He nodded at the cat. "Come on. We're going to see your mama."

Jean-Luc returned to his ghost form and leaped from Birdie's arms to Remy's shoulder.

"I can't see him anymore. Does that mean he did what you wanted?" Birdie asked.

"He did. Let's go."

The drive took too long, even though Remy drove faster than he should have. Birdie was on her phone most of the time. Texting, from the look of it, although Remy was trying to keep his eyes on the road. She also told him that Ephie's mother had been called and was on her way, and that the other woman Remy had pulled from the fire was also in critical condition. She had been identified as Desiree Turner.

Abraham Turner's daughter.

"If you dig into her," Remy said, "you'll probably find Dee Mills is an alias. She's the woman who was in the SUV down from my house. The second plate I had you run."

When they arrived, they parked and went straight in. He flashed his badge at the visitors desk. "Ephelia Moreau's room, please."

The older man behind the desk checked the badge, then pecked at the keyboard in front of him. "412."

The ride up in the elevator took too long. Jean-Luc rubbed his head on Remy's hat. The three of them stepped off the elevator to dim lighting, the quiet hum of machines, and the smell of antiseptic.

Birdie pointed left. "That way."

They walked down the hall until they came to Ephie's room. Remy paused outside, his heart hurting, knowing that what he was about to see was only going to break it into pieces. He flattened his hand against the door and pushed.

Ephie lay lifeless in the bed, most of her body bandaged, tubes running out of her, machines softly beeping, another one breathing for her. What he could see of her skin looked like one continuous scab.

The muscles in his jaw constricted. Tears filled his eyes. He rubbed his hand across his mouth. For Ephie's sake, he would not break down. He would be positive and give off good energy. Healing energy.

Jean-Luc jumped down to the floor and then back up again, onto Ephie's bed. He curled up next to her, looking at her expectantly. Like any moment she would acknowledge his presence with a little scratch on his head.

Remy's vision blurred.

Birdie pressed a tissue into his hand and patted his arm. "I'll give you some time."

She left, and Remy tipped his head back until the tears stopped. He pulled a chair alongside the bed and sat, slipping his hand under Ephie's. "Hello, sweetheart. I don't know if you can hear me or not, but I'm right here, at your side. Jean-Luc is here, too."

There was no response but the machines.

He lost track of time. At some point, Birdie came back in. She took the other chair, saying nothing. Just being there.

Finally, after how long he didn't know, Birdie got to her feet. "Sun will be up soon."

"I know," Remy said. "I can feel it. But I don't want to leave her."

"I know you don't. But you can come back tomorrow. Soon as possible."

Remy stood and leaned in to kiss her cheek. The faint smell of smoke still lingered. He straightened. "I could fix all this, you know. I could turn her."

"Do you think she's strong enough to survive that?"

He frowned and, after a moment, shook his head.

"No. Probably not." He hesitated. "Maybe ... maybe there's something Alice could do? A healing spell. Something."

Birdie touched his arm, her voice almost breaking. "Already been done."

Remy nodded reluctantly. The pain in his chest was nothing compared with the pain of the fire. "Come on, Jean-Luc. Time to go home."

33

On the second night of visiting Ephie, Remy entered her room to find Leonie there. A man roughly her age sat next to her. She stood as Remy came in.

He braced himself for the attack that had to be coming. Hopefully, Jean-Luc, who was perched in his usual place on Remy's shoulder, would stay invisible.

But there was no attack. Instead, Leonie sniffed and whispered, "Thank you." She cleared her throat. "I've been told what happened. That if it wasn't for you, she would have died. So thank you for saving my daughter's life."

"I just did what had to be done."

The man with Leonie stood as well. He stuck his hand out. "Darryl Tyson, New Orleans Police Commissioner. Thank you for what you did for Ephie."

"You don't need to thank me." Remy shook the man's hand.

"If Turner's daughter pulls through, she'll face the consequences of her actions. My men have already arrested the men working with her." Darryl stuck his hands in his pockets. "That other woman you pulled out of the fire was Abraham Turner's daughter. She was the one behind the letters. We linked one of the janitors to her, and he's since been arrested."

"That's good news." Remy looked at the woman he loved. There didn't seem to be any change in her status. Several large vases of flowers sat on the windowsill, perfuming the air. A better smell than smoke and soot.

He moved closer to Ephie's bedside.

Leonie picked up her purse. "We should go. Give you some time with her. We've been here all day."

"I'm glad she wasn't alone." Remy gave Leonie and Darryl a nod, then pulled a chair close to the bed and sat, slipping his hand underneath Ephie's bandaged one. "Hey, sweetheart. It's me. And I have Jean-Luc with me."

The cat jumped down and settled into the same spot as the night before, curled against Ephie's side.

And just like the night before, there was no sign that she knew either of them were there.

It broke his heart. He felt helpless sitting there, and the frustration of not being able to do anything only made things worse.

"I thought I'd find you here."

He turned to see Alice walking in. He stood. "Hello."

"Sit." She came to stand beside him.

He stayed on his feet, too many years of etiquette embedded in him to do otherwise. "No change that I can see since last night."

Alice reached out and rested her hand on Ephie's leg. Even through the blanket, it was easy to see the bandages that wrapped her. "There won't be a change for a long time unless you do something."

He looked at her. "There isn't anything I can do."

"Yes, there is. You can turn her."

"I wish I could. I don't know if you understand that process, but it's not exactly gentle on the human body. She's in no shape to go through that."

Alice took her hand off of Ephie's leg and turned toward him. "She doesn't need to be turned in the ordinary way. She's dhampir. All she needs is an adequate infusion of strong vampire blood. Yours should do nicely."

He shook his head, wondering how a witch this powerful couldn't recognize one of her own. "She's not dhampir. She's not any part vampire, let alone half. She's a witch with some basic fire magic. Always has been. She'd tell you that herself if she could."

"Her mother's a witch?"

"Yes, but from what Ephie's told me, it generally skips a generation. Her grandmother's magic is a lot stronger."

"Then her father was the vampire."

Remy sighed. "She doesn't know her father. Never has. He died before she was born, from what I remember. And her mother hates vampires, so I don't think she'd have had a kid with one."

"Perhaps that's *why* she hates vampires."

Remy fell silent, thinking about that. "I don't know. What makes you think Ephie's a dhampir?"

"I sensed something darker in her the night of the

coven meeting. I touched her, and that confirmed my suspicions. You must give me credit for knowing when there's a vampire about. I've been rather closely associated with them for some time now. But the hair you gave me was the final bit of proof I needed. I tested it. She is, indeed, dhampir."

Half vampire. He stared at Ephie, trying to see that side of her, but all he could see were bandages and tubes and a few bits of skin that had somehow, miraculously, escaped being singed. "If that's true, why isn't she healing better? Why have I never seen any signs of that in her? She has no problem being in the sun. And she doesn't like the sight of blood, I can tell you that much."

"She doesn't like it? Or she finds her interest in it unsettling?"

He thought back to her reaction when he'd taken a bottle from the fridge. "I don't know the answer to that."

"As for why she's not healing as quickly as you might expect, it's simple. Her two halves have been at war with each other so long that they now damper each other, nearly canceling each other out. She's getting very little benefit from either side. In truth, her magic could be much stronger. And I suspect it will be once she's become fully vampire."

"So turning her won't take away her abilities?"

Alice shook her head. "On the contrary, it will finally enable that side of her to bloom into its own fullness. And because of her dual nature, she will never have a problem being in the sun. Dhampirs are born, not made, and as a result, they can usually daywalk. I'm sure Ephelia is no exception."

His mouth came open in surprise. Hope trickled through him. "She could live a normal life. Without worrying about sunrise."

Alice nodded. "Indeed."

"And she'd heal? With the same speed and precision that any other vampire does? She'd be whole in a matter of days, not weeks or months."

"She would."

He touched Ephie's hand. "Her mother won't like it."

"I imagine her mother would prefer her daughter whole and healthy more than she would care about a change in her daughter's supernatural status."

"You don't know Leonie."

"True. I don't. But if she has a problem with any of this, I will gladly speak to her."

Remy would pay good money to see that. "What do I need to do? You said it would require an infusion of vampire blood."

"That's correct. Normally, I'd say one large syringe, but given her condition, two might be more beneficial." Alice looked around. "Syringes shouldn't be too hard to find. We are in a hospital, after all."

Jean-Luc let out a little chirp as he rolled closer to Ephie, his head slightly upside down, his paws extended and kneading the air.

Alice nodded her head at the little animal. "You and

Ephie can both see the cat when others can't, correct? Unless, of course, he chooses to be invisible."

"That's right. But you can see him." Jean-Luc was translucent and tended to stay that way when they were in the hospital. It was like he understood he wouldn't be allowed if he were seen.

"No, I can't see him, but I can sense his presence. Just like when he was in my practice. But you and Ephie can see him because your status as vampires allows you to access the realm of death in a way other supernaturals can't."

"Being half-blooded is enough to do that for her?"

"Yes."

He didn't need to weigh the decision. If turning Ephie could save her and bring her back to full health, there was no question that it should be done. Leonie would hate it. She'd hate him. He just had to pray she wouldn't also hate Ephie.

If that happened, Remy feared he'd lose Ephie. But he was facing that now. She was badly burned. People with fewer burns had succumbed.

He nodded. "I'll see if I can find some syringes."

Ephie drifted. At times, she was vaguely aware of voices. Of purring. Singing. Laughter. Tears. Music. Prayers. All kinds of sounds filled her consciousness. Most of them good. Most of them made her want to wake up and join in.

No matter how hard she tried, that never happened.

The tears made her sad. Sadder. She knew from the pain that leaked through the heavy fog of medication that she had been gravely injured. That knowledge was a weight that rested on top of everything else.

Sometimes, she slept. Truly slept, not the involuntary blackout brought on by the drugs in her system. The blackouts were just that. Blackness. Nothingness. Floating through a void that had neither time nor shape nor meaning. No dreams, either.

The dreams came with genuine sleep. Jean-Luc and his silly antics. Her mother. Alphonso. Her grandmother. But mostly Remy. Proud, handsome, sweet, funny, wonderful Remy.

In one of her dreams, he rescued her from the inferno that had raged about her. In another, they were back at Tulane, walking hand in hand across the campus on a warm, starry spring night. Once, she'd dreamed of them having ice cream, but they'd eaten it in the middle of the frozen foods aisle at the Shop-n-Save.

Those were the good ones.

Most of her dreams were much darker. Snippets of images that swirled through her mind like a terrible storm. Being burned alive. Unable to escape the flames. Sometimes her mother was with her. Or her grandmother. In the worst of her dreams, Jean-Luc had run into a burning building and Remy had gone after him, then the building had collapsed.

The sense of loss felt like a crushing weight.

Now and then, hot, heavy air seared her skin, the rushing growl of the fire filling her ears like a freight train bearing down on her.

She had dreams about pain. About her skin bubbling and blistering. About the heat. About melting like she was made of wax. She dreamed she was in an oven and couldn't find a way out as the temperature grew higher and higher.

She even dreamed about waking up once and finding that Remy had moved on. In her dream, he was married with three handsome sons who looked just like him. His wife was the woman who'd held Ephie hostage, Abraham Turner's daughter.

Ephie imagined looking in the mirror and being unable to identify herself. Her face was scarred beyond recognition. Marked by hard, marbled flesh that frightened her. Sometimes, in that dream, Remy would show up and hold her, telling her he would always love her no matter what. But in the worst version, he cringed in horror and ran from her while Jean-Luc hissed, back arched.

In her dreams, Ephie cried a lot. There was so much that upset her. She wanted only the good dreams, but there was no way to control what went on in her head.

Maybe she cried in real life, too, but she wasn't sure that still existed.

Had she died? She didn't know, and she wasn't sure how to find out. When she tried to talk, nothing happened. Her body didn't respond to her commands, and neither did her voice. She felt trapped in a kind of limbo.

Maybe that was death. Maybe this was all she would ever know for as long as time went on.

Thankfully, about the time she didn't think she could take anymore, the medicated abyss would return. She'd fought it at first, but now she welcomed it. Better to be numb and unaware than to succumb to the terrors of her mind.

Somewhere in the distance, a machine hummed and ticked, and she sank back into the thick fog of nothing, drifting off once again.

35

Remy found the syringes he needed by accessing an area he had no permission to be in, but that didn't bother him. Ephie's health and well-being were at stake here. He would have done anything for her, legal, illegal, or otherwise.

It occurred to him he could have asked. As a sheriff's deputy, there was every chance they'd have given him anything he requested. But how long would that have taken? He was in no mood for paperwork or waiting on approval.

When he returned, Alice was sitting by Ephie's bedside with her hand on Ephie's arm. Jean-Luc was barely visible, his little body so still that he had to be sleeping. Alice's eyes were closed, and she was whispering in Latin.

It had been a few years since Remy'd had to use his knowledge of the language, but it sounded like a spell to him. He picked out enough words to know it was something for comfort and healing and a long future.

He approved. He stood by, patiently waiting.

Alice finished and opened her eyes. Her gaze went to his hands before meeting his eyes. "Did you get them?"

He pulled two large syringes out of his back pocket and showed them to her. "Good enough?"

"Those will do nicely." Alice glanced at the chart on the wall, which mostly read like gibberish to Remy due to the incomprehensible handwriting. "She's due for a visit from her doctor in the next half hour or so. After that, you'll have time to do what needs to be done."

For a moment, he worried Alice was leaving. "You're going to stay with me, aren't you? Please. In case ... I'd just feel better if you were here."

Alice nodded, smiling softly. "Your love for her is a beautiful thing. Of course I will stay."

"Thank you." Remy wasn't sure how they were allowed to be here at all because visiting hours weren't twenty-four-seven. Someone with pull had intervened. For that he was eternally grateful.

They sat with her until the doctor came and went. Jean-Luc, still thankfully translucent, hissed at the man, then swatted at the ID card clipped to his white coat. None of which had any effect, as the doctor was apparently human with no secret ability to see ghosts.

The doctor was also quick and made very little small talk. For that, Remy was glad. His head was in no place for such things. He was fixated on what he was about to do. The path Ephelia was about to take.

Without her knowledge.

That part unsettled him. She ought to have some say in this.

The doctor left. Still, Remy sat, his mind filled with what-ifs.

"Something's bothering you."

He looked over at Alice. "What's that?"

"You're frowning. Your brow is furrowed. Something's bothering you."

He nodded, a feeling of bleakness coming over him. "What if Ephie doesn't want this? She never has before."

"You asked her?"

"Yes. Twelve years ago. I asked her to be my bride and to let me turn her so that she and I could spend eternity together." He looked at his hands. "Not only didn't she want that, she ran from me. That was the last I saw of her until this trip to New Orleans."

It had cost him so much.

"And yet she still wears the ring you gave her."

He raised his head. "Yes. How did you know that?"

"Educated guess. I saw it on her hand at the coven meeting. It's a very old ring. Not necessarily the style a woman of her age would wear unless it was sentimental." Alice smiled gently. "Also, it carries the scent of vampire."

He let out a quick, humorless laugh. "It was from my share of my grandfather's hoard, one of the many pieces of bounty he collected in his days of privateering. I thought it was a good sign that she still wore it, too."

"A sign that she still loves you. Never stopped, most likely," Alice said. "I understand that you'd prefer to talk this over with her, to include her in the decision, but if that were possible, this decision wouldn't be necessary."

He sighed, the weight of the decision heavy even in the face of Alice's logic. "That is true."

"This turning will not only save her life, it will give her a brand-new one. And just because you turn her, it doesn't mean she has to choose to be with you for the remainder of her days. She may not. You have to accept that as a possible outcome."

He was frowning again but couldn't stop himself. "I'm aware. Just like I'm aware that if she comes out of this and hates what I've done to her, she'll hate me for doing it."

And once again, he'd be the reason for his own broken heart.

Alice nodded solemnly. "That is another possibility. But not one I foresee."

Did she mean that she'd had an actual vision of the future? Or was she just projecting? He wasn't sure.

Alice stood. "Are you ready? Dawn will be here before you know it."

He wasn't ready, but putting it off another night or two would only mean prolonging Ephie's suffering. It might also mean she'd get worse and he'd lose the opportunity altogether. That was not an outcome he wanted to risk. He got to his feet and walked to her bedside.

He laid the syringes on the bed. "I've never drawn my own blood before. Or anyone's, for that matter. Not like this, anyway."

Alice held her hand out. "If you'll permit me."

He picked the syringes up and placed them in her

palm, then pushed up his sleeve as he walked around to her. "What if we get interrupted?"

"We won't. For the next hour or so, this room will cease to exist."

"How is that— Oh. Thank you. Good idea."

"A small spell, nothing much." Alice removed the cap from the first syringe. "This won't hurt."

"Won't bother me if it does."

"I'm sure. But you needn't endure more than you already have."

As Alice sank the needle into his arm, he watched Ephie. At times, she looked peaceful. But now and then her expression changed, and she seemed to be distraught or in pain. He hurt then, too.

Jean-Luc twitched in his sleep, whiskers quivering, but he never woke.

After a few long minutes, Alice patted his arm. "All done. Would you like me to administer it?"

He knew why she was asking him that. She was offering him the option of not shouldering all the blame, should Ephie not approve of this decision. "No, I'll do it. No reason for her to hate you, too."

Alice gave him a quick smile. "Directly into the port on the IV."

"Okay. How long will it take to work?"

"I'm not sure. In her condition, it might be another twenty-four hours before she wakes up. Maybe longer." Alice shrugged. "It will take as long as it needs to."

"But it *will* work."

"It will."

He inserted the needle of the first syringe into the port and depressed the plunger, hoping that he was doing the right thing. Praying Ephie would understand. No, that she would do more than understand.

That she would welcome this new life. That she would still love him.

He administered both syringes before kissing Ephie's cheek. "Rest and heal. I love you."

Then he woke Jean-Luc. "Time to go, little man."

Alice walked with them on their way out of the hospital. She didn't say a word, which was fine with him.

In the parking lot, Alice said goodbye and went to her car. He stopped and stared back at the building, calculating where Ephie's room was and sending her every bit of positive energy and all the good thoughts he could muster.

All while praying he hadn't just made the biggest mistake of both their lives.

Ephie woke bleary-eyed and groggy but feeling better than she'd thought she would. The pain was gone. She was tired, and the fog of the pain meds remained, although nothing like what it had been.

Was she dreaming again? No, she was actually awake and coherent. Something that hadn't happened since ... before the fire.

The fire.

It all came rushing back to her. Ephie stared at the dim light filtering through the blinds on the window. Several beautiful bouquets of flowers sat on the sill, the scent of them lovely but not enough to stop the images from playing out. The soft beep and hum of the machines she was hooked up to provided the soundtrack to her memories.

Tears trickled down her face. So much of what had happened was a blur, but there were parts she remembered vividly. The smell of the smoke. The deafening sound of the fire. The intense heat. And the pain. She turned her head away from the window.

A nurse was coming in. She stopped, and her brows went up. She quickly smiled at Ephie. "You're awake. I ... wasn't expecting that." The older woman went straight to

Ephie's chart, flipping through it with concern on her face. "How are you feeling?"

"All right. Not bad, I guess. A little groggy."

"Not bad? Do you have any pain? Any stiffness?"

Ephie thought about that, trying to really listen to her body. "No, neither of those."

The nurse momentarily stopped reading the chart to stare at Ephie. "You're *sure*?"

"Yep." Ephie did her best to sit up, but between the blankets, the tubes, and the bandages, it was like fighting some kind of land octopus.

"Whoa, now!" The nurse started forward. "I can raise the bed for you a bit if you'd like, but too much movement can loosen the bandages and—"

The end of the dressing on Ephie's left hand already dangled free. She pulled it loose as the nurse looked on.

The skin underneath looked very new. It was different shades of pink, the outline of the burn still visible, but there was no hard scarring, no scabs, no dying or burned skin. Ephie shrugged one shoulder and lifted her hand up a little. "Do I really need to cover this?"

The nurse's mouth was open, her eyes narrowed. She shook her head, but the gesture felt more like it was for herself than Ephie. "I'll, uh, be right back."

The nurse scurried off, passing someone at the door.

Smiling big, Birdie strode in with a full tote bag in one hand and her purse over the other shoulder. "Hello there, doll face. How are you? Causing trouble?"

Ephie shook her head. "I'm not trying to." She smiled. It was so good to see a friendly face. "How are you?"

"I'm just peachy." Birdie rested the tote bag against the edge of the bed, then lowered her voice. "Jean-Luc's not in here, is he? I don't want to put the bag on top of him."

"No." Ephie laughed. "How would Jean-Luc get here?"

"Well, Remy's been bringing him."

"He has?" Figured. The two of them were as thick as thieves. She loved it.

"Sure," Birdie said. "As soon as Remy was able, he's been coming to see you. And I have it on good authority that since he helped you get better, you're going to be getting out of here soon. How are you feeling, by the way? You look pretty good."

"He helped me get better?" Ephie searched her memory, trying to figure out what Birdie was referring to. Her last dreams had been good. Really good. Her and Remy and Jean-Luc strolling through the French Quarter on a balmy evening as happy music played. They'd been dressed in beautiful, old-fashioned clothing. Like they were in period costumes from the early days of Louisiana.

But then, so had everyone else they'd passed.

"He did." Birdie leaned in, taking a closer look at Ephie. "Don't you feel better?"

"I do feel pretty good." In the few minutes since she'd woken up, the last of the medicated fog had lifted.

"That's because he gave you a blood transfusion. I guess that's the best term for it. Anyway, a few of us were told so that we could keep an eye out for you in case you got discharged during daylight hours. I figured I'd come and check on you and bring you a change of clothing for when that happened. So you'd be ready."

Ephie was still stuck on the blood transfusion part. "When did that happen? I don't even remember him being here."

"I'm sure you don't. They've kept you pretty doped up. For the pain, I'm sure. Every time I've been here, you've been completely out of it."

Ephie glanced at her hand again. If she'd been that badly burned, she shouldn't be this healed. Something was going on.

Before she could figure out what that was, her mother and Darryl came in. Her mother gasped. "You're awake."

Ephie nodded. "Hi, Mom. Hi, Darryl. I didn't know you guys were here."

Leonie rushed to Ephie's bedside as Birdie stepped back. "We came as soon as we heard about the fire. How are you, sweetheart? How are you feeling? Is the pain awful? Should you be up?"

It was a bit overwhelming to be barraged with questions, but Ephie did her best. "I'm good. I feel fine. There's no pain. And why shouldn't I be up?"

"Your mother's just worried," Darryl said. "We both were. Glad to see you're doing better."

Birdie leaned in and stuck her hand out. "Birdie Caruthers. I'm a friend of Ephie's. Friend of Remy's, too.

You could say we work together. I'm the receptionist at the sheriff's department."

Leonie shook Birdie's hand. "Nice to meet you, Birdie. Thank you for looking out for Ephie. That's very kind of you."

Darryl shook Birdie's hand, too. "Darryl Tyson. Police commissioner. Always nice to meet someone else in law enforcement."

Birdie grinned. Ephie understood. Birdie liked that Darryl had included her as a member of a very special group, even though she was only a receptionist. After hearing Birdie's stories and seeing how capable she was, Ephie had pretty quickly concluded that Birdie was way more than just a receptionist.

Ephie cleared her throat, no longer raw from the smoke. "What happened to the woman who kidnapped me?"

Darryl shook his head. "She didn't make it. She passed a few hours ago."

A doctor strode in, white coat flapping out behind him. "Ms. Moreau. I understand you're feeling better today?"

Leonie, Darryl, and Birdie all stepped aside so the doctor could have access.

Ephie nodded. "I am. Feeling better by the minute, actually."

"Mm-hmm." The doctor just nodded and looked at her chart. Then he checked the machines monitoring her vital signs and sighed. "I fear you might be experiencing a temporary euphoria brought on by a buildup of pain medication in your system."

Ephie frowned. "I don't think so."

"Ms. Moreau, I am a trained medical professional. You have second- and third-degree burns on over forty-seven percent of your body. There is no way you—"

"Okay, but ..." Ephie held up her left hand, still unbandaged. "How do you explain this?"

He took her hand, turning it over to inspect the skin. He slipped on a pair of gloves and carefully unwrapped the bandages that remained around her wrist and up her arm.

The skin underneath was the same as the skin on her hand—several shades of fresh pink, with some lines where the worst of the burns had been, but no blood, no oozing, no scabs, no burned skin. No real sign that she'd been burned at all except for the small, still-healing marks that remained.

He frowned, muttering to himself. "This is highly unusual."

The idea that Ephie might be getting out of here and back to Remy's motivated her. She started unwrapping more of her bandages.

"No," the doctor said. "Don't do that."

"Why not?" She didn't stop.

Her mother put her hand on Ephie's ankle. "Sweetheart, listen to the doctor."

"What are the bandages for?" Ephie asked. "If they're

to protect my burns, but the burns are healed, then I don't need them, right?"

The doctor sputtered. "There's no way your burns are healed."

Ephie kept unwrapping. The pile of discarded dressings began to grow. "Doctor, I appreciate everything the hospital has done for me. I'd like to be discharged." She glanced at Birdie. "You can take me back to Remy's, right?"

"Sure," Birdie said. She looked tickled with the situation.

Ephie smiled at the doctor. "Can you send someone in to unhook me from all these machines? Or should I do that myself?

"What? No. I— You can't— Please don't." He sighed and, still muttering to himself, started for the door. "Nurse. *Nurse!*"

Ephie's stomach rumbled.

"Hungry?" Birdie asked.

Ephie nodded. "Yeah, I am. And you know what I want?"

"A big juicy steak? Rare?"

Ephie grinned. "I don't know how, but you read my mind."

"Ephelia." Leonie looked horrified. "I think something simpler would be a better idea."

Darryl had taken a seat. He smiled. "Leonie, the girl's hungry. Let her eat what she wants to eat. What's so wrong with that?"

Birdie winked at Ephie. "The way hospitals go, it'll be an hour or two before they let you get out of here. I'll go get you some food and be right back."

"Thank you." Ephie couldn't explain it, but her craving for meat, the rarer the better, seemed to occupy her entire thought process.

Birdie left. But Leonie came closer. "What's going on with you? Something's different. Something's ... off."

"Nothing's off." Ephie moved the pile of bandages to the little bedside table. She contemplated removing the IV line, but she wasn't sure how much it would bleed, and that might get messy.

Leonie inched closer. "You don't look like someone who's been in the hospital because of severe burns."

"No? What do I look like then?"

Leonie stared harder. "Darryl, get me a cup of coffee, would you?"

He got up from the chair. "All right. Be right back."

As soon as he left, Leonie leaned in and inhaled. She reared back, horror in her eyes. "You look and smell like a *vampire*."

Remy anxiously read Birdie's text message. He'd found it waiting for him when he woke up. Relief flooded him. Ephie was better. Well enough to come home. They were just waiting for her to be discharged.

The turning had worked. So far. He wasn't clear if Ephie understood everything that had happened to her, and he didn't want to take the time to ask Birdie for all the details.

He'd find out for himself soon enough.

He showered and dressed, then texted the department to let them know he'd need at least one more night off. No one expected him back yet, but he felt duty-bound to keep them in the loop all the same.

Jean-Luc was waiting at the door as if he knew it was time to go visit Ephie again.

"This time," Remy told him, "she'll be coming home with us." Hopefully.

He got Jean-Luc in the car, and they sped to the hospital, Jean-Luc riding shotgun, his front paws on the dashboard.

Remy's emotions warred with one another. He couldn't wait to see Ephie. To hold her and kiss her and share the joy that she was no longer in mortal danger.

But he worried about her reaction to what he'd done. There was no way she wouldn't be angry at him. It felt like a foregone conclusion.

He only hoped that anger wouldn't last long. That she'd understand his reasons. Understand that the decision had been made out of love for her. Out of his need to have her in his life.

He couldn't imagine an existence without her now. This brief taste of domestic life with her had been paradise. It had shown him that his life wasn't complete any other way. He wished he'd thought to bring her flowers or something, but he had the rest of their lives to give her flowers.

If all went well.

If not, he'd spend the rest of his life trying to apologize. His gut was in knots at the thought.

"Please understand," he whispered.

Jean-Luc meowed.

Remy nodded. "Maybe you can talk some sense into her."

With Jean-Luc on his shoulder, Remy walked into her room, expecting it to be just him and Ephie. Maybe Birdie. Instead, he was greeted by Birdie and Alice, who both seemed happy, a clearly upset Leonie, and Darryl, who looked like he'd just been told the secret of the universe and didn't like it one bit.

Jean-Luc jumped down and ran straight to Ephie, who greeted him with open arms. "*Bebe*," she cooed, petting him.

Remy was glad he'd brought Jean-Luc. Ephie couldn't be completely mad while also loving on the little cat. Could she?

"Hi," he said softly, making his way to the bed. "You look great."

She did, too. The deathly pallor of her skin was gone, replaced by a healthy flush. Her eyes were bright, her skin glowing. Her entire being seemed new. Which it was. Thanks to the blood he'd given her.

Birdie interjected. "They're supposed to be discharging her any second."

"Good," Remy said.

Ephie cut her eyes at him. "I know what you did."

He nodded. "I hope you also know I didn't think there was any other choice."

The tiniest hint of a smile played on Ephie's lips. "I know. Alice told me everything."

He looked at the elder witch. "Thank you."

Alice nodded. "I pushed you to do it. Seemed only fitting that I share my part in things." She took a step toward him. "If I might have a moment of your time? In the hall perhaps?"

He braced himself. What now? "Of course."

"Be right back." He stepped outside with Alice, who led him down the hall to a small, uninhabited waiting area. "What's going on?"

She tucked her hands into the pockets of her cardigan. "I've spoken to the Ellinghams. Elenora, especially. Told them about your part in all of this, most of which they already knew. But they've agreed with me that you deserve something for your heroism."

He shook his head. "That's very kind of you, but I did what I did out of love and duty. Not because I hoped to gain anything."

"We all know that. It's part of what helped make the decision." She pulled one hand from her pocket and held out a small leather pouch. "Wear this, and you will never fear the sun again. But protect it. There are those who would do terrible things for such power."

He took the pouch, staring at it. It had weight, and the soft clink of metal against metal was easily heard. "You mean it will enable me to daywalk?"

"It will. You'll need it if you're going to be with Ephie. And you've earned it."

This was monumental. It was well known that all the Ellinghams could daywalk. He had a feeling whatever was in the pouch gave them that power. "Thank you. That is incredibly generous. And kind."

Alice nodded. "Like I said, you earned it. Now, I am going home. Go be with her. The mother is not happy. I wish you luck."

"Thank you." As Alice walked away, he opened the pouch. A chain of white metal links, weighty enough to be platinum, held a curious amulet, a blood-red stone set in the center with filigree around the edges. He brought the amulet closer. There appeared to be words worked into the pattern. The back bore more engraving.

Could this really protect him from the sun? He tucked the empty pouch into his pocket and put the chain on, slipping the amulet under his shirt. He'd have to test it at some point. Right now, he needed to be with Ephie.

And deal with Leonie.

As he was about to go back in, Birdie came out. "I'm going to head home, unless you want me to stay."

He hesitated. He did want Birdie to stay, but at the same time, she'd done so much for both of them lately. She'd even been injured because of them. He didn't want to take advantage of her kind nature. "Thank you for everything. I owe you."

She smiled. "You can pay me back in Zombie Donuts and iced mochas from the Hallowed Bean."

He laughed. "Consider me your personal delivery service." He hugged her. "Thanks again."

She gave him a good squeeze. "Someday soon, I'd like for the four of us to go to dinner."

He nodded as she released him. "Tell Jack we're on. Also, it's going to be my treat."

"I'll let him know. Talk to you soon. Take care of our girl. And that crazy cat."

"I will." He went back into the room.

Leonie was straightening the blanket that covered Ephie. Darryl was still sitting in the same chair, staring at nothing.

Remy approached the side of the bed Leonie wasn't on. "What happened to Darryl?"

Leonie answered before Ephie could say anything. "He just found out some truths about the world we live in."

"Witches," Darryl murmured. He looked at Remy. "And vampires."

Remy nodded solemnly. He could only imagine what such a realization must be like.

Leonie came around to Remy's side of the bed, jabbing her finger at him. "You turned my daughter against her will."

He held his hands up. "I did what I felt was necessary to save her life."

"Mom," Ephie said. "Don't. Not here. Not now."

Jean-Luc meowed and flopped down on Ephie's lap.

But Leonie wasn't so easily silenced. "He's ruined your life, Ephie. Ruined it. He's turned you into a monster."

"See here," Remy said. "I don't appreciate you calling the woman I love a monster. I don't care for you implying that I'm one, either. If I wasn't who I am, I never would have been able to save her. You get that, right?"

Leonie fumed. "She would have healed."

"Maybe," Remy said, noticing how she'd ignored the part about his supernatural abilities making it possible for him to save Ephie. "And maybe she would have succumbed to the burns and died. If she'd made it out of that motel room."

Ephie frowned, looking teary-eyed. "Mom, I know

you hate vampires, but you're going to have to get over that, because now I am one."

Leonie shook her head. "No. I refuse to acknowledge what he's done to you."

Remy had to ask, even if it was a hard question. "Is that because of what Ephie's father did to you?"

Leonie turned on Remy. "You be quiet. You don't know what you're talking about."

"Don't talk to him like that." Ephie didn't like the harsh tone of her mother's voice, especially not directed at the man who'd saved her life. But there was pain in her mother's voice, too. Deep pain. "Mom, what does he mean? What about my father? What did he do to you? What haven't you told me?"

Leonie shook her head, the pain in her eyes clear.

Hands stuffed in his pockets, Remy cleared his throat. "Darryl, what do you say we go get some coffee and you can ask me anything you want."

Darryl looked up. "Anything?"

Remy nodded.

The man got up and walked with Remy to the door. "I have a lot of questions."

"I'm sure you do," Remy said as he let Darryl go ahead of him. He glanced back at Ephie and gave her a supportive nod.

She already knew he was on her side. He'd saved her life. Twice. She appreciated him understanding her need for some private time with her mother. "Mom, what haven't you told me?"

Jean-Luc yawned, then went back to sleep.

Leonie sank into a chair near the bed, her face crumpling into an expression of anguish. "All my life, I tried to protect you."

"I know," Ephie said softly. "And you did a great job."

"I did a terrible job. Everything I tried to protect you from ..." Leonie shook her head, wringing her hands in her lap. "All of it happened. And now this. You've become the creature I most despise."

Ephie let out a soft breath. This wasn't news. Leonie had always loathed vampires. "Why, Mom? What's so awful about vampires? There has to be a reason you feel that way. What are you keeping from me?"

Leonie took a tissue from the box on Ephie's rolling table and dabbed at her eyes. After a moment's pause, she sighed. "Your father wasn't Owen Larose. He didn't die right before you were born. Well, Owen did, actually. He was a nice boy at my college who was killed in a car accident, and he was convenient. May he rest in peace. But he wasn't your father. I don't think he would have minded being part of my story."

Ephie shook her head. "I don't understand."

Leonie looked up, her eyes suddenly hot with anger. "Your father was a vampire who seduced me and left me."

Ephie needed a second to process that. "What? My father was a vampire?"

Leonie nodded. "Yes. A terrible, heartless, despicable creature who used his allure to turn my no into a yes."

She twisted the tissue until it began to shred, then

balled it up. "I didn't want anything to do with him, but that just spurred him on. No matter how many times I turned him down, he kept hounding me."

Her mother dropped her gaze to her hands again. "On three occasions, after vehemently refusing him, I found myself in his bed. Against my will. But he had the ability to charm a person into doing his bidding if he held their gaze long enough. Something I learned too late. I could have armed myself against his power if I'd realized it sooner."

Ephie felt sick at what her mother had endured. "I'm so sorry that happened to you. No wonder you hate vampires. But Remy's nothing like that."

Leonie nodded, still not making eye contact. "I guess he's not, but I can't help what I feel."

"After what you went through, you're entitled."

Leonie exhaled, a long, tired breath. "The only good thing that came from that devil was you. I'd always hoped your maternal bloodlines would be stronger than his side, but apparently, I was wrong."

"I don't think that's true," Ephie said. "From what Alice told me, your half of me is probably what kept me from turning sooner. Remy giving me his blood just sort of tipped the scales. I'm still very much your child, though. I still have my gifts. The change did nothing to take them away from me." Ephie knew her mother needed the reassurance that things weren't going to be any different. Even though they would be.

"That's good," her mother said softly.

What Ephie couldn't say to her mother was how she would gladly give those gifts up, if the chance arose.

After the fire, she never wanted to use them again.

She would never live down that fire. She hadn't meant for it to happen. She'd only been trying to save herself. Instead, she'd caused an incredible amount of destruction and taken a life. Didn't matter that it was the life of the woman who meant to harm her. It was still a life.

She would carry that loss for the rest of hers.

How she'd created such a fireball, she had no idea. All she could guess was that the sunstone around her neck had focused her abilities so intensely that it had resulted in a super-boost of her skills.

No more sunstones. No more magic. No more terrifying accidents. She didn't know where her necklace was anyway. Lost in the fire maybe. She had no intention of replacing it. In fact, she'd be very careful what stones she wore from now on.

She glanced down at her hand where her pansy ring usually sat. Birdie had told her the ring had been taken off her finger when she'd arrived at the hospital and stored with anything else that had been saved to be returned to her upon her discharge.

At least she knew the diamonds and sapphires were safe. She couldn't wait to put that ring back on. It meant so much to her.

Which would hopefully be soon. She wanted to go. To put all of this behind her and start her new life with Remy. Here. In Nocturne Falls.

New Orleans felt like her past now. Nocturne Falls felt like her future. Jean-Luc would be happy. He loved Remy's backyard so much.

Ephie glanced at her mother, who seemed to be lost in her own thoughts. Now was not the time to share her decision. Her mother wouldn't take it well regardless of when Ephie told her, but Leonie wasn't in any kind of shape to hear it now. Adding to what she was dealing with would just be cruel.

No, Ephie would let her mother believe she was just going to stay here with Remy a while longer, to convalesce and learn how to manage life as a vampire. Then, when the time was right, she'd tell her mother she'd decided to stay on permanently.

Ephie sat back, content to let her mother be. She had plenty to think about herself. Like what life would be like as a vampire.

She didn't feel much different. Her vision might have been a little crisper, her hearing more acute, but nothing else seemed to have changed. Being stuck in a hospital bed was no place to test out such a change anyway.

She was sure that over the next few weeks, Remy would give her all the information she needed.

She smiled. She owed Remy. He had been so obviously uncertain about what he'd done, but Alice—and Birdie—had explained everything. Ephie understood he'd done it to save her, not for his own reasons.

She wasn't sure she'd have cared if he had. The darkness and pain that had taken over her mind had been horrific. The nightmares had been even worse. She was glad all of that was over with.

And being a vampire wasn't such a bad thing, was it? Remy was one, and he was everything that was right in the world. In Ephie's world, anyway.

Her smile got a little bigger as she tucked her fingers under Jean-Luc's translucent sleeping form. Would Remy ask her to marry him again?

It seemed the logical conclusion now that they were both the same species and they had a better understanding of what they wanted out of life.

At least she did. What she wanted was to be happy. To do her job well. To make the world a better place whenever possible. And to have Remy at her side. Whatever else that entailed, she'd figure it out.

Or rather, they would, together, if all went well.

Jean-Luc shifted, opening his eyes and looking up at her. He gave her a slow blink. She slow-blinked back.

"I love you, *bebe*," she whispered.

A soft knock at her door was followed by a nurse coming in. She had a tablet in her hand and a small clear plastic bag with the hospital's name imprinted on it in the other. "Ms. Moreau, I have your discharge paperwork all ready. Just a few forms to sign, some instructions, and we'll have you out of here in the next hour or so."

"Great," Ephie said. "Because I am definitely ready to go."

The small self-serve refreshment area of the hospital was pretty much just a large room with a few couches, several tables and chairs, vending machines that offered everything from sandwiches to candy bars to soft drinks and coffee, and two flat-screen TVs that displayed the weather channel and an all-news station.

Soft music played in the background, and one of the walls was painted with a mural of the falls, a pretty rainbow over the water, flowers everywhere, and lots of wildlife gathered around the water. A note near the bottom said it had been done by Mrs. Dwyer's art students from Nocturne Falls High School.

The space wasn't as comfortable as the main cafeteria, but that was closed. And this room was thankfully empty, except for Remy and Darryl.

They'd gotten coffee from one of the machines and taken a table in the corner.

Darryl turned his coffee cup counterclockwise every so often. A nervous habit, Remy assumed. Darryl seemed like a good, upstanding man, but Remy admitted he might be a little prejudiced, seeing as how they were both law enforcement.

Remy leaned in. "You said you had questions."

"I do." Darryl shook his head. "Hard to know where to start."

"Just ask whatever comes to mind first. Doesn't matter to me. Nothing you ask will upset me."

"You sure?"

"We're brothers-in-arms, you and I," Remy said. "We've seen people at their worst, haven't we?"

Darryl nodded. "That we have."

"Nothing you can ask me will bother me. I promise you."

Darryl sipped his coffee, then set the cup back on the table. "Do you, uh, like the taste of ... you know."

"Blood?" Remy supplied. He stifled his smile. It was a valid question and not the first time he'd been asked it. He'd have been more surprised if Darryl *hadn't* brought it up. "Well, it does keep me alive, so I've grown accustomed to it."

"Right, right." Darryl turned the cup again. "When you look at someone like me, a human, I mean, do you get a craving to ... That is, how do I know you won't ... Maybe never mind."

"I don't want to bite you or drink your blood. I feed on a regular basis, so that is never an issue. It's also pretty frowned upon in civil vampire society to drink from anyone who isn't a willing participant. Most areas, Nocturne Falls included, have blood banks that provide vampires with what they need."

"That's good to know." Darryl exhaled, letting out a

long, slow, *relieved* breath. "Can you turn into anything else?"

"Like a bat?" This time Remy smiled. "No, but that would be something. There have been a couple times in my life being able to fly away would have been pretty useful."

"So you can't fly either?"

"No, but I can jump pretty high, and long drops don't bother me."

Darryl seemed to consider that. "What's the longest drop you've made?"

"So far, four stories."

Darryl's eyes rounded. "And you weren't hurt?"

Remy shook his head. "Landed on my feet like a cat."

"Holy smokes." Darryl appeared suitably impressed with that. "And you're real fast, too, right?"

"I am. Fast enough that human eyes can't track me."

"Get out." Disbelief filled Darryl's gaze.

Never one to disappoint, Remy used his speed to get up, grab two sugar packets and sit back down. He held the packets up. "Did you see me get these?"

"I ... no. Did you just— Wait. How?"

"Told you. I'm fast. Vampire speed is something else. Our hearing and sense of smell are pretty sharp, too, but the shifters beat us at that. Although the shifters can't move as fast as we can."

"Shifters?" Darryl's brows pulled together. "Leonie told me about vampires and witches. Are you saying there are more kinds of people I don't know about?"

Remy drank some of his coffee before answering. It wasn't as good as what he made at home, but it wasn't bad. "Let me put it to you this way. Most legends and myths and fairy tales all have some basis in reality."

Darryl's eyes went big again, and a grave expression settled over his face. "Are you telling me the rougarou is real?"

"As real as you and I are sitting here having this conversation. Shifters of all kinds are very real. You've already met one."

Darryl frowned. "I have?"

"Sure. Birdie."

Darryl laughed. "Come on now. What is she? A real bird?"

"No, she's a werewolf. Not a rougarou. Those are a different breed. She's a wolf shifter. So is my boss, the sheriff."

"I'll be." He was quiet for a moment. Lost in thought maybe. Then he tapped his finger on the table. "You know, this explains a few things I've run across in my time as a cop."

Remy snorted softly. "Considering the town you work in, I bet it does."

Darryl rubbed his chin. "What else don't I know?"

"Let me think." Remy hesitated, not sure how to answer that.

"You know what?" Darryl swirled his coffee around. "Don't answer that. Better let me just sit a while on what I already know."

"I'm sure it feels like a lot to process."

"It does. But Leonie and I aren't about to stop being friends, so I'll come to terms with it soon enough." He tipped his coffee cup and peered inside. "Just about gone. Probably should get back soon before they think we've run out on them. I appreciate you talking to me."

"Anytime. I mean that." Remy shrugged. "Who knows, you might end up being my father-in-law one of these days. Unless I'm wrong and you don't like Leonie the way I think you like her."

Darryl's smile was suddenly a little shy, giving him the look of a much younger and very lovestruck man. "I've been in love with that woman a long time. Married someone else, who I cared for, but she couldn't take being a cop's wife. Anyway, Leonie has always done something to me no other woman has."

Remy nodded. "Boy, do I know that feeling. Ephie's been in my head since the first day I met her."

Darryl's eyes sparkled, and he pursed his lips for a moment. "Maybe they put spells on us."

Remy laughed. "No maybe about it."

Darryl's phone buzzed on his hip. He reached for it and checked the screen, then looked at Remy. "Leonie says they're about ready to let Ephie go. A little more paperwork to sign and she's free."

Remy closed his eyes for a second, his gratitude deep. He looked at Darryl. "That night at the hotel when I pulled her out of those flames …" He swallowed. "I had a moment where I thought, 'I'm going to put her in that ambulance and never see her again.' Now she's ready to come home."

Darryl nodded. "I understand. It's been a rough few days. For all of us. But for you and Ephie, especially."

They got up and tossed their cups in the trash.

Remy stuck the sugar packets back in the dispenser. "It has been. I'm ready for some downtime. A few uneventful shifts, a few nice quiet evenings, just some peace and simplicity."

"Well, you'll get it. Now that Ephie's all right, I'm sure Leonie will want to head back soon."

They walked back to Ephie's room. Remy liked the man. He wasn't just a good guy; he was someone who could be a great influence on Leonie. "Be nice if you stayed around long enough to see the town a bit. Maybe come over to my place for dinner. Or we could go out. Whatever you want."

"That's a very nice offer. Thank you. But it's really up to Leonie. It's hard for a justice to take time off when court's in session."

"I'm sure."

They reached Ephie's room. Darryl stopped. "I'll see what I can do as far as getting Leonie to stick around a little longer. It would be good for her to see more of you and Ephie together. It would help her not be so afraid. I know she is. I also know, after talking to you, that she doesn't need to be. Heck, I didn't even need to talk to you to know that. Not after what you did for that girl."

Remy smiled. "Thanks."

"You saved that young woman's life. You didn't do that just to ruin it in some other way." Darryl put his hand on Remy's shoulder. "I'll talk to her."

"I appreciate that." Remy did, too. But he didn't hold out a lot of hope that Leonie was going to magically have a change of heart when it came to him or vampires.

Maybe a few years would make a difference. Or maybe it wouldn't. But as long as Ephie was happy, that was all that mattered to Remy.

While the men, Jean-Luc excluded, waited outside, Ephie changed into the clothing that Birdie had brought her. Leonie helped, although Ephie could have managed just fine on her own. She thought it was more important that her mom felt useful.

The outfit wasn't fancy, but it was the perfect thing to go home from the hospital in. A pair of leggings, a T-shirt with a rendering of Jean-Luc on it that Ephie had done herself using a graphics program, and her long cardigan. Comfy and forgiving.

Leonie tied Ephie's new sneakers, something she probably hadn't done since Ephie was five. "You have everything?"

"I think so. Hang on." She dug into the bag the nurse had brought.

Jean-Luc sneezed. Could he smell the smoke? Ephie could as soon as she'd opened it up.

There wasn't much in the bag, because very little had survived the fire. There was no sign of the sneakers or cardigan she'd worn that day. Inside the bag were the top and jeans she'd had on, which reeked of smoke, and a small bundle of things in a separate bag. She was sure that contained her jewelry.

It did. The few pieces were all wrapped in a length of gauze. Her earrings, the sunstone pendant on its chain, a little bracelet, and her precious pansy ring.

She left everything in the gauze but the pansy ring. She inspected it, but it seemed untouched by the fire. She put it on, feeling complete again, then patted her shoulder. Jean-Luc jumped up. "Good boy," she whispered.

"Who are you talking to, sweetheart?"

"Just Jean-Luc." She looked at her mom, who now probably thought she was having some kind of mental episode. "Okay. I have everything. We can go."

As she and her mom walked out into the hall, Remy pulled Ephie into a gentle hug. "Ready to go?"

"So ready."

He took her bag and held her hand on the way to the parking lot. At some point, Jean-Luc jumped to his shoulder.

Ephie was just going to have to get used to the fact that her cat liked Remy better. The stinker. It was pretty sweet, though, seeing Remy with Jean-Luc. Made her wonder what he'd be like with an actual child.

Remy had his SUV and Darryl had his rental, so they stopped when they reached the edge of the parking lot.

"Why don't you come over for a bit," Remy said. "It's only seven o'clock. I'd love to show you my house. If you're hungry, we can order some pizza or something."

"Oh, *pizza*," Ephie breathed as she found herself craving the food. "That sounds amazing, and now I won't be able to sleep until I have some."

Remy smiled. "Pizza it is then."

"Sounds good to me," Darryl said. "You want us to pick it up?"

Remy shook his head. "I'll order it on the way to the house and have it delivered. Any preferences?"

Leonie didn't look happy, but that didn't surprise Ephie. Her mother wasn't generally a fan of food eaten without utensils. "Something with veggies, maybe? Do they have salad?"

"They do. I'll get you one," Remy said. "I'll wait for your car at the exit so you can follow us home."

"Roger," Darryl said.

They parted company. Remy took Ephie's hand again. "I am so happy that you're coming home, but I'm even happier you don't hate me."

"I could never hate you."

"No one would blame you if you did, after I made such a big decision for you."

"You're right, I could have hated you. If I was an idiot. But I'm not. I know you saved my life. Thank you."

"You don't need to thank me."

She'd spend the rest of her life doing just that, if he let her. She released his hand to wrap her arm around his, tugging him closer. A razor-thin sliver of moon shone down on them, the stars sparkling in the night sky like the diamonds in her ring. "You know you're going to have to teach me how to be a vampire now."

He smiled. "I'm all right with that. I don't think I'll have to teach you much, though."

"If it's all right with you, I'd like to stay a while. Unless you'd rather have your space back. I can rent a—"

"There is nothing I want more than more of *you* in my space."

She laughed. "You're about to be a very happy man, then."

He patted her arm as they reached his car. "I already am." He walked around to the passenger side with her, unlocked her door and opened it. "You know the only thing that would make me happier than a few more weeks with you would be spending the rest of my life with you."

She leaned in and kissed him. "I love you, Remy. I owe you my life. I think sharing it with you sounds like a very good idea."

"Yeah?" He grinned.

She nodded, too emotional to speak.

Jean-Luc meowed and jumped into the car, taking over the front seat, paws on the dashboard.

She laughed. "Hey, little man, that's my seat."

"He likes to sit there," Remy said with a shrug.

"He's spoiled."

Remy kissed her, then leaned his forehead against hers. "Nothing wrong with spoiling the person, or cat, you love."

She smiled and looked into his eyes. "Are you trying to steal my cat from me?"

"No, never, I swear. But he does seem to like me."

"He adores you." She slipped into the passenger seat,

Jean-Luc going to stand on the console as she did. "I think we should probably consider him *our* cat."

Remy's grin went ear to ear. "I'd like that."

He shut her door, then put her bag in the backseat before coming around and getting behind the wheel. He started the car, pulled out, waited for Darryl to get behind him, then drove them home.

On the way, he called Salvatore's and ordered three pizzas. A meat lovers', a veggie supreme, and a plain cheese, plus two garden salads and four orders of tiramisu.

"That's a lot of pizza," Ephie said.

"You're craving it, and it's good pizza. Nothing wrong with some leftovers, right?"

"Sure." But she also wondered if he wasn't trying to impress her mom and Darryl just a little bit. She had no problem with that. In fact, it was sweet.

When they arrived home, he parked on one side to make room for the other car in the driveway. With Jean-Luc on his shoulder again, Remy got out, came around and got her door, then retrieved her bag from the backseat.

Together, they went up the front porch steps. Standing in the glow of the porch light, he unlocked the door as Darryl and Leonie joined them.

"Nice house," Darryl said.

"Thank you." Remy pushed the door open. "Pizza should be here in about fifteen or twenty minutes."

"Great," Darryl said. He stood to one side. "Ladies first."

Ephie stepped inside. It was so good to be back. Her mother came in behind her, Darryl and Remy following.

"Let me get the light," Remy said. He flipped it on.

That's when Ephie realized they weren't exactly alone. "Um, Remy?"

"Hmm?"

She pointed toward the man sitting on the back deck. "Please tell me that's a friend of yours and not one of Turner's men?"

"I'll take care of this." Remy's body tensed, and a steely look came into his eyes. Jean-Luc hissed and arched his back. Remy rushed to the sliders, unlocked them, and yanked them open. "Who are you and what are you doing at my house?"

The man stood up, unfolding his lanky form with exceptional grace. He smiled at them, revealing gleaming white fangs, but his attention seemed directed at Leonie, who now stood with Ephie and Darryl behind Remy.

He stepped in front of Ephie like he intended to shield her from any danger. Ephie shivered, already imagining the worst.

Beside Ephie, her mother let out a gasp when she saw the stranger's face. "You. What are you doing here?"

The man nodded at Leonie. "Nice to see you, too. You look well, considering you've aged." He shrugged. "I could have done something about that, but you were too stubborn."

"Get out of here," Leonie warned. "I want nothing to do with you."

"Yes, you made that abundantly clear over the years." He strode toward them, stopping just shy of the threshold. "But this isn't about you, Leonie. It's about me paying my daughter a visit." He looked at Ephie. "You certainly have grown into a lovely creature."

Ephie grabbed her mother's arm, already knowing the answer to the question she was about to ask but hoping she was wrong. "Mom, who is this guy?"

Leonie answered, her voice so tight it sounded like it might crack. "Solomon Lang. Your father."

Remy kept Ephie behind him. Ephie's father. Unbelievable. He knew the man wasn't here for any good reason. Bad intentions wafted off him like smoke. "I don't care who you are. You're trespassing. You need to leave now."

Solomon stuck his hands in the pockets of his leather jacket, looking amused in the most annoying way. "Really? You don't care that I'm both the father *and* the maker of the woman you claim to be in love with? Rather disrespectful, considering I am your elder."

Remy shook his head. At the moment, he didn't give two figs about vampire etiquette. He'd like to punch the smugness off the man's face. "You didn't turn her. I did. And I don't care how old you are. This is my house and my property. You are not welcome here."

At least he couldn't get in without an invite.

Solomon's laughter held an air of condescension. "Your opinion doesn't matter, and I don't need your permission. Nor do I care about what you want or don't want. That is my daughter. I have every right to see her."

"No, you don't," Leonie hissed.

Remy realized they were getting nowhere fast with this egotistical intruder. It was time to put an end to this nonsense. "Well, you've seen Ephie. You've had your visit. You can leave now."

Solomon shook his head. "Not without my daughter."

Ephie snorted. "I'm not going anywhere with you."

"Oh, but you are," Solomon said. "You see, you've made your choice to become a vampire. I knew you would eventually. Now I've come to take you home with me and educate you in the ways of our kind. You are the heir to my throne, so to speak. I am quite a wealthy man with a great deal of influence. The life that awaits you is beyond your dreams."

"I couldn't care less," Ephie muttered, lip curled in disgust.

Solomon held his hand out. "We really should go."

Darryl stepped forward. "Not while there's breath in my body, you aren't taking her anywhere."

Remy cringed inwardly. Darryl meant well, but Solomon wasn't going to like being challenged by a mortal. Darryl would be safe so long as he stayed inside the house, though.

Solomon's eyes narrowed into cold slits, his voice just as icy. "Is that a request? If so, I will gladly grant it. Just step outside and –"

"Enough," Remy spat. Anger coiled in his body like a cobra about to strike. He let his fangs down and gave himself over to his true nature. "You touch any of them and I will turn you to ash before you can speak my name."

Solomon leaned forward, his face inches from the

invisible wall keeping him out. "Remy Lafitte." Then he laughed. "Such spirit. I find it highly amusing. Ephelia, that's quite a young man you've chosen for yourself, but you'll soon see there are so many more, shall we say, interesting choices. I will introduce you to men that will make this one look like the rustic he is." He sniffed. "A pirate's grandson. How very droll."

He gestured toward Ephie again. "Come."

"*No.*" Ephie moved out from behind Remy to stand beside him, her shoulder touching his. "First of all, Remy is an *amazing* man. Stop trying to run him down. I don't like it. And you're only making yourself look like a moron."

Darryl grinned.

"Secondly," Ephie went on, "I don't care who you are or what part you think you played in my life, but I'm not going anywhere with you. You took advantage of my mother, then you abandoned us both. You *chose* not to have a relationship with either of us. If you think suddenly showing up changes any of that, you're not just a moron; you're a brain-dead moron."

Solomon's eyes glittered with a steely, supernatural glow. "I will overlook your insolence this time, but you have a lot to learn. Exactly the reason I'm here. Let me start by teaching you a very important rule. I am your maker, and I am in charge. This decision isn't up to you."

"Of course it is," Ephie said. "It's my life. I make my own choices."

Solomon arched his brows, lips pursed in a moment

of frustration. Then he smiled. "You are a treasure. You have your mother's stubbornness, but as I'm sure you're aware, I overcame that. This is going to be fun." He pulled a pocket watch from the interior pocket of his jacket. "Plenty of time before the sun comes up, but we need to get going all the same."

He put the watch away. "Say your goodbyes, Ephelia."

Remy took a step toward the man, stopping just shy of stepping outside. "Are you so old that your hearing has failed? She's not going anywhere with you. The only one who needs to leave is you. I'm done discussing this. Get off my property before I really get angry."

Solomon sighed like he was bored. "Such strong words for a man with a cat on his shoulder. It's quite a look, by the way." He shook his head and looked past Remy toward Ephie, Leonie, and Darryl. "This younger generation. Who can keep up?"

Leonie clicked her tongue. "I see you never stopped being an idiot. I guess a leopard can't change its spots."

Solomon scowled. "You could have had an amazing life with me, Leonie. Sad how bitter you've become. Is that from living with so much regret?"

"You need to go," Remy repeated. "Ephie is not coming with you. You have no relationship with her and never will."

"That's right," Ephie said, linking her arm through Remy's.

"Neither of you seem to grasp the reality of this situation," Solomon said. "She's coming with me. It would have happened sooner, but she took quite a while to finally decide she wanted to be a vampire. Now that you're turned, Ephie, you belong to me."

"I don't belong to you." Ephie practically snarled the words out. "I don't belong to anyone."

Solomon shrugged. "You've left me no choice." His eyes took on the vampire glow again. "*Ephelia, come here. Now.*"

Remy heard a strain of power in Solomon's voice that hadn't been there before. It wasn't something anyone but another vampire would have picked up on. It made his skin prickle and the little hairs on the back of his neck stand up. He didn't know how old Solomon was, but he definitely had power.

Ephie walked toward Solomon.

Remy grabbed her hand before she stepped across the threshold. "Ephie, no. Block him out."

Ephie kept moving forward, her eyes never leaving Solomon.

Remy tugged her back.

The man lifted his chin. "She's under my sway, Lafitte. She always will be. She has no choice but to obey the one who made her."

The doorbell rang, followed by three short knocks. Ephie shook herself before moving closer to Remy. She pointed at Solomon. "Stay out of my head."

"Must be the pizza," Darryl said. "You want me to get rid of him?"

"No." Remy pulled money from his wallet. "Here, pay him."

Darryl took the money and went to take care of things.

Solomon inched back a few steps, glancing anxiously at the front of the house. "You have twenty-four hours to say your goodbyes, Ephelia. Running won't make a difference. I can find you anywhere. Remember that."

Then he left, vanishing off the deck in a blur. Remy closed the sliders and locked them, then joined Darryl at the front door.

Remy took the three pizza boxes Darryl was holding and nodded at the young man who still had the bag with the salads and desserts hooked on his arm. "Don't worry about the change. That's all yours."

"Thank you, sir." The young man pocketed the money and handed over the bag to Darryl. "Y'all have a good night."

"You, too," Remy said. He nudged the door shut with his foot.

Darryl turned, looking toward the backyard. "Solomon's gone? Where'd he go? He was right there."

"He's gone. I guess he wasn't sure who was at the front door and it spooked him," Remy said. He pulled his cap off and ran a hand over his head. The spot where he'd been burned was almost fully healed. "Unfortunately, he'll be back."

"Vampire speed," Darryl whispered.

"That's right." Remy nodded. Darryl was dealing

pretty well with all the new information he'd recently gotten. The man would make a great vampire, but Remy wasn't about to mention that.

A soft sob escaped Leonie's throat. She put her hand over her mouth. "What are we going to do? We can't let him take Ephie."

"I won't go with him," Ephie said. "I won't. Remy, how do we stop him from having control over me?"

Remy didn't have an answer, but there had to be someone in this town that did. He had a pretty good idea who that might be. "I don't know. Yet. But we'll figure it out. I'll figure it out. This isn't a town that takes kindly to people like him."

Ephie shook her head. "I can't go with him, Remy. I can't."

"You won't have to. I swear." He put his hand on her shoulder. "I will do everything in my power to make sure that doesn't happen." He meant that, too. If it meant battling Solomon in a duel to the death, so be it.

Ephie came first. In everything.

"How?" Leonie cried. She pointed at the door, her finger trembling. "He told me once that he'd come back for Ephie someday. I thought it was just a threat. I thought he'd forgotten about both of us. Obviously, I was wrong."

Remy carried the pizza boxes to the dining room table and set them down. "I need to make some calls. Go ahead and eat. You might not feel like it, but we're all going to need our strength."

"I have no appetite now," Ephie said. She wrapped her arms around herself.

Leonie shook her head. "Neither do I."

"I understand how you both feel," Remy said. "But Ephie, you need sustenance. You're still healing. Your body needs energy and resources for that. Please eat. All of you." She'd also need blood, but he'd get her that after Leonie and Darryl were gone.

Leonie ignored him, going to her daughter instead. She hugged Ephie, her voice weak with worry. "I'm so sorry."

Darryl looked lost. He took the rest of the food to the table and just stood there a moment, clearly feeling for the two women but not knowing what to say.

Remy understood. "It's going to be all right." He wasn't sure how just yet, but he'd find a way to make it all right. Whatever he had to do. Someone in this town would have an answer. He'd start with the oldest vampire he knew, Elenora Ellingham.

Darryl nodded. "I believe him, ladies, and so should you. Look what he did to save Ephie from the fire." He went to them. "You think he's going to let another vampire take you away, Ephie?"

Ephie smiled weakly and shook her head. "No. But you don't understand the control Solomon had over me. I was powerless. It was terrifying. I couldn't do anything *but* obey him."

"That was exactly what he did to me," Leonie said.

There was fear in Ephie's eyes when she looked at

Remy. "Do you really think you can figure out a way to keep me here?"

He hated that she was scared. He loved her. It was his job to protect her. "I do. I just need a little time."

Leonie looked less convinced. "Well, then, you'd better get started. You only have twenty-four hours."

"This might be the craziest night I've ever had," Ephie whispered as they approached the impressive front doors of Elenora Ellingham's estate. There were some incredible mansions in the Garden District, but this place made them look like guesthouses. Very nice guesthouses, but still.

"That might be true for me, too," Remy said. "But don't be nervous. Elenora might be intimidating, but she's a good woman. Kind, generous, and deeply protective of her town and its citizens."

Ephie exhaled. "I hope she can help me." Hope was all she had right now. The way Solomon had been able to control her with his voice had shaken Ephie to her core.

"She will. If she's at all able." He knocked.

A butler answered. "Remy Lafitte?"

Remy nodded. "And Ms. Ephelia Moreau."

"Ms. Ellingham is expecting you. Right this way." He led them through to a sitting room, where Elenora and Alice were already seated in matching chairs. They each had a cup of tea beside them. Nearby was a two-tiered cart bearing a full tea set and plates of cookies and small cakes.

Remy nodded at them. "Thank you for seeing us, Elenora. I appreciate your time."

She smiled. "Anything for one of Nocturne Falls' finest." She gestured toward the sofa. "Please, have a seat. Would you like something to eat or drink?"

"I'm fine," Remy said, looking at Ephie.

Ephie shook her head as she and Remy took seats on the couch. "I'm good. We just ate dinner before we came here. It's very nice to meet you, Elenora. And nice to see you again, Alice."

"Nice to see you again, too," Alice said. "I didn't think it would be quite so soon. You seem to be recovering very well."

"I'm still a little bit weak, but the change has been remarkable."

"And now you're one of us," Elenora said.

Ephie smiled. "I suppose I am."

Elenora folded her hands in her lap. The hand on top bore an enormous gumdrop-size amethyst surrounded by diamonds. "Alice has apprised me of the adventure you've had since arriving in our little town. Not exactly the vacation you imagined, I suppose."

"No, not exactly," Ephie confessed. "I'm really sorry about the fire at the motel. I don't have much money, but if you want me to pay for that, I'll do whatever I can."

Elenora's smile expanded. "That is so generous of you to offer, but as I see it, you were in a fight for your life and were only acting in self-defense. The motel has been appropriately compensated."

Ephie's mouth opened. "Oh. Thank you. Did you, I mean, for me? I feel so bad. That had to be so expensive."

Elenora arched one brow as her gaze shifted to Remy. "You didn't tell her?"

He shook his head. "It didn't come up. We've had other things to deal with."

"I guess you have," Elenora said.

"Tell me what?" Ephie looked from Elenora to Remy.

He rubbed his chin. "I took care of things with the motel."

"*You* did?"

"We can talk about it later, if you want."

"Okay." Now wasn't the time, but they were definitely going to talk about it at some point.

Elenora sipped from a teacup as delicate as a hummingbird. "I understand your maker wishes to take you home with him."

Ephie quickly nodded. "He does. He's also my father, not that he was in my life or anything. He basically used his magic to take advantage of my mother, got her pregnant and then disappeared."

Alice tipped her head slightly. "He has the power of compulsion?"

"He does," Remy said. "I suspect it's exceptionally strong when it comes to Ephie because of their blood bond, but we already know he used it on Ephie's mother."

"Who is a witch," Alice stated.

Ephie nodded. "She is, but the true power tends to skip a generation, so my grandmother has a good deal of it, but my mother really doesn't. A tiny bit but nothing spectacular."

"Even so," Alice said. "His power must be considerable to have used it on someone with their own gifts, however minor." She looked at Elenora. "We might need to consult Allard."

"As it happens, I already have. About this very thing." Elenora smiled. "My grandson, Sebastian, and his wife, Tessa, adopted a child recently. Her name is Ellie." Elenora's smile widened. "Short for Elenora."

"Congratulations on the addition," Ephie said. "That's wonderful."

"I agree," Elenora said. "And thank you. Ellie is a dhampir, like yourself, Ephelia."

"So she's half vampire and half witch, too?" Ephie asked.

"She's half vampire," Elenora replied. "But we don't know the rest of her makeup. Perhaps one day it will make itself known, but for now, nothing has presented itself, and we haven't concerned ourselves with tests."

Alice reached for her tea. "I doubt her other half is witch or I would have picked up on it."

Remy nodded. "I'm sure you would have."

Elenora touched the saucer her cup rested on. "Naturally, I had some questions and concerns. Not because I was in any way against the adoption. I was overjoyed. Ellie is a delightful child, and I love her as I love all my great-grandchildren. But my instincts drove me to find out more about dhampirs and their characteristics. Also, what would happen if the child's maker came for her someday."

"Wow," Ephie breathed out. "That was so thoughtful on your part." She was full of hope. Elenora was on top of things. "That means you must know what I need to do."

"I believe I do." Elenora picked up her tea, sipped it, then set it back on the saucer. "First, I should tell you that my information comes from Allard Desmarais. He is an *ancient* vampire. He was turned more than eight centuries ago. Thankfully, unlike some, age has made him wiser. He is my maker, and so, accordingly, his bloodline runs through my grandsons, as I turned them. I tell you all of that because I want you to understand I trust him implicitly."

"Of course." Ephie nodded. Eight hundred years was an incredible amount of time. This vampire would be a great resource about all kinds of things.

Elenora glanced at Alice. "You know something of dhampirs as well."

Alice leaned forward. "Dhampirs are unique creatures. The only real prerequisite to becoming one is that one parent is a vampire. The other might be anything from human to shifter or, in your case, witch. So long as they are magically and biologically compatible with their partner, of course. There is no explanation as to why some pairings produce offspring and others do not. Magic is capricious that way."

Ephie had an odd feeling that she was about to get

bad news. She reached over and took Remy's hand, glad he was close. "I understand."

Elenora chimed in. "Of course, you are no longer technically a dhampir. You're a full-fledged vampire. With the powers of a fire witch." She took a deep breath, something Ephie interpreted as a means of bracing herself for what came next, because Elenora clearly didn't need to breathe.

Ephie swallowed, anticipating whatever Elenora was about to say.

The woman glanced at her hands, moving her fingers to adjust the giant amethyst ring, then looked up at Ephie. "Forgive me for not getting to the point. There is only one tried and true method for breaking the bond between a vampire and their maker."

Remy's hand tightened around Ephie's. "And that is?"

Elenora interlaced her fingers. "Either the vampire, or their maker, must die."

The chill that went through Remy felt otherworldly. Like he'd stepped on a fresh grave under the light of a full moon. "I would happily turn Solomon Lang to ash, but that is the only outcome in the scenario you mentioned that I'd be all right with."

"Obviously," Alice said. "We would never imply that anything should happen to Ephelia. But we're in a tenuous position. I'm certain that were we to contact the appropriate authorities, Lang would be of great interest to them. The fact that he uses his powers for such unsavory and criminal means needs to be dealt with."

"Agreed," Remy said. He'd take Lang out himself if given the word.

"Unfortunately," Elenora continued, "those authorities don't always move with the speed vampires have been endowed with. By the time they arrived to take him into custody, he would most likely be gone. Ephelia along with him."

"Unacceptable." Remy couldn't stop the anger building inside him. "I would never see her again. No. I will not go along with that."

Elenora held her hands up. "I understand. We both

do. Which is why we'd like to propose the next best thing."

Alice nodded. "We make him *believe* Ephelia is dead. Once that's done, we take him into custody ourselves, confining him in the Basement."

Ephie made a face. "You're going to put him in a basement? That doesn't sound very safe to me."

Remy squeezed her hand. "It's not a basement like you're thinking of. In this case, it's a private underground area of the town that also happens to contain some top-notch, supernatural-proof holding cells."

"Oh. In that case, it might be all right."

"It will be fine," Alice said. She got up and went to the tea cart for the pot.

Ephie nodded. "I believe you. How are we going to make him think I'm dead? He claims he can find me wherever I am. Like he's got some way of homing in on me."

"He does," Elenora said. "From what Allard's told me, the bond between a dhampir and their vampire parent is extremely strong. Greater than the bond between a maker and their vampire child. Even Remy should have some sense of you, since his blood is what caused you to turn."

Ephie glanced at him, brows raised in question.

He nodded. "I can definitely sense you. Not like I could find you, exactly, but I'm aware of you. The same way you're aware of one of your limbs. Sort of."

"I see," Ephie said. He knew she probably didn't, but they could talk about that some more later.

"Anyway," Elenora said, "this is where Alice comes in."

Alice refilled her cup and Elenora's. "I will cast a disconnection spell over you, Ephelia. A temporary one. It will seal you off from everything. With that spell on you, he won't be able to detect you. No one will. Then, once the bond is broken, I'll release you from that spell and his ability to find you and control you will be gone."

"And that's how we're going to convince him that I'm dead?"

"That's part of it." Alice returned the teapot, then sat down. "There has to be proof. For that, we'll need your blood. And your abilities."

Ephie frowned. "My abilities?"

Alice nodded. "Your gift of fire."

Ephie shook her head and sat back. "I don't want to do that. I don't want to use them. Not after …"

"I understand, but you must," Alice explained. "We need a portion of your blood turned to ashes. That will be the proof Remy gives Lang. He'll tell Lang that you were so distraught, you decided to leave despite his threat to hunt you down. When you went outside and stepped into the sun, you burst into flames and that was the end of you."

Remy cringed at the very thought.

"Okay, but …" Ephie hesitated. "Why do you need me

to use my abilities to burn that blood to ash? Can't we just use a blowtorch or something?"

Alice took a breath. "Because he'll detect anything else. Your magic is part of you. It will only enhance his belief that those ashes are all that's left of you."

Remy lifted his finger to interrupt. "One possible flaw in that plan. Doesn't Lang know she can daywalk?"

Alice nodded. "He will assume that, yes, which is why you need to be convincing when you tell him what happened. Can you do that?"

Remy thought for a second. "Can I convince him that it's his fault Ephie died?" He looked at Ephie. There was nothing he wouldn't do for her. A little acting was nothing. He nodded. "I can do that."

"Excellent," Elenora said. "You'll have the proof of her ashes, of course. That should help sell it."

"I hope," Remy said. "But how does that break the bond?"

Elenora answered. "We're counting on him to be distraught, for his guard to be down. Alice has been working on something that will subdue him."

A curious light came into Alice's eyes. "My own version of the zombie dust based on the sample Sheriff Merrow gave me. Very effective. But I've tweaked it a bit to increase that effectiveness against vampires without harming humans. Someone, preferably a non-vampire, will need to blow it into Lang's face. Once he's paralyzed, some of Ephie's ashes must be sprinkled on his tongue. He needs to taste her death. Those ingested ashes, once

The Vampire's Former Flame

they enter his system, will sever the bond, and she'll be free."

"Ew," Ephie said. "But if it works ..."

Alice chuckled. "Perhaps not the most pleasant thing, but it's what Allard has assured us is necessary."

"And," Elenora began, "while he's unconscious thanks to Alice's zombie dust, he'll be cuffed and put into one of the Basement cells. I'm sure Sheriff Merrow will make himself available to assist with that."

Remy nodded. "I'm sure he will."

Ephie sat back. "Can this really work?"

"We believe so," Elenora said.

Remy raised his finger again because he had a question. "Have you already contacted the vampire council?"

"I have not," Elenora said. "I wanted to discuss the plan with both of you first."

Ephie looked at him. "I don't see another way."

"Neither do I." He returned his attention to Elenora. "Please contact them. The sooner we can get him extradited, the better."

Elenora gave a little nod. "I will do that right away." She glanced toward Ephie. "You should go with Alice. Get the ashes taken care of so Remy can take them back to his house. And Remy, you'll need the dust, too. Do you have someone who can blow the dust onto Lang?"

Ephie answered before he could. "My mother or Darryl will do it. My mother would probably enjoy it, if I'm being honest."

Remy narrowed his eyes at Elenora. "You're talking like Ephie's not coming back with me."

Alice glanced at Elenora. "We think it's best if she stays here. If anything goes wrong, she'll be better protected here."

He couldn't argue that. Reluctantly, he nodded. "I guess I'm going home alone." He sighed as he spoke to Ephie. "Your mother isn't going to like that at all."

Ephie reached out and grasped his hand, giving him a quick smile. "She can always call me, but she'll be fine once you tell her what's about to happen."

"I hope," Remy said.

Suddenly, Ephie gasped and turned to look at Alice. "Wait a minute. If you cast a spell over me that cuts me off from the world, what will happen to Jean-Luc? What if he thinks I really did die and somehow gets recalled to the cemetery where I found him? Or, worse, he ceases to exist because he no longer has a connection to this life?"

Alice frowned. "That's a valid concern. Both of those things are possible. While you're covered by that spell, you will technically be dead to this world."

Ephie shook her head. "No. I can't do that. Jean-Luc means everything to me. I know he's just a ghost and you probably think that's silly, but no. I won't do it. There has to be another way."

"Eph, please," Remy said. "I don't want anything to happen to Jean-Luc, either, but losing you would be worse. Lang will take you with him if you don't do this."

She looked close to tears. "Jean-Luc is part of my heart. There has to be another way. I can't lose him."

"Now, now," Alice said patiently. "No tears. There is a simple solution."

"There is?" Ephie perked up.

Alice nodded. "We'll just include him in the spell with you."

Ephie sniffed. "And that will keep him safe?"

"It will," Alice assured her.

Ephie smiled, still clearly emotional. "Thank you. Sorry."

Elenora shook her head. "Nothing to apologize for."

Remy exhaled in relief. He got to his feet. "In that case, I'll run back to the house and get him while you and Alice work on the ashes." He turned to Elenora and Alice. "Thank you both. We are in your debt."

Elenora stood, as did Alice and Ephie. "There is no debt. We must protect our own. If you'll excuse me, I must send a message to the vampire council."

"Thank you," Ephie said as Elenora left. She took Remy's hand. "Alice, if you don't mind, I'd like to walk Remy out to the car, then I'll be right back."

"Fine with me," Alice said. "I'll be in my practice preparing. The butler will show you back." She left as well.

Ephie and Remy saw themselves out, but Ephie didn't say a word until they reached the SUV. "I'm scared something will go wrong. Or that he won't believe I'm dead or that he'll do something to you or my mom or Darryl. I know I need to do this, but it's how I feel."

He pulled her into his arms. "I will protect them with my life. I know it's scary, but we don't have any other choice."

She leaned into him and sighed. "I know." She held him a moment longer, cherishing the closeness. "I just want this all to be over so we can get on with our lives."

"So do I." He held on to her and kissed her. As he did, he inhaled her scent, memorizing the softness of her skin and the sound of her sighs. All because, while he was unwilling to believe it might be for the last time, he also knew it was a very real possibility.

44

Remy had brought Jean-Luc back to Elenora's, collected the zombie dust from Alice, and reassured her and Ephie that Leonie had agreed to handle it with Darryl as a backup. He'd also confirmed that Sheriff Merrow was on call, prepared to respond the moment they were ready for him.

Ephie had taken the opportunity to kiss him one more time, then returned with Alice to her practice, Jean-Luc trotting along with them. Nervous energy buzzed over her skin like a swarm of tiny, annoying insects.

Alice shut and locked the door of her practice, then aimed her hand toward the fireplace and turned her palm in the air as though gently scooping something up. The fire increased.

"You make that look so easy," Ephie said.

"Because it is," Alice replied. "With years of practice, the impossible becomes possible. The difficult simple."

"So you're saying I need to get over myself and practice."

Alice shook her head as she walked behind the big worktable. "I'm not saying anything of the kind, merely stating the truth. Repetition is the key to mastery. That and learning to overcome one's fear."

"What happened at the hotel definitely scared me."

"Understandable." Alice took a large bowl of cast iron from one of the shelves, carrying it with both hands back to the table. She went back to the shelves, looking for something else. "It was a frightening situation."

"So is this one."

Alice searched through a few boxes. "Everything and nothing are terrifying. It's how you perceive events and their outcomes that shapes your views."

Ephie went closer to the table. "You don't think Lang wanting to basically kidnap me is something I should be afraid of?"

"Concerned? Yes. But you're actively working to prevent that from happening, so now?" Alice came back to the table with a slim silver blade in her hand. The hilt was mother-of-pearl. "No, I don't think you should be afraid of him or what he might do. He is only one vampire, as are you, but you have the strength of many around you. He has already lost."

Ephie just nodded. She wasn't that confident. After all, Turner's daughter had bested her, and all she'd had was a little voodoo magic and the element of surprise.

"Have faith," Alice said softly. "In large amounts, fear will weaken the magic."

Jean-Luc sat by the fire, batting at the occasional spark that leaped out.

Ephie watched him for a second, wishing she could be that carefree. "I'm trying."

"I know you are." Alice glanced toward the door. A

moment later, someone knocked on it. She went to answer it and came back with a bottle of blood just like the ones Remy had in his fridge.

"I thought we needed my blood."

"We do." Alice set the bottle on the table. "This is to replenish you once we've collected what we need."

"Is this going to hurt?"

"Will the pain stop you from doing it?"

"No."

"Good," Alice said. She held her hand out. "Your arm."

Ephie stuck her arm out, cringing in anticipation of what was to come. "I might not be cut out to be a vampire."

Alice smiled gently. "Too late." She offered Ephie the hilt of the dagger. "The blade is silver. It will prevent the wound from closing immediately, which should allow us to collect enough for our purposes."

Ephie shook her head. "You do it. I don't think I can."

Alice didn't argue, just turned the blade around to hold it properly, whispered a few words over Ephie's arm, then drew the blade across her wrist.

Surprisingly, Ephie didn't feel a thing. After a few long moments, the wound healed, disappearing like it had never happened. A small amount of blood filled the bowl. Ephie peered in. "Is that enough?"

Alice nodded. "It should be. How do you feel?"

"A little lightheaded, but that's probably more from the experience than the lack of blood."

Alice let go of Ephie's arm and stepped back. "We're almost done. Set fire to what we've gathered now. Burn it until it's ash."

"You trust me?"

"More than you trust yourself, I think." Alice smiled. "Go on. You can do it. Focus on the bowl and its contents."

Ephie nodded, staring into the bowl. Calling on her power scared her. What if she accidentally sent a giant fireball into the room like she'd done at the motel? She slanted her gaze at Alice's shelves. So much wood and paper.

"It will be fine," Alice whispered. "You can do this. You must do this."

"I know. I just don't want to hurt you or your things."

"You think I can't control a little fire?" Alice smiled at her. "The blood has already begun to age. Do it now or we'll have to start over."

Ephie didn't want that. She focused on the bowl and its contents like Alice had told her to. She sent fire into the bowl. A few sparks fizzled midair, but that was all. "Maybe I need the sunstone..."

Jean-Luc, ever curious, came closer.

"You don't," Alice said. "You might have before but not now. Stop holding back. Dig deep within yourself."

Ephie took a breath and concentrated harder, thinking about fire and flames and turning that blood into the ash that would fool Solomon into believing she really was gone.

The bowl erupted in a whoosh of flame that shot upward, dying back a little as Ephie jumped out of the way. Jean-Luc went scurrying off, staring back at the inferno like it had been a personal attack.

"Sorry, sorry." Ephie looked for something to quench the fire with. "That was too much. I'll—"

"You'll do nothing. That was perfect. Stay focused so that it burns completely."

"Okay." Ephie inched toward the bowl again. Heat radiated from it as the fire continued to devour the bowl's contents. Had Alice really thought that was perfect? Or had she just said that? Alice didn't seem like the kind of woman who gave false praise. Either way, the elder witch's words gave Ephie's confidence a boost.

When the fire seemed like it might go out, she boosted it with an extra dose of her magic. Jean-Luc kept his distance, although there was no way the fire could have hurt him.

When only a few flickering flames remained, Alice stood at the table again to have a better look at the bowl's contents. "Just about there."

Ephie joined her on the other side of the table. The blood was gone. Only ash remained. It still burned in three spots. One of those petered out while she watched. The other two weren't far behind. "So it's done then? We did it?"

"You did it," Alice said. "And yes, it's done. I'll have these delivered to Remy. You should drink that bottle now, too."

"I'll drink it in a moment. Are you going to cast the spell on me then?"

"Not until morning. It's important that Lang senses your presence until then. Things need to fit into the timeline properly to be the most believable."

"Won't he sense that I'm not at Remy's though?"

"Hopefully not. Unless he was lying about giving you twenty-four hours. In that case, you're still safest here. I'll show you to a guest room."

"All right." Ephie turned. "Come on, Jean-Luc." He scampered to her, getting up on her shoulder in one big leap. She picked up the bottle that would be her dinner, grabbed the bag Remy had brought her, then followed Alice.

Didn't matter how nice the room was, this was going to be a very long night.

45

Remy stood at the sliding glass doors, staring out at his backyard. The lights were off, but he could see just fine. No sign of Lang and there had better not be. With Ephie gone, Remy no longer felt the same constraints on his civility.

Lang might be older and therefore stronger or more powerful in some ways, but had he trained in hand-to-hand? Did he know all the techniques Remy did for taking down a difficult suspect? More importantly, Lang knew nothing about the special security lights Remy had installed years ago when he'd first arrived in Nocturne Falls.

They were a precaution against other vampires, something he'd anticipated before he'd understood what life in Nocturne Falls was really like. Now, he knew better. The vampires here weren't out for themselves as they were in most cities. Here there was a sense of community, a willingness to help others unlike anything he'd known before.

The danger he'd expected just didn't exist here.

Despite that, Remy tested the lights often enough to know they were in perfect working condition. The remote that operated them was in his pocket now, next to the pouch of Ephie's ashes that had been delivered by messenger just a few hours ago. Both would remain there until Lang was a memory.

But if Lang showed up and things didn't go according to plan, if he struck out against Leonie or Darryl, or even at Remy himself, the lights would go on.

They would bathe the backyard in UV. And Lang, without the protection that Remy now had around his neck, would cease to be a problem.

"I figured you'd still be up."

He turned at the sound of Leonie's voice. She was sleeping in Ephie's room, Darryl in Remy's. He'd thought it better that they stay with him than return to their hotel where they were more vulnerable.

Surprisingly, Leonie hadn't argued. Darryl had gone back to the hotel to get their things, returning without incident, thankfully.

Remy nodded. "This is my daytime, you know."

"I know." She wrapped her robe a little tighter and came to stand by him. "You're looking for Lang, aren't you?"

"Just checking."

"Anything?"

"No."

"Thank God." Leonie sighed and stared out into the darkness.

"I'm very sorry for what he did to you. That he took advantage of you."

Leonie nodded. "I ended up with Ephie, though."

"You did an incredible job raising her. She's the most amazing woman I've ever met. You're pretty impressive, too."

Leonie snorted, looking at him sideways. "You're a terrible liar, but I appreciate the effort."

"I'm not lying. You raised her as a single mother, moving through the ranks of the judicial system, fighting for what's right and good, standing up to men like Turner, and now you're on the state supreme court. What's not impressive about that?"

Her expression grew more skeptical. "I know you don't like me."

"We've had our differences, but I respect you deeply."

She studied him like she was trying to find his tell. After a moment, she went back to looking out the window. "You're not as bad as I thought you were."

He smirked. "Thanks."

"You going to stand here all night?"

"If I'm not outside, taking a walk around the house, I'll be keeping watch from inside."

"Do you really think Lang is going to come back?"

"He might. And if he does, I want to be ready."

She eyed him curiously. "To do what?"

"To do whatever's necessary to keep us safe."

She reached out tentatively and laid her hand on his arm. "I approve of that plan. Thank you."

He couldn't recall her ever touching him before. Maybe she was softening toward him. "Get some sleep, Leonie."

She headed for the bedroom. "*Bonne nuit*, Lafitte."

"*Bonne nuit*." He went back to watching the backyard. The sun would be up in a few hours. For once in his life, he couldn't wait.

EPHIE YAWNED as it grew closer to the time when Lang was due to return. She hadn't slept much last night. She'd already napped once today, and she was still tired, but that no longer mattered. In a few minutes, Alice would cast the spell over Ephie that would make her disappear from the world.

She sat in Alice's practice, smiling down at Jean-Luc, who lounged half-asleep on the rug in front of the fire. Must be nice to sleep wherever and whenever you wanted. "At least I'll have you with me in the spell."

Jean-Luc, intoxicated by the warmth of the fire, rolled onto his back, stretched out his front and back legs, and continued to snooze.

With Alice's guidance, Ephie had worked on her magic today. Nothing big. It had been more about gaining control, and now that Ephie knew how to practice that, she'd promised Alice she'd continue. Just like she'd promised Alice to attend the next coven meeting. That hadn't been hard to do.

Ephie had really enjoyed the meeting. It was something she looked forward to doing more of as part of her life here in Nocturne Falls.

Provided that life went on.

Alice came in. She was dressed in a simple navy-blue caftan. "It's nearly time. Are you ready?"

"I am." Nervous, but ready. She'd never been the subject of a spell before. Unless she counted the one her grandmother claimed to have put on her right before her high school prom to keep boys away.

"Then let's begin. Help me roll this rug up."

Together they moved the furniture off the rug, which caused Jean-Luc to move, too, then they rolled the rug away from the fireplace, leaving a large open area of bare floor.

Alice cast a large circle of salt and wood ash, then selected a candle from the shelves. Pure beeswax, no color. She stepped over the circle line and walked to the center. "Join me. Bring the cat if you want him with you."

"I do." Ephie clicked her tongue to get his attention and called for him. "Come on, *bebe*. Come to mama."

He trotted over and leaped onto her shoulder. Ephie stepped over the salt line and joined Alice.

The elder witch sat, crossing her legs as nimbly as a teenager, then gestured to the place across from her. "Sit."

Ephie did.

Alice set the candle between them and nodded at it. "We need it lit."

With her newfound confidence, Ephie brought fire to the wick easily. The flame flickered, then steadied into an easy, wavering pulse, lengthening until the light it created was hard to look away from. The pleasing scent of honey drifted up.

"That's it," Alice said softly. "Watch the flame. Study it. Become the flame. Rest in its light as it warms you."

The undulating movement was mesmerizing. Ephie had no problem doing exactly as Alice asked.

Jean-Luc slipped from her shoulder onto her lap and wound himself into a little ball, his purrs vibrating through her.

Alice's voice grew softer still, her words no longer English, but Latin. The words blended into the flame, becoming part of the magic that Ephie could feel surrounding her. It was warm and bright, encompassing her entire being.

Around her, the air shimmered silver like glassy water. It ebbed and flowed, a seamless orb of perfect tranquility. Alice's voice was a whisper now, miles away.

The gentle thrum of Jean-Luc's purring felt like bubbles on Ephie's skin. His fur was silk under her fingertips. Peace filled her. On some plane, in the distant part of her that was disconnected, she knew Remy was about to face danger on her behalf.

But Ephie floated above that, her gaze suffused with light as her entire being rested in the nothingness that Alice had created.

This was it. Lang would be here any moment. Remy stood on his back patio. Darryl and Leonie were nearby. They'd taken the seats at the table. They knew nothing about the UV lights, but he didn't need them to. All they had to worry about was their part in the proceedings.

And if things went wrong, Remy would hopefully live long enough to turn those lights on and save them from Lang's wrath.

He scanned the property's perimeter. Any second he expected to see Lang.

Then the air to his right shifted, just a subtle change in the currents. He turned to find Lang standing there, smiling like he'd come to collect his prize. He was in for a shock.

Remy lifted his chin slightly. "Lang."

"Lafitte." Lang looked at Leonie and Darryl for a moment, then appeared to dismiss them as insignificant. He scanned the back deck and seemed to be peering into the house. His nostrils flared. "Where is she?"

"About that. I have some bad news." Remy had played this scene over and over again in his head, trying out the different ways it could go. Working on what the most convincing delivery would be.

Lang had to buy this, or their plan would deteriorate quickly.

It wasn't hard to pretend Ephie was truly gone. He'd lost many friends over the years, and for the last twelve of those years, he'd believed she was one of them. But for the last half hour, Remy could no longer sense her as he'd been able to since the turning.

It was unsettling, to say the least.

Lang frowned. "What now?"

Remy swallowed, thinking about the pain of actually losing Ephie. Of seeing her in that fire and thinking she was gone. Then he focused on reaching out to her now and finding nothing there. Whatever spell Alice had cast had worked. "She couldn't accept going with you. She hated the idea so much that ... that she ..."

His voice broke at the very idea. Panic rose up in him. He let it, knowing it would only help convince Lang.

"She *what*," Lang growled as he stalked closer to Remy.

"She couldn't deal with it. Or you. She decided ... death would be better. She met the dawn this morning. Before I could stop her. She's gone." He pointed back to the deck where earlier he'd sprinkled the ashes Alice had sent. He could smell them from where he was. "Right there. Her ashes are still ..." Remy shook his head.

Lang stood still. "You're lying." But there was genuine anxiety in his voice. "She should have been able to daywalk."

"You're right," Remy said. "She should have been able

to." He blew out a breath and looked away, the pain of his imagined reality giving him the sincerity he hoped would be enough.

Behind Remy, Leonie had begun weeping. Soft, barely audible sobs. Remy had to hand it to her; she was good. There was no doubt she was helping.

Remy turned back to Lang and held his gaze as he shook his head, his expression full of the disgust he felt for the man. "You can't sense her, can you? I can't. But if you don't believe me, see for yourself. Her ashes are still on the deck."

Lang sped past Remy and up the steps. He fell to the deck's surface, hands splayed on the boards, eyes wild. Little puffs of ash drifted up around him, stirred by his movements. "No," he muttered. "*No*. This can't be true."

Leonie charged after him, Darryl following. "Yes," she hissed. "It is true. And all because of you. This is your fault, you murderous monster. You did this. *You!*" she screamed at him, all while reaching into her pocket and pulling out the vial of zombie dust. She pulled the stopper out with her teeth.

Lang, still bent over, clutched at his chest. He started to cry, which reflexively made him take in air. "I can't feel her."

Leonie grabbed a handful of his hair and yanked his head back. "Maybe this will help." She dumped the vial onto him.

He coughed, sucking in more of the dust. A choking

sound gurgled in his throat. He reached out, clutching at the air, then he went limp.

Leonie let go of him. Lang fell to the decking, landing on his face, since he'd already been on his knees. "Darryl, Remy. Now."

Remy had already ascended the stairs. Darryl ran up behind him, cuffs in his hands. While he cuffed Lang, Remy sent the text he had waiting, letting Sherriff Merrow know they were ready for him.

Darryl rolled Lang over. His eyes were still open and filled with panic, but he wasn't moving. Strangled, inarticulate sounds emanated from his throat. He was fighting the zombie dust but not effectively.

Remy reached into his pocket for the pouch of ashes he'd saved back from those he'd scattered on the deck. Red and blue lights flashed in the distance, coming down the street. Remy loosened the drawstring on the pouch, then pried Lang's mouth open and upended the bag into it. A plume of ash rose into the air.

Lang made a soft gagging sound, then his eyes rolled back in his head.

Remy rocked back on his heels. The scent of Ephie's ashes was almost unbearable. "It's over."

"Now, Darryl," Leonie said.

Darryl reached into his jacket and pulled out a wooden stake. Where he'd gotten that, Remy had no idea.

He jumped up and grabbed Darryl's hand. "Don't. The sheriff will be here any moment, and the vampire council representatives are on their way to collect Lang. Let him face the consequences of his actions."

Darryl's eyes narrowed, but his hand didn't move. He was a big man, but he couldn't overcome Remy's strength. "Will he, though? You and I both know that far too often the bad guys don't get what they deserve."

"He will. I promise you." Remy held the man's gaze. "Or I'll hunt him down and take care of it myself. I swear it on these ashes."

Darryl glanced at Leonie.

"I want him dead," she grumbled.

"So do I," Remy said, looking up at her. "But I'd rather have his blood on the hands of the vampire council than any of us."

Reluctantly, she nodded.

Darryl exhaled. "Fine."

Remy let go of him. Darryl tucked the stake back into his jacket just as Sheriff Merrow came through the gate.

He looked at Remy, the question of the night in his gaze.

Remy pushed to his feet and greeted his boss with a nod. "It's done."

Merrow nodded. "Cell's ready and waiting." He came up the steps, surveyed the scene, nose wrinkling. "Smells like dead vampire up here."

"That was the plan," Remy said. It was an awful smell and not one Remy ever wanted to experience again.

Merrow bent at the knees, scooped Lang up under his armpits, and hauled him to his feet. Then Merrow dropped the man over his shoulder and straightened. "I've got this. You go get Ephie."

Remy smiled. "Thanks." He looked at Darryl and Leonie. "You two all right if I—"

"Go," Leonie said, clinging to Darryl's arm. "We'll be right here, waiting. Bring her home."

Remy broke every speed limit getting to Elenora's.

The enveloping calm surrounding Ephie vanished like smoke. She blinked rapidly, trying to remember where she was. Jean-Luc was on her lap. Then it all came back to her. She was in Alice's practice.

But so was Remy. He was right in front of her, a big goofy grin on his face.

"Hey," she said, shaking off the last of the spell's euphoria.

"Hey." The word came out of him filled with relief and happiness. "How are you feeling?"

"Um ..." She thought a moment. "Honestly, like I just had a spa day. I feel great. Although I feel a little disconnected from things. You know, the way you do after a great nap?" She laughed.

Alice, standing by the worktable, smiled. "The disconnection will fade soon. You did very well."

Ephie inhaled. "I was ... under a spell, right?"

"Yes," Alice said. "You were completely immersed in one, to be precise."

"I feel like I've been gone for days. How long was I in there for?"

Remy looked at Alice.

She answered. "Not quite an hour."

"Wow." Ephie tried to equate that amount of time with how long it had felt like. But there was no meshing the two. Being in the spell had seemed timeless. Literally as though time no longer existed.

She smiled at Remy. "Did you just get here?"

He nodded. "I did."

"Oh! You and Mom and Darryl were tricking Lang into thinking I was dead." Concern filled her, both that she'd forgotten what was going on and to ask how it had all played out. "Are they okay? Are you okay? Did you get him?"

"We're all fine, and yes, we got him. By now, I'm sure he's locked up in one of the special supernatural-proof cells. A pair of representatives from the vampire council should be here by the end of the week to transport him."

"To where?"

Remy shook his head. "That's not information they'll share, but we'll be made aware of the outcome of the trial. We may even be called to testify, but we've been told that can be done by video conferencing." He took her hand. "I'm so glad that's behind us."

"Me, too."

Jean-Luc stretched, blinking lazily up at them. *Let's go home now, Mama.*

Ephie squinted at Remy. "What did you say?"

"I didn't say anything."

"I just heard you say something. About going home."

"Wasn't me, but I'm all for that."

It was me, Mama. Jean-Luc.

Ephie's jaw fell open, and she glanced at the cat in her lap. "That can't be right."

Jean-Luc reached a paw toward her. *I want to roll around in the grass in the backyard, Mama.*

Ephie tipped her head at Jean-Luc. Could that really be him talking? "Um, Alice?"

"Yes?"

Ephie looked at her. "This is going to sound crazy, but I can hear Jean-Luc's thoughts in my head."

"What?" Remy said. "You can *hear* Jean-Luc's thoughts?"

"Yes," Ephie said. "Crazy, right?" She turned toward Alice again. "That can't really be possible, can it?"

Alice crossed one arm over her body, resting her other elbow on her hand as she seemed to contemplate the possibility. "Well ... Jean-Luc's a ghost. And you're technically dead, seeing as how you're now a full-fledged vampire." She paused. "It's possible that the spell I cast could have seen you as one entity, so when I broke the spell, it released you both at the same time and somehow linked you."

She shook her head. "Nothing like that has ever happened before with my magic. I apologize. I will consult my library and find a way to fix it."

Ephie laughed. "No, don't. I love being able to communicate with my little *bebe*. It's a gift. Thank you."

She scooped Jean-Luc up and kissed his head. "You sweet thing. Yes, we will go home now, and you can roll around in the grass all you want."

Also, I would like some tuna.

Ephie chuckled. "We'll make the tuna happen, too. Get up on my shoulder, and we'll go out to the car. I just have to collect my things."

Jean-Luc climbed up onto her shoulder. *I want to go to Remy.*

Ephie got to her feet. "He wants you."

Remy leaned one shoulder forward. "Come on."

Jean-Luc hopped across and rubbed his head on Remy's.

"I wonder ..." Ephie shook her head. It was silly. "Never mind."

"You wonder what?" Remy asked.

"I was just thinking it would be nice if you could hear Jean-Luc, too. I mean, seeing as how we're both going to be around you for a while, but maybe you wouldn't want to, and Alice is probably busy and—"

"I'd love it," Remy said.

"The recipe for zombie dust has eluded me for years," Alice said. "I only have it now because of you two. If you want me to repeat the isolation spell in an attempt to bond Remy and Jean-Luc, I will absolutely do it."

"Let's try it," Remy said.

Alice nodded. "You'll have to step out, Ephelia. Even if you're not in the circle, I worry the magic would recognize you and potentially include you again."

"No problem. I need to pack up my things."

"Then we'll see you in about twenty minutes."

Ephie winked at Remy and Jean-Luc. "See you boys then."

She went to the guest room where she'd spent the night, keeping an eye on the time while she packed. Twenty minutes later, she returned to the practice, knocking softly on the door.

"Come in," Alice called out.

Remy was sitting cross-legged in the same spot Ephie had just occupied. Jean-Luc was sitting in Remy's lap looking pleased with himself, although Jean-Luc often looked like that. Remy was blinking like he was still coming out of the spell.

"How did it go?" Ephie asked.

"I don't know yet," Alice answered.

"Jean-Luc, say something to Remy."

Jean-Luc meowed and flopped over in Remy's lap.

"Hey," Remy said, looking from the cat to Ephie. "I can hear him. Wow, that's incredible. Alice, your talent surpasses your reputation."

Alice's smile was demure. "I can't take credit for something that was merely a side-effect, but I am happy to have learned something in the process."

Jean-Luc went to his usual spot on Remy's shoulder, and Remy stood. "Thank you for your part in this. We couldn't have done it without you."

Alice nodded. "Pleased I could help. Be well, both of you."

Jean-Luc chirped from his shoulder perch.

"All three of you, that is," Alice corrected.

They said their goodbyes and left the practice. The butler appeared at the door, opening it for them. He bowed as they approached. "Good night."

"Good night," Remy and Ephie replied.

Remy went ahead of her and opened the SUV's door, then went around to the driver's side and let Jean-Luc get in, then followed after him. Remy and Ephie buckled up, then he started the SUV and headed for home. "Quite a night, huh?"

"I'll say. But probably more for you than it was for me. All I did was veg out in magical limbo."

He smiled. "I'm glad that's all you had to do."

"How did it really go?" Ephie asked. Jean-Luc sat on the console, staring out the windshield. "Did he fight?

Remy shook his head. "It was all fairly smooth. Other than Darryl's plan to stake Lang once he was knocked out."

Ephie's jaw dropped. "He did not."

"No, he didn't, but there were a few seconds where I wasn't sure what was going to happen. Your mother was all for it."

"That doesn't surprise me." Ephie could imagine that her mother would be far happier with Lang completely removed from the picture. "Are they still at your house?"

"They are. They want to see you and know that you're all right."

"Okay." She reached in front of Jean-Luc and wrapped her hand around Remy's forearm. "I love you,

you know. Thank you for helping me deal with all of this."

"I love you, too. And Jean-Luc. I'm so glad I'm not going to lose you again."

"The same goes for me. About that. I'm not going to tell my mother just yet that I'm staying, but soon. Like, after she's back in New Orleans and can't pitch a fit that wakes the neighborhood."

Remy laughed. "I support that decision."

"Somehow, I knew you would."

The next morning, Remy carefully tested the amulet around his neck to be sure it would keep him safe in the sun. It did. Ephie tested her daywalking abilities by sticking her fingertips into the sun. Also good to go.

With that done, they jumped in his car, with Jean-Luc, of course, and went by the hotel to pick up Darryl and Leonie for breakfast.

Once they were in the car, Remy headed for Main Street. "I've always wanted to do this, you know."

"Do what?" Leonie asked from the seat behind him.

"Go to Mummy's Diner for breakfast. You can get it anytime, but having breakfast at breakfast time was never something I could do before."

"How are you able to do it now?" Darryl asked. "Be out in the daylight, I mean."

"I can't tell you," Remy said. "It's a secret that isn't mine to share, but if I just say magic, is that good enough?"

Visible in the rearview mirror, Darryl nodded. "All the answer I need. I probably wouldn't understand it anyway."

"You can still ask me anything you want to. If I can answer, I will. If I can't, I'll tell you that much."

"All right," Darryl said. "Here's another one for you. What's this diner known for?"

"Just some of the best food you'll ever eat. Pancakes and cinnamon buns are two of their best breakfast items, though."

"I'm in," Darryl said.

Leonie sniffed. "Those sound rather heavy."

Ephie turned to look at her mother. "Mom, you eat grits and rice on a regular basis. Pancakes and cinnamon buns are just different forms of carbs. You'll be fine."

Remy smiled to himself. Ephie sure wasn't bothered by standing up to her mother anymore. It was interesting to see.

He found a parking spot, and they went in, managing to snag a booth after only a few minutes. Darryl and Leonie sat on one side, Ephie and Remy on the other. Jean-Luc sat between them. Fortunately, he took up very little space.

A server dropped off menus and waters, then left them to peruse the options.

"This place must be good," Darryl said. "It's crowded. And a deputy just came in to pick up an order. Always a good sign if the police like it."

"I've had the cinnamon bun," Ephie said. "Ah-mazing."

Remy turned, saw Deputy Jenna Blythe, and gave her a wave. She waved back. He'd sent an email to the sheriff's department loop before going to bed, letting them know they'd be seeing him during the day from now on and not to be alarmed.

Maybe it was a cliché, but today really was the first day of the rest of his life, and he was thrilled to be sharing it with Ephie.

The server returned with coffee, filling everyone's cups, and they placed their orders. Ephie picked blueberry pancakes with a side of bacon, Leonie had a veggie omelet with grits, Darryl had the special—devil's food pancakes with strawberries and whipped cream—and Remy had the bananas foster pancakes. He also ordered a cinnamon bun for the table.

Tuna, Jean-Luc said, his voice loud and clear in Remy's head.

Remy glanced down at the cat and whispered, "I am not ordering tuna just so you can smell it."

Hearing Jean-Luc was pretty cool, but having to answer him in a crowded, public place was not something Remy had taken into consideration.

The server gave him an odd look but said nothing. Ephie snorted, covering her face with her menu.

Fortunately, he and Ephie had explained the new development to Darryl and Leonie last night.

As the server left, Leonie got a curious gleam in her eyes. "I have a question for you, since you said to ask."

His guard was already up. "I did. What would you like to know?"

"What your intentions are toward my daughter."

He should have seen that one coming.

"Mom," Ephie started. "I really don't think this is the time or place."

"Why not?" Leonie asked. "It's a perfectly reasonable question."

Ephie sighed, but Remy wasn't bothered. "You're right. It is. I'll tell you what my intentions are. My intentions are to marry her and spend the rest of our lives giving her the royal treatment like the queen she is. Are you all right with that?"

Darryl and Ephie were all smiles. Leonie, not so much. She frowned. "On a deputy's salary?"

"Mom." Ephie's voice held a warning.

Remy doubted that would have much effect on Leonie.

It didn't. Leonie stirred her coffee. "It's a valid concern."

Ephie leaned forward. "When I accidentally destroyed a good part of that motel with my magic, who do you think compensated the owners? Because it wasn't me."

Remy put his hand on her arm. "Eph, you don't have to—"

"Yes, I do." Ephie's brow furrowed. "She needs to know. I don't want this to be a thing our entire marriage, her believing you don't make enough to take care of me the way she thinks I should be. I mean, let's just ignore the fact that I make my own money. For a liberated woman, my mother has some very old-fashioned ideas. You'd think she'd love you because of that, but no, no man's good enough for me. Heaven forbid." Ephie punctuated her words with a dramatic roll of her eyes.

Darryl laughed, then quickly stopped when Leonie shot him a look. "She's not wrong, Leonie. You've never thought a man good enough for Ephie. Now she's got one who's saved her life not once but twice. If that's not good enough, no man ever will be."

Remy could have kissed Darryl, but he refrained. He spoke to Leonie. "Would you like to see my bank statement? Or have a peek into my safety deposit box? I assure you I am able to fulfill any need Ephie might have."

Leonie sat quietly for a few moments, her gaze downcast. Tension spread across the table like a dark cloud. She lifted her chin, and Remy braced for the storm that was about to break.

Leonie took a breath and looked at Ephie. "You're not coming back to New Orleans, are you?"

Ephie shook her head. "Not permanently, no." Her voice was soft, the tone gentle. "I want to be here, Mom. With Remy. I've already fallen in love with this place."

Leonie nodded. "I can see that." She swallowed. "Will you at least let me help you plan the wedding?"

Ephie grinned. "No, because I want us to stay friends. But you can go with me when I shop for the dress. How's that?"

Leonie smiled. "That sounds wonderful." She glanced across the table at Remy, her smile tightening a bit. "You did save Ephie's life. And paying her debt to the motel was ... exceptionally generous. Thank you for all you've done for her. I will do my best to not be the mother-in-law you think I'm going to be."

Remy relaxed. "I appreciate that. We're going to be great friends. You just wait and see."

Leonie snorted. "Don't get ahead of yourself, Lafitte." She sipped her coffee before looking at Ephie again. "How soon can I expect to be a grandmother?"

Jean-Luc sat up, glaring at Leonie. *I'm the* bebe.

"Mom!"

"*Leonie*," Darryl said. "Good heavens, woman. Let them at least have a honeymoon first."

With utterly perfect timing, the server arrived with their food, completely oblivious to the fact that Jean-Luc was now perched gargoyle-style on Darryl's head, staring down at Leonie.

While Darryl and Leonie chatted with the server about how good the food looked, Remy reached over to take Ephie's hand in his and kept his voice low, for her ears only. "Is that something you're interested in? Kids, I mean? You were at one time."

Ephie grinned and gave him a shy nod. "Still am. But maybe we could just practice for a year or two first."

He kissed her cheek. "You have the best ideas. Besides, I don't think Jean-Luc is ready to be an older brother just yet."

Smirking, she glanced at the cat. "Definitely not." Her gaze turned pensive as she looked at Remy again. "Do you really think children will be possible for us?"

"A few days ago, I thought you were out of my life for

good. Now look at us." He'd never felt so alive, so ready for what came next. Ephie really was the most beautiful woman he'd ever seen. "Whatever we set our minds on, we'll make it happen. You have to admit, the two of us are a pretty incredible team."

Jean-Luc meowed.

"Pardon me," Remy said. "The three of us."

"That's right." Ephie laughed. "Then here's to whatever comes next. So long as it's together."

"That's all I've ever wanted." Remy lifted his coffee cup. "And what comes next is ring shopping."

"Remy, I have a ring." She smiled at the sapphire and diamond pansy on her finger. "One I love very much."

"Don't worry, we'll find another one that you love, too. A ring that complements that one." He winked at her. "And leaves your mother speechless."

Want to be up to date on all books & release dates by Kristen Painter? Sign-up for my newsletter on my website, www.kristenpainter.com. No spam, just news (sales, freebies, and releases.)

If you loved the book and want to help the series grow, tell a friend about the book and take time to leave a review!

PARANORMAL WOMEN'S FICTION

Midlife Fairy Tale Series:

The Accidental Queen

The Summer Palace

First Fangs Club Series:

Sucks To Be Me

Suck It Up Buttercup

Sucker Punch

The Suck Stops Here

Embrace The Suck

Code Name: Mockingbird (A Paranormal Women's Fiction Novella)

COZY MYSTERY:

Jayne Frost Series:

Miss Frost Solves A Cold Case: A Nocturne Falls Mystery

Miss Frost Ices The Imp: A Nocturne Falls Mystery

Miss Frost Saves The Sandman: A Nocturne Falls Mystery

Miss Frost Cracks A Caper: A Nocturne Falls Mystery

When Birdie Babysat Spider: A Jayne Frost Short

Miss Frost Braves The Blizzard: A Nocturne Falls Mystery

Miss Frost Chills The Cheater: A Nocturne Falls Mystery

Miss Frost Says I Do: A Nocturne Falls Mystery

Lost in Las Vegas: A Frost And Crowe Mystery

Wrapped up in Christmas: A Frost And Crowe Mystery

Mystified In Magic City

HappilyEverlasting Series:

Witchful Thinking

PARANORMAL ROMANCE

Nocturne Falls Series:

The Vampire's Mail Order Bride

The Werewolf Meets His Match

The Gargoyle Gets His Girl

The Professor Woos The Witch

The Witch's Halloween Hero – short story

The Werewolf's Christmas Wish – short story

The Vampire's Fake Fiancée

The Vampire's Valentine Surprise – short story

The Shifter Romances The Writer

The Vampire's True Love Trials – short story

The Dragon Finds Forever

The Vampire's Accidental Wife

The Reaper Rescues The Genie

The Detective Wins The Witch

The Vampire's Priceless Treasure

The Werewolf Dates The Deputy
The Siren Saves The Billionaire
The Vampire's Sunny Sweetheart
Death Dates The Oracle
The Vampire's Former Flame

Shadowvale Series:

The Trouble With Witches
The Vampire's Cursed Kiss
The Forgettable Miss French
Moody And The Beast
Her First Taste Of Fire
Monster In The Mirror
A Sky Full Of Stars

Sin City Collectors Series

Queen Of Hearts
Dead Man's Hand
Double or Nothing

Standalone Paranormal Romance:

Dark Kiss of the Reaper
Heart of Fire
Recipe for Magic
Miss Bramble and the Leviathan

All Fired Up

His Maker's Mark

URBAN FANTASY

The House of Comarré series:

Forbidden Blood

Blood Rights

Flesh and Blood

Bad Blood

Out For Blood

Last Blood

The Crescent City series:

House of the Rising Sun

City of Eternal Night

Garden of Dreams and Desires

Nothing is completed without an amazing team.

Many thanks to:

*Cover design: Janet Holmes using images under license
from Shutterstock.com
Interior Formatting: Gem Promotions
Editor: Chris Kridler*

ABOUT THE AUTHOR

USA Today Best Selling Author Kristen Painter is a little obsessed with cats, books, chocolate, and shoes. It's a healthy mix. She loves to entertain her readers with interesting twists and unforgettable characters. She currently writes the best-selling paranormal romance series, Nocturne Falls, and award-winning urban fantasy. The former college English teacher can often be found all over social media where she loves to interact with readers.

For more information go to www.kristenpainter.com

Made in the USA
Las Vegas, NV
26 November 2024